Shakespeare on the Double!™

Hamlet

Shakespeare on the Double!™

Hamlet

translated by

Mary Ellen Snodgrass

Wiley Publishing, Inc.

For general information on our other products and services or to obtain technical support please contact our Customer Care Department within the U.S. at (800) 762-2974, outside the U.S. at (317) 572-3993 or fax (317) 572-4002.

Wiley also publishes its books in a variety of electronic formats. Some content that appears in print may not be available in electronic books. For more information about Wiley products, please visit our web site at www.wiley.com.

Library of Congress Cataloging-in-Publication data is available from the publisher upon request.

ISBN:13: 978-0-470-04155-0

ISBN-10: 0-470-04155-2

Printed in the United States of America

10 9 8 7 6 5 4 3 2 1

Book design by Melissa Auciello-Brogan
Book production by Wiley Publishing, Inc. Composition Services

Contents

ABOUT THE TRANSLATOR

Mary Ellen Snodgrass is an award-winning author of textbooks and general reference works, and a former columnist for the *Charlotte Observer*. A member of Phi Beta Kappa, she graduated magna cum laude from the University of North Carolina at Greensboro and Appalachian State University, and holds degrees in English, Latin, psychology, and education of gifted children.

Introduction

*S*hakespeare on the Double! *Hamlet* provides the full text of the Bard's play side by side with an easy-to-read modern English translation that you can understand. You no longer have to wonder what exactly "To be or not to be" means! You can read the Shakespearean text on the left-hand pages and check the right-hand pages when Shakespeare's language stumps you. Or you can read only the translation, which enables you to understand the action and characters at an even pace. You can also read both, referring easily between the original text and the modern translation. Any way you choose, you can now understand every line of the Bard's masterpiece!

We've also provided you with some additional resources:

- **Brief synopsis** of the plot and action provides a broad-strokes overview of the play.
- **Comprehensive character list** covers the actions, motivations, and characteristics of each major player.
- **Visual character map** displays who the major characters are and how they relate to each other.
- **Cycle-of-death** pinpoints the sequence of deaths in the play, including who dies, how they die, and why they die.
- **Reflective questions** help you delve even more into the themes and meanings of the play.

Reading Shakespeare can be slow and difficult. No more! With *Shakespeare on the Double! Hamlet,* you can read the play in language that you can grasp quickly and thoroughly.

Hamlet Synopsis

ACT I

Scene 1

Two months after a state funeral for King Hamlet at Elsinore Castle in Denmark, Prince Hamlet remains at home. Horatio, his fellow student at Wittenberg, investigates a late-night apparition reported two consecutive nights by the watch, Bernardo and Marcellus. Shortly before cock-crow, the spirit of King Hamlet returns decked out in the battle armor he wore during his war with Old Fortinbras of Norway. Horatio ponders the unrest of the former king's spirit.

Scene 2

Hamlet, dressed in funereal black, appears in the council hall in low spirits. His uncle Claudius, King Hamlet's successor, has married the old king's wife Gertrude. Hamlet chooses not to return to school. He suppresses his dismay at the widow's remarriage only one month after her husband's death. Horatio, Bernardo, and Marcellus inform Hamlet about the spirit's pacing on the battlements. Hamlet promises to join the trio that night to await the ghost's return.

Scene 3

Laertes, son of Polonius, the lord chamberlain, packs to attend school in Paris. Laertes warns his sister Ophelia to guard her reputation by avoiding Hamlet's courtship. Laertes suspects that Hamlet is merely toying with Ophelia. Polonius gives parental advice on a young man's behavior, then warns Ophelia about encouraging Hamlet's interest in her.

Scene 4

Around midnight, Hamlet joins Horatio and Marcellus on the castle battlements. The ghost appears. Hamlet recognizes the disturbed spirit and inquires about its return to earth. The ghost beckons Prince Hamlet to one side.

Scene 5

In private, the spirit of King Hamlet confides to his son the necessity of expiating sins in purgatory. The ghost tells Prince Hamlet how Claudius, the brother of King Hamlet, poured yew sap in his ear and killed him with his sins unforgiven. Claudius then seized the crown and married Gertrude, King Hamlet's widow. Prince Hamlet swears to avenge his father's murder. On his sword, Hamlet pledges Horatio and Marcellus to secrecy while the prince investigates the truth of the ghost's accusations.

ACT II

Scene 1

Several weeks later, Polonius instructs Reynaldo on how to spy on Laertes and learn about his behavior in Paris. Ophelia reports to her father that Hamlet's behavior is bizarre. Polonius diagnoses Prince Hamlet's strangeness as love-sickness rather than insanity.

Scene 2

Claudius and Gertrude question Guildenstern and Rosencrantz about their schoolmate Hamlet's peculiarities. Polonius informs Claudius on the effrontery of young Fortinbras, whom the king of Norway scolds for raising an army. Set to attack Poland, young Fortinbras requests permission to march peacefully through Denmark on his way to war. Claudius grants the request. Polonius offers Hamlet's love letters as proof that the prince is love-sick. Claudius and Polonius plot to hide behind an arras to eavesdrop on Hamlet's conversation with Ophelia.

ACT III

Scene 1

Hamlet paces the foyer reading a book. Polonius speaks to him, but misunderstands the prince's nonsensical replies. Rosencrantz and Guildenstern try to diagnose their boyhood friend's mental illness. Hamlet realizes that Claudius has enlisted his schoolmates to spy on him. The prince confuses the men with daft oratory. Rosencrantz and Guildenstern report that Hamlet's favorite acting troupe is approaching Elsinore castle.

Scene 2

Hamlet welcomes the players and asks for a recitation of his favorite passage about Pyrrhus's slaughter of King Priam during the Trojan War. Hamlet assigns Polonius to aid the troupe while they set up their evening performance. To the company's manager, Hamlet requests a performance of *The Murder of Gonzago*. In solitude, Hamlet reveals his doubts that the ghost on the battlements was really his father. He suspects that a demon misleads him. To substantiate King Hamlet's charges against Claudius, Prince Hamlet plans to observe Claudius's reaction to the dramatization of his crime against his brother.

Claudius questions Rosencrantz and Guildenstern about the prince's insanity. The king and Polonius lurk behind a curtain to spy on Hamlet's wooing of Ophelia. Hamlet ponders suicide as the best solution to his dilemma. When Ophelia enters, the prince charges her with immodesty. After Hamlet departs, Claudius fears that he can't allow an insane prince to endanger others. Claudius decides to send Hamlet on an embassy to the king of England to collect a tax owed to Denmark. Polonius urges Gertrude to question her son about his mental unrest.

The next night, the acting troupe discusses with Hamlet the correct delivery of dramatic lines. After the players depart for the stage, Hamlet assigns Horatio to watch Claudius for proof that he is guilty of poisoning King Hamlet. The court assembles for the play, which Hamlet calls "The Mousetrap." He plops his head in Ophelia's lap and pretends to summarize the play while complaining of the court's disrespect for King Hamlet.

The players perform a pantomime of Baptista's loving relationship with King Gonzago. After a nephew poisons Gonzago, Baptista allows the killer to console her. Immediately after Gonzago's corpse is carried away, the murderer seduces Baptista. Claudius asks Hamlet if the rest of the play is offensive. Hamlet assures him that anyone with a clear conscience has no reason to object to the story. Nonetheless, Claudius is so guilt-ridden that he rushes out. The play comes to an abrupt end as the court follows him.

Hamlet confers with Horatio and exults that Claudius displayed guilt by bolting from the play. Rosencrantz and Guildenstern carry a summons from Gertrude to her son. When Polonius delivers a similar command, Hamlet resolves not to harm the queen for her disloyalty to King Hamlet. Polonius hurries to get in position behind the drape to eavesdrop on the queen's conversation with the prince.

Scene 3

Claudius attempts to ease his guilty conscience by praying for forgiveness. Hamlet observes the king at prayer, but decides against stabbing Claudius to death. Because Claudius killed his brother without giving him an opportunity to confess his sins, Hamlet chooses to wait until Claudius has damned himself through drunkeness, quarreling, or adultery with Gertrude.

Scene 4

In her chamber, Gertrude scolds Hamlet for willful behavior. He upsets her by retaliating with charges against Claudius for killing his brother. At Gertrude's outcry, Polonius replies from behind the drape. Hamlet, who suspects that Claudius is hiding in the room, thrusts his rapier through the drape and kills Polonius. Without pause, Hamlet continues berating the queen for adultery. The ghost appears to remind Hamlet not to harm his former wife. The queen grows agitated at Hamlet's apparent discussion with an invisible person. Hamlet drags Polonius's remains from the room in preparation for an embassy requiring a sea voyage to England.

ACT IV

Scene 1

Gertrude, trembling with the night's events, reports them to Claudius, who is conferring with Rosencrantz and Guildenstern. Claudius realizes that Hamlet thought he was stabbing the king when he unintentionally killed Polonius. Claudius sends the two spies to locate Polonius's corpse.

Scene 2

Hamlet pretends to help the spies search for Polonius's body. The prince tells his old friends that Claudius is using them in a plot against Hamlet.

Scene 3

Claudius questions Hamlet about Polonius's death. The prince mocks the investigation and claims that everyone will soon smell the decomposing corpse, which is hidden in the foyer under the steps. The king sends Hamlet on assignment to England. In private, Claudius reveals that the sealed diplomatic pouch that Hamlet carries condemns him to execution.

Scene 4

Before leaving Denmark, Hamlet encounters young Fortinbras. The prince asks about the army that is marching toward Poland. He pities the soldiers who will die for a pointless gesture of honor requiring the seizure of a small plot of land lost in battle. Hamlet then ponders his failure to avenge his father's murder.

Scene 5

Days later, Gertrude learns that Ophelia has suffered an emotional collapse following her father's sudden death. Ophelia wanders into the hall. Disheveled and disoriented, she sings snatches of old songs and ballads. She calls for Laertes, who intends to avenge his father's murder. Danish rebels support Laertes's claim to the throne. Claudius cajoles Laertes to convince him that the king had no part in Polonius's murder.

Scene 6

Hamlet sends a letter to Horatio reporting an attack at sea by pirates. The prince returned to Denmark with the pirates' aid. Horatio carries the letter to the king.

Scene 7

Later, Claudius manipulates Laertes into the role of Hamlet's killer. Laertes is so enraged at Polonius's death and Ophelia's madness that he vows to fight a duel with Hamlet. To assure the prince's death, Laertes produces poison that he bought from a quack. Claudius promises to poison a wine cup to kill Hamlet when he pauses during the duel for a drink. Gertrude interrupts to report that Ophelia has drowned. The king surmises that the news will redouble Laertes's fury at Hamlet.

ACT V

Scene 1

Outside the castle, gravediggers finish Ophelia's burial place and discuss the church's duality in burying aristocratic suicides, but not commoners who take their own lives. Hamlet and Horatio muse on the rapid deterioration of corpses. A gravedigger tosses up the skull of Yorick, the court jester of King Hamlet. The prince learns that the grave awaits Ophelia's remains. When Laertes leaps into the clay pit to embrace his sister's corpse, Hamlet jumps in and grapples with his old friend. Gertrude scolds her son for his rash behavior. Claudius resolves that Laertes must kill Hamlet in the duel.

Scene 2

Hamlet informs Horatio of Claudius's royal dispatch to the king of England to execute Hamlet. The prince exults in stealing the message from the diplomatic pouch, forging a royal order to have Rosencrantz and

Guildenstern executed, and sealing the message with King Hamlet's signet ring. Horatio fears that Hamlet is too over-wrought to commit to a duel. The prince insists that he fight Laertes. Before the face-off begins, Hamlet apologizes for harming Laertes's father and sister. Claudius bets six Arabian horses on his stepson and offers him a pearl in a wine cup. Hamlet scores the first points against Laertes. The Queen mops Hamlet's brow and drinks from the poisoned cup.

At the second round, Laertes stabs Hamlet with the poisoned rapier. The duel continues. After exchanging swords, the prince strikes his opponent with the poisoned tip. When Gertrude collapses and claims that the wine is poisoned, Hamlet orders servants to secure the exits. Laertes admits his guilt and reveals that his opponent, too, is dying. Hamlet stabs Claudius with the poisoned foil and forces him to drink from the wine cup.

As Laertes sinks toward death, he exonerates the prince for the deaths of Polonius and Ophelia. Hamlet, growing weaker, commissions Horatio to remain alive to defend the prince's reputation. Cannon fire alerts the court to young Fortinbras's victory over the Poles. English messengers report that Rosencrantz and Guildenstern were executed in England. Hamlet supports Fortinbras's claim to the Danish throne. As Fortinbras looks in amazement at the bodies lying in the hall, he is shaken by the carnage that has ended the Danish dynasty. Horatio promises to explain. Fortinbras orders honors and military music for prince Hamlet.

List of Characters

HAMLET, PRINCE OF DENMARK The crown prince of Denmark who returns from the university in Wittenberg, Germany, to find his father dead, his mother married to the king's brother Claudius, and Claudius newly self-crowned King.

CLAUDIUS, KING OF DENMARK Dead Hamlet's brother who has usurped the throne and married his sister-in-law.

GERTRUDE, QUEEN OF DENMARK Prince Hamlet's mother, King Hamlet's widow, King Claudius's wife.

THE GHOST Spirit of the late King Hamlet, condemned to walk the earth until his soul is cleansed of its sins.

POLONIUS The elderly Lord Chamberlain, chief counselor to Claudius.

HORATIO A commoner, who went to school with Hamlet and remains his loyal best friend.

LAERTES A student in Paris, who is Polonius's son and Ophelia's brother. He returns from school because of King Hamlet's death, leaves to go back to Paris, and then returns again after his own father's murder.

OPHELIA Daughter of Polonius, sister of Laertes, who is beloved of Hamlet.

ROSENCRANTZ AND GUILDENSTERN Classmates of Hamlet's in Wittenberg whom Claudius summons to Elsinore to spy on Prince Hamlet.

FORTINBRAS King of Norway, who is bound to avenge his father's death by Danish forces.

OSRIC Affected courtier who plays a minor role as the King's messenger and as umpire of the fencing match between Hamlet and Laertes.

VOLTIMAND AND CORNELIUS Danish courtiers who are sent as ambassadors to the court of Norway.

MARCELLUS AND BERNARDO   Danish officers who guard the castle of Elsinore.

FRANCISCO   Danish soldier who guards at the castle of Elsinore.

REYNALDO   Young man whom Polonius instructs and sends to Paris to observe and report on Laertes's conduct.

PLAYERS (actors)   A troupe of actors who put on a play at Hamlet's command at Elsinore Castle.

TWO CLOWNS (the Gravediggers)   Two rustics (identified as clowns) who dig Ophelia's grave.

Character Map

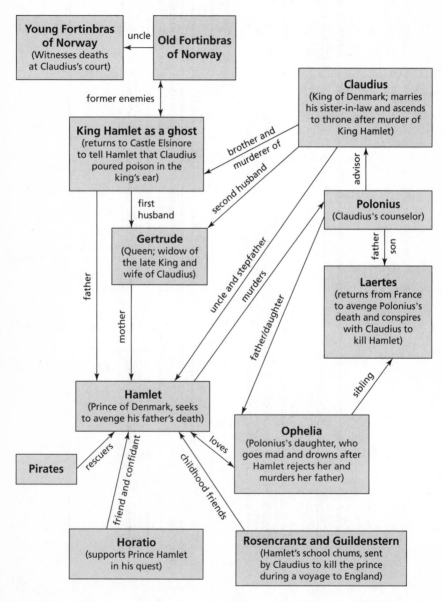

Cycle of Death

One of Prince Hamlet's main motives is to avenge his father's murder, which causes the ensuing cycle of death. The graphic below outlines the sequence of deaths that spur the play's plot.

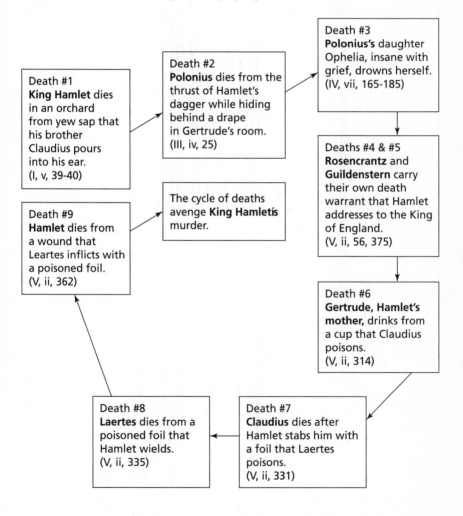

Death #1
King Hamlet dies in an orchard from yew sap that his brother Claudius pours into his ear. (I, v, 39-40)

Death #2
Polonius dies from the thrust of Hamlet's dagger while hiding behind a drape in Gertrude's room. (III, iv, 25)

Death #3
Polonius's daughter Ophelia, insane with grief, drowns herself. (IV, vii, 165-185)

Deaths #4 & #5
Rosencrantz and **Guildenstern** carry their own death warrant that Hamlet addresses to the King of England. (V, ii, 56, 375)

The cycle of deaths avenge **King Hamlet's** murder.

Death #9
Hamlet dies from a wound that Leartes inflicts with a poisoned foil. (V, ii, 362)

Death #6
Gertrude, Hamlet's mother, drinks from a cup that Claudius poisons. (V, ii, 314)

Death #8
Laertes dies from a poisoned foil that Hamlet wields. (V, ii, 335)

Death #7
Claudius dies after Hamlet stabs him with a foil that Laertes poisons. (V, ii, 331)

Shakespeare's
Hamlet

ACT I, SCENE 1

Elsinore. A platform before the castle.

[FRANCISCO at his post. Enter to him BERNARDO]

BERNARDO	Who's there?	
FRANCISCO	Nay, answer me. Stand and unfold yourself.	
BERNARDO	Long live the king!	
FRANCISCO	Bernardo?	
BERNARDO	He.	5
FRANCISCO	You come most carefully upon your hour.	
BERNARDO	'Tis now struck twelve; get thee to bed, Francisco.	
FRANCISCO	For this relief much thanks; 'tis bitter cold, And I am sick at heart.	
BERNARDO	Have you had quiet guard?	
FRANCISCO	Not a mouse stirring.	10
BERNARDO	Well, good-night. If you do meet Horatio and Marcellus, The rivals of my watch, bid them make haste.	
FRANCISCO	I think I hear them. Stand, ho! Who is there? *[Enter HORATIO and MARCELLUS]*	
HORATIO	Friends to this ground.	
MARCELLUS	And liegemen to the Dane.	15
FRANCISCO	Give you good-night.	
MARCELLUS	Oh! farewell, honest soldier: Who hath reliev'd you?	
FRANCISCO	Bernardo has my place. Give you good-night. *[Exit]*	
MARCELLUS	Holla! Bernardo!	
BERNARDO	Say, what! is Horatio there?	
HORATIO	A piece of him.	
BERNARDO	Welcome, Horatio; welcome, good Marcellus.	20

ACT I, SCENE 1

A sentry post before the castle at Elsinore, a port city of Denmark.

[Bernardo joins Francisco at the sentry post]

BERNARDO	Who is standing guard?
FRANCISCO	No, speak the password to me. Stand up straight.
BERNARDO	Long live the king!
FRANCISCO	Is that you Bernardo?
BERNARDO	Yes.
FRANCISCO	You arrive promptly for your watch.
BERNARDO	It is midnight. Go to bed, Francisco.
FRANCISCO	Thanks for taking over. It's a bitterly cold night and I'm depressed.
BERNARDO	Have you had any disturbances on your watch?
FRANCISCO	I haven't even seen a mouse.
BERNARDO	Well, have a good night. If you meet up with Horatio and Marcellus, my watch partners, tell them to hurry.
FRANCISCO	I think I hear them approaching. Halt! Who is coming? *[Enter HORATIO and MARCELLUS]*
HORATIO	Friends of Denmark.
MARCELLUS	And loyalists of the Danish king.
FRANCISCO	I bid you good night.
MARCELLUS	Goodbye, worthy guard. Who is taking your place?
FRANCISCO	Bernardo has relieved me. Good night. *[He goes out]*
MARCELLUS	Hello! Bernardo!
BERNARDO	Hey, is that Horatio coming?
HORATIO	Part of him.
BERNARDO	Welcome, Horatio and Marcellus.

TRANSLATION

HORATIO	What! has this thing appear'd again to-night?
BERNARDO	I have seen nothing.
MARCELLUS	Horatio says 'tis but our fantasy, And will not let belief take hold of him Touching this dreaded sight twice seen of us: 25 Therefore I have entreated him along With us to watch the minutes of this night; That if again this apparition come, He may approve our eyes and speak to it.
HORATIO	Tush, tush! 'twill not appear.
BERNARDO	Sit down awhile, 30 And let us once again assail your ears, That are so fortified against our story, What we two nights have seen.
HORATIO	Well, sit we down, And let us hear Bernardo speak of this.
BERNARDO	Last night of all, 35 When yond same star that's westward from the pole Had made his course to illume that part of heaven Where now it burns, Marcellus and myself, The bell then beating one,— *[Enter GHOST]*
MARCELLUS	Peace! break thee off; look, where it comes again! 40
BERNARDO	In the same figure like the king that's dead.
MARCELLUS	Thou art a scholar; speak to it, Horatio.
BERNARDO	Looks it not like the king? mark it, Horatio.
HORATIO	Most like: it harrows me with fear and wonder.
BERNARDO	It would be spoke to.
MARCELLUS	Question it, Horatio. 45
HORATIO	What art thou that usurp'st this time of night, Together with that fair and war-like form In which the majesty of buried Denmark Did sometimes march? by heaven I charge thee, speak!

HORATIO	Tell me, has the ghost appeared again tonight?
BERNARDO	I haven't seen it.
MARCELLUS	Horatio doesn't believe our sighting and refuses to accept an apparition that we have seen twice. So I asked him to join us to watch through the night. If the ghost returns, he can verify our sighting and speak to the apparition.
HORATIO	Nonsense! It won't appear.
BERNARDO	Though you reject our story, listen once again while we tell you about our two nightly encounters with the ghost.
HORATIO	Okay, let's all sit and listen to Bernardo's story.
BERNARDO	Last night, when the North Star shone in the sky at the same point where it now stands, Marcellus and I, about one o'clock A.M. — *[The GHOST enters]*
MARCELLUS	Silence! Stop talking. See, it is coming again!
BERNARDO	It looks like our dead King Hamlet.
MARCELLUS	You're an educated man, Horatio, speak to it.
BERNARDO	Look, Horatio. Doesn't it look like the old king?
HORATIO	It does. It terrifies me.
BERNARDO	It wants us to speak to it.
MARCELLUS	Horatio, ask it a question.
HORATIO	What are you that appears at this time each night in the handsome, warlike shape of our dead king? By God, I demand that you speak!

MARCELLUS	It is offended.
BERNARDO	See! it stalks away. 50
HORATIO	Stay! speak, speak! I charge thee, speak! *[Exit GHOST]*
MARCELLUS	'Tis gone, and will not answer.
BERNARDO	How now, Horatio! you tremble and look pale: Is not this something more than fantasy? What think you on't? 55
HORATIO	Before my God, I might not this believe Without the sensible and true avouch Of mine own eyes.
MARCELLUS	Is it not like the king?
HORATIO	As thou art to thyself: Such was the very armour he had on 60 When he the ambitious Norway combated; So frown'd he once, when in an angry parle He smote the sledded Polacks on the ice. 'Tis strange.
MARCELLUS	Thus twice before, and jump at this dead hour, 65 With martial stalk hath he gone by our watch.
HORATIO	In what particular thought to work I know not: But in the gross and scope of my opinion, This bodes some strange eruption to our state.
MARCELLUS	Good now, sit down, and tell me, he that knows 70 Why this same strict and most observant watch So nightly toils the subject of the land, And why such daily cast of brazen cannon, And foreign mart for implements of war, Why such impress of shipwrights, whose sore task 75 Does not divide the Sunday from the week, What might be toward, that this sweaty haste Doth make the night joint-labourer with the day: Who is't that can inform me?

ORIGINAL

MARCELLUS	You insulted it.
BERNARDO	See, the ghost is stalking away.
HORATIO	Stay! Speak, I command you! *[The GHOST goes out]*
MARCELLUS	It left without answering.
BERNARDO	Horatio! You are pale and trembling. Now do you believe that this apparition is more than our imagining? What do you think of it?
HORATIO	By God, if I hadn't seen it with my own eyes, I would not believe it.
MARCELLUS	Doesn't it look like the king?
HORATIO	Just like you look like yourself. He was dressed in the armor he wore when he fought the ambitious king of Norway. He frowned that way when, after an angry conference, he attacked Polish troops approaching by sled over the ice. This is strange.
MARCELLUS	The past two times at this very hour he has stalked past our sentry post like a warrior.
HORATIO	I don't know what to think about this apparition. In my opinion, it indicates some disturbing upheaval in Denmark.
MARCELLUS	Sit down, Horatio, and tell me, if you can, why this timely night watch protects the people of Denmark. And why every day bronze cannons are being molded and weapons are being purchased abroad. Why are ship builders working seven days a week? What is the purpose of this constant hard labor that forces night workers to continue their toil into the next day. Who can answer me?

HORATIO   That can I;
At least, the whisper goes so. Our last king,   80
Whose image even but now appear'd to us,
Was, as you know, by Fortinbras of Norway,
Thereto prick'd on by a most emulate pride,
Dar'd to the combat; in which our valiant Hamlet—
For so this side of our known world esteem'd him—   85
Did slay this Fortinbras; who, by a seal'd compact,
Well ratified by law and heraldry,
Did forfeit with his life all those his lands
Which he stood seiz'd of, to the conqueror;
Against the which, a moiety competent   90
Was gaged by our king; which had return'd
To the inheritance of Fortinbras,
Had he been vanquisher; as, by the same co-mart,
And carriage of the article design'd,
His fell to Hamlet. Now, sir, young Fortinbras,   95
Of unimproved mettle hot and full,
Hath in the skirts of Norway here and there
Shark'd up a list of lawless resolutes
For food and diet to some enterprise
That hath a stomach in 't; which is no other—   100
As it doth well appear unto our state—
But to recover of us, by strong hand
And terms compulsative, those foresaid lands
So by his father lost. And this, I take it,
Is the main motive of our preparations,   105
The source of this our watch and the chief head
Of this post-haste and romage in the land.

BERNARDO   I think it be no other but e'en so;
Well may it sort that this portentous figure
Comes armed through our watch, so like the king   110
That was and is the question of these wars.

HORATIO   I can. At least I can tell you what is being rumored. King Hamlet, whose ghost just appeared to us, received a challenge from the proud King Fortinbras of Norway to fight. As a result, our brave King Hamlet—much admired by the world—killed King Fortinbras. By their agreement, according to law, the loser forfeited his land to the winner. As a result, King Hamlet was pledged to receive a sizeable portion of the land from Fortinbras's inheritance if Denmark won the battle.

Therefore, according to the agreement, Fortinbras's land passed to King Hamlet. Now, young Fortinbras, an inexperienced hothead, has hired mercenaries from the outskirts of Norway. Obviously, he intends to recapture the land that his father lost in combat. His challenge is the main reason that Denmark prepares for war. We are posted each night to watch for him. His threat is the cause of the hurried work of our military.

BERNARDO   I think you are right. That explains why this ominous ghost comes in armor in the night. It looks as though the old king is preparing for an attack.

HORATIO	A mote it is to trouble the mind's eye.
	In the most high and palmy state of Rome,
	A little ere the mightiest Julius fell,
	The graves stood tenantless, and the sheeted dead 115
	Did squeak and gibber in the Roman streets;
	As stars with trains of fire and dews of blood,
	Disasters in the sun; and the moist star
	Upon whose influence Neptune's empire stands
	Was sick almost to doomsday with eclipse; 120
	And even the like precurse of fierce events,
	As harbingers preceding still the fates
	And prologue to the omen coming on,
	Have heaven and earth together demonstrated
	Unto our climatures and countrymen. 125
	[Re-enter GHOST]
	But, soft! behold! lo! where it comes again.
	I'll cross it, though it blast me. Stay, illusion!
	If thou hast any sound, or use of voice,
	Speak to me:
	If there be any good thing to be done, 130
	That may to thee do ease and grace to me,
	Speak to me:
	If thou art privy to thy country's fate,
	Which happily foreknowing may avoid,
	O! speak! 135
	Or if thou hast uphoarded in thy life
	Extorted treasure in the womb of earth,
	For which, they say, you spirits oft walk in death,
	Speak of it: stay, and speak! *[Cock crows]* Stop it, Marcellus.
MARCELLUS	Shall I strike at it with my partisan? 140
HORATIO	Do, if it will not stand.
BERNARDO	'Tis here!
HORATIO	'Tis here!
	[Exit GHOST]
MARCELLUS	'Tis gone!
	We do it wrong, being so majestical,
	To offer it the show of violence;
	For it is, as the air, invulnerable, 145
	And our vain blows malicious mockery.

ORIGINAL

HORATIO	The same thing happened in the Roman Republic just before the assassination of Julius Caesar. Graves gave up their dead. Moaning corpses wandered the streets of Rome. Comets trailing fire and red dewdrops, omens in the sun, and the moon, which controls the ocean tides, disappeared in an eclipse as though it were the end of the world. It is the same in Denmark that terrible events in heaven and earth warn us of danger to our country and people. *[The GHOST returns]* Hush, look! The ghost is returning. I'll stand in its way, even if it strikes me. Stop, ghost! If you can talk, speak to me. If I can do anything to ease you without disgracing myself, speak to me. If you can predict what will happen to Denmark to avoid catastrophe, tell me! If you buried treasure that draws you back from death, tell me about it. Stop and speak. *[A rooster crows, indicating the approach of morning]* Halt the ghost, Marcellus.
MARCELLUS	Shall I attack it with my spear?
HORATIO	If it refuses to stop, strike it.
BERNARDO	It's here!
HORATIO	It's here! *[The GHOST departs]*
MARCELLUS	It's gone! We were wrong to threaten the spirit of a king. It was foolish to strike at a ghost, which is as light as air.

BERNARDO	It was about to speak when the cock crew.
HORATIO	And then it started like a guilty thing
	Upon a fearful summons. I have heard,
	The cock, that is the trumpet to the morn,
	Doth with his lofty and shrill-sounding throat
	Awake the god of day; and at his warning,
	Whether in sea or fire, in earth or air,
	Th' extravagant and erring spirit hies
	To his confine; and of the truth herein
	This present object made probation.
MARCELLUS	It faded on the crowing of the cock.
	Some say that ever 'gainst that season comes
	Wherein our Saviour's birth is celebrated,
	The bird of dawning singeth all night long;
	And then, they say, no spirit dare stir abroad;
	The nights are wholesome; then no planets strike,
	No fairy takes, nor witch hath power to charm,
	So hallow'd and so gracious is that time.
HORATIO	So have I heard and do in part believe it.
	But look, the morn in russet mantle clad
	Walks o'er the dew of yon high eastern hill;
	Break we our watch up; and by my advice
	Let us impart what we have seen to-night
	Unto young Hamlet; for, upon my life,
	This spirit, dumb to us, will speak to him.
	Do you consent we shall acquaint him with it,
	As needful in our loves, fitting our duty?
MARCELLUS	Let's do't, I pray; and I this morning know
	Where we shall find him most conveniently.
	[Exeunt]

150

155

160

165

170

175

BERNARDO   It was about to reply when the rooster crowed.

HORATIO   And then it flinched as though it were being called to answer for its wrongdoing. I have heard that roosters summon the morning. At the rooster's crow, ghosts disappear from sea, land, fire, and air, and go back to the grave. The ghost's disappearance proves this belief about roosters.

MARCELLUS   The spirit disappeared at the sound of the rooster's crow. Some people say that, on Christmas Eve, roosters sing all night to announce the Savior's birth. Christmas night is safe from harm in the heavens, fairy thefts, and witches' charms. It is a holy, blessed time.

HORATIO   I've heard the same thing and I at least partly believe it. Look, sunrise is lighting up the hill to the east. Let us end the night watch and report to Prince Hamlet what we have seen tonight. I am certain that the ghost that refused to speak to us will talk to the prince. Do you agree that we should report the ghost to him as a part of a sentry's duty?

MARCELLUS   Let's tell Hamlet. I know where we can find him. *[They depart]*

TRANSLATION

ACT I, SCENE 2

The council chamber.

[Enter CLAUDIUS, King of Denmark, GERTRUDE, the Queen, Councillors, POLONIUS and his son LAERTES, VOLTIMAND and CORNELIUS, HAMLET and Attendants]

KING   Though yet of Hamlet our dear brother's death
The memory be green, and that it us befitted
To bear our hearts in grief, and our whole kingdom
To be contracted in one brow of woe,
Yet so far hath discretion fought with nature   5
That we with wisest sorrow think on him,
Together with remembrance of ourselves.
Therefore our sometime sister, now our queen,
Th' imperial jointress to this war-like state,
Have we, as 'twere with a defeated joy,   10
With one auspicious and one dropping eye,
With mirth in funeral and with dirge in marriage,
In equal scale weighing delight and dole,
Taken to wife: nor have we herein barr'd
Your better wisdoms, which have freely gone   15
With this affair along: for all, our thanks.
Now follows, that you know, young Fortinbras,
Holding a weak supposal of our worth,
Or thinking by our late dear brother's death
Our state to be disjoint and out of frame,   20
Colleagued with the dream of his advantage,
He hath not fail'd to pester us with message,
Importing the surrender of those lands
Lost by his father, with all bands of law,
To our most valiant brother. So much for him.   25
Now for ourself and for this time of meeting.
Thus much the business is: we have here writ
To Norway, uncle of young Fortinbras,
Who, impotent and bed-rid, scarcely hears
Of this his nephew's purpose, to suppress   30
His further gait herein; in that the levies,
The lists and full proportions, are all made
Out of his subject; and we here dispatch
You, good Cornelius, and you, Voltimand,
For bearers of this greeting to old Norway,   35
Giving to you no further personal power
To business with the king more than the scope
Of these delated articles allow.
Farewell and let your haste commend your duty.

ACT I, SCENE 2

The castle's conference room.

[Enter CLAUDIUS, King of Denmark, GERTRUDE, the Queen, Councillors, POLONIUS and his son LAERTES, VOLTIMAND and CORNELIUS, HAMLET and Attendants]

KING   The memory of King Hamlet's death is still painful. It is appropriate that we grieve and that Denmark join us in our sorrow. Yet, necessity forces us to temper our grief with wisdom. For the sake of Denmark, I have married my sister-in-law and made her queen and joint ruler of a country that is preparing for war. I arranged this marriage at the time of a state funeral and moderated my sorrow with joy. I did not violate your advice, which supported this plan to marry so soon after the former king's death. For your kindness, I thank you. At the moment, young Fortinbras underestimates my power. He may think that King Hamlet's death has left Denmark unprepared for war. Assuming that he has the advantage, young Fortinbras has ordered me to surrender the land that his father lost to King Hamlet in their war. Fortinbras is wrong in his assumptions. At the moment, I have business to attend to. I have written to the current king of Norway, who is young Fortinbras's uncle. Even though the old man is an invalid who can't superintend his nephew's plot or control his actions. I have mustered soldiers from Norway. I assign you, Cornelius and Voltimand, to carry my greetings to the aged king of Norway. You have the power to carry out my orders. Goodbye. Hurry and do what I command.

TRANSLATION

CORNELIUS AND VOLTIMAND	In that and all things will we show our duty. 40

KING   We doubt it nothing: heartily farewell.
[Exeunt VOLTIMAND and CORNELIUS]
And now, Laertes, what's the news with you?
You told us of some suit; what is 't, Laertes?
You cannot speak of reason to the Dane,
And lose your voice; what wouldst thou beg, Laertes,   45
That shall not be my offer, not thy asking?
The head is not more native to the heart,
The hand more instrumental to the mouth,
Than is the throne of Denmark to thy father.
What wouldst thou have, Laertes?

LAERTES   Dread my lord,   50
Your leave and favour to return to France;
From whence though willingly I came to Denmark,
To show my duty in your coronation,
Yet now, I must confess, that duty done,
My thoughts and wishes bend again toward France   55
And bow them to your gracious leave and pardon.

KING   Have you your father's leave? What says Polonius?

POLONIUS   He hath, my lord, wrung from me my slow leave
By laboursome petition, and at last
Upon his will I seal'd my hard consent: 60
I do beeseech you, give him leave to go.

KING   Take thy fair hour, Laertes; time be thine,
And thy best graces spend it at thy will.
But now, my cousin Hamlet, and my son,—

HAMLET   *[Aside]* A little more than kin, and less than kind.   65

KING   How is it that the clouds still hang on you?

HAMLET   Not so, my lord; I am too much i' the sun.

QUEEN   Good Hamlet, cast thy nighted colour off,
And let thine eye look like a friend on Denmark.
Do not for ever with thy vailed lids   70
Seek for thy noble father in the dust:
Thou know'st 'tis common; all that live must die,
Passing through nature to eternity.

ORIGINAL

CORNELIUS AND VOLTIMAND	In this assignment and all others we will be dutiful.
KING	I trust you completely. A hearty goodbye. *[VOLTIMAND and CORNELIUS depart]* And now, Laertes, what can I do for you? You informed me of a petition. What do you want, Laertes? Anyone who requests reasonably from the king will receive an answer. What do you want, Laertes? Whatever you ask, I will grant. My respect of your father Polonius is certain. What do you need, Laertes?
LAERTES	Esteemed king, I ask your permission to return to France. I came home to Denmark willingly to attend your crowning. Now that my duty is done, I am eager to return to France. Please grant me leave to depart.
KING	Does your father give his permission? What do you say, Polonius?
POLONIUS	He has worn me down with his begging. Finally, I begrudgingly consented. I ask the king to let him go.
KING	Enjoy your youth, Laertes. This is your time. Do whatever you want. But now, my nephew Hamlet, my stepson—
HAMLET	*[To himself]* A little more than uncle, and not very affectionate.
KING	Why are you still moping under a cloud?
HAMLET	I'm not, my lord. I am often in the sun.
QUEEN	Dear Hamlet, stop grieving for your father and welcome the new king. Don't look downward in your sorrow for your father. You know that everything living must die in the passage from life to eternity.

HAMLET　　　　Ay, madam, it is common.

QUEEN　　　　　　　　　　　　　If it be,
　　　　　　　　Why seems it so particular with thee?　　　　　75

HAMLET　　　　Seems, madam! Nay, it is; I know not 'seems'.
　　　　　　　　'Tis not alone my inky cloak, good mother,
　　　　　　　　Nor customary suits of solemn black,
　　　　　　　　Nor windy suspiration of forc'd breath,
　　　　　　　　No, nor the fruitful river in the eye,　　　　　80
　　　　　　　　Nor the dejected haviour of the visage,
　　　　　　　　Together with all forms, modes, shows of grief,
　　　　　　　　That can denote me truly; these indeed seem,
　　　　　　　　For they are actions that a man might play:
　　　　　　　　But I have that within which passeth show;　　85
　　　　　　　　These but the trappings and the suits of woe.

KING　　　　　'Tis sweet and commendable in your nature, Hamlet,
　　　　　　　　To give these mourning duties to your father:
　　　　　　　　But, you must know, your father lost a father;
　　　　　　　　That father lost, lost his; and the survivor bound　　90
　　　　　　　　In filial obligation for some term
　　　　　　　　To do obsequious sorrow; but to persever
　　　　　　　　In obstinate condolement is a course
　　　　　　　　Of impious stubbornness; 'tis unmanly grief:
　　　　　　　　It shows a will most incorrect to heaven,　　　95
　　　　　　　　A heart unfortified, a mind impatient,
　　　　　　　　An understanding simple and unschool'd:
　　　　　　　　For what we know must be and is as common
　　　　　　　　As any the most vulgar thing to sense,
　　　　　　　　Why should we in our peevish opposition　　　100
　　　　　　　　Take it to heart? Fie! 'tis a fault to heaven,
　　　　　　　　A fault against the dead, a fault to nature,
　　　　　　　　To reason most absurd, whose common theme
　　　　　　　　Is death of fathers, and who still hath cried,
　　　　　　　　From the first corse till he that died to-day,　　105
　　　　　　　　'This must be so.' We pray you, throw to earth
　　　　　　　　This unprevailing woe, and think of us
　　　　　　　　As of a father; for let the world take note,
　　　　　　　　You are the most immediate to our throne;
　　　　　　　　And with no less nobility of love　　　　　　110
　　　　　　　　Than that which dearest father bears his son
　　　　　　　　Do I impart toward you. For your intent
　　　　　　　　In going back to school in Wittenberg,
　　　　　　　　It is most retrograde to our desire;
　　　　　　　　And we beseech you, bend you to remain　　　115
　　　　　　　　Here, in the cheer and comfort of our eye,
　　　　　　　　Our chiefest courtier, cousin, and our son.

ORIGINAL

HAMLET   Yes, madam, it is the way of things.

QUEEN   If you understand the laws of life and death, why do you seem to grieve so much for your father?

HAMLET   Madam, I don't just appear to grieve. I am sorrowing. I'm wearing black for a reason, mother. My black suit is not just a polite custom. I'm not sighing, weeping, or wearing a sad face just for the sake of appearances. My sorrow is slow to ease. Inside, I am truly sad.

KING   You are sweet and dutiful to mourn your father, Hamlet. But your father mourned his father and your grandfather mourned your great grandfather. It is proper for a son to sorrow for a time. But to continue grieving is willful and unholy. Grown men don't carry sorrow to such lengths. Such behavior is ungodly, a display of a weak heart, a stubborn mind, and a child's thinking. We know that death is a necessary end to even the simplest living beings. Why should you carry grief to such extremes? Shame on you. You dishonor heaven, your father, and all life to carry sorrow for a father to such absurd lengths. Every person who has ever lived has accepted the inevitability of death. Please stop your grieving and accept me as a substitute parent. The world must know that you are crown prince of Denmark. I tell you this with the royal affection that a father feels for his son. I regret that you want to return to school in Wittenberg, Germany. I beg you to stay here and comfort me as son, nephew, and courtier.

QUEEN	Let not thy mother lose her prayers, Hamlet:
	I pray thee, stay with us; go not to Wittenberg.

HAMLET	I shall in all my best obey you, madam.	120

KING	Why, 'tis a loving and a fair reply:
	Be as ourself in Denmark. Madam, come;
	This gentle and unforc'd accord of Hamlet
	Sits smiling to my heart; in grace whereof,
	No jocund health that Denmark drinks to-day,
	But the great cannon to the clouds shall tell,
	And the king's rouse the heavens shall bruit again,
	Re-speaking earthly thunder. Come away.
	[Exeunt all except HAMLET]

125

HAMLET	O! that this too too solid flesh would melt,
	Thaw and resolve itself into a dew;
	Or that the Everlasting had not fix'd
	His canon 'gainst self-slaughter! O God! God!
	How weary, stale, flat, and unprofitable
	Seem to me all the uses of this world.
	Fie on 't! Ah fie! 'tis an unweeded garden,
	That grows to seed; things rank and gross in nature
	Possess it merely. That it should come to this!
	But two months dead: nay, not so much, not two:
	So excellent a king; that was, to this,
	Hyperion to a satyr; so loving to my mother
	That he might not beteem the winds of heaven
	Visit her face too roughly. Heaven and earth!
	Must I remember? why, she would hang on him,
	As if increase of appetite had grown
	By what it fed on; and yet, within a month,
	Let me not think on't: Frailty, thy name is woman!
	A little month; or ere those shoes were old
	With which she follow'd my poor father's body,
	Like Niobe, all tears; why she, even she,—
	O God! a beast, that wants discourse of reason,
	Would have mourn'd longer,—married with mine uncle,
	My father's brother, but no more like my father
	Than I to Hercules: within a month,
	Ere yet the salt of most unrighteous tears
	Had left the flushing in her galled eyes,
	She married. O! most wicked speed, to post
	With such dexterity to incestuous sheets.
	It is not nor it cannot come to good;
	But break, my heart, for I must hold my tongue!
	[Enter HORATIO, MARCELLUS and BERNARDO]

130

135

140

145

150

155

ORIGINAL

QUEEN	Don't make me waste my prayers, Hamlet. Stay here. Don't return to Wittenberg.
HAMLET	I shall obey, mother, as best I can.
KING	That was a loving and tender answer. Carry the king's authority in Denmark. Madam, this agreement with Hamlet pleases me for its courtesy and honesty. Therefore, no toast that I drink today shall lack the firing of a cannon. When the king lifts his cup, the echo shall sound in the sky like thunder. Let's depart. *[All exit except HAMLET]*
HAMLET	I wish that my body could turn to liquid. Or that the Church had not condemned suicide! Oh, God! God! Everyday life seems tedious, boring, uninteresting, and pointless. Drat it! Oh, damn. My life is like a garden gone to weeds that overrun it. How could this happen? My father has been dead less than two months. He was so excellent a king. In comparison to Claudius, he was the sun god and his replacement is a goatish lecher. My father loved my mother so much that he would not per-mit the wind to chap her face. Heaven and earth! Must I recall these painful thoughts? She embraced him as if her desire grew from their daily affection. Yet, she remarried within a month. I must stop thinking about it. Women are so unreliable! She remarried within a month after she had followed my father's corpse to the grave. Even though she had wept like Niobe, a mythic Greek mother who was turned to stone for mourning her dead chil-dren. My own mother! Oh God! An animal would have sorrowed longer. She married my uncle, my father's brother. Claudius is no more similar to my father than I am to Hercules, the Greek strong man. Within a month, before her tears had stopped falling, she remarried. It was wicked of her to hurry into an incestuous marriage with her brother-in-law. No good can come of this union. But my heart must break in silence while I say nothing. *[HORATIO, MARCELLUS and BERNARDO come in]*

HORATIO	Hail to your lordship!
HAMLET	I am glad to see you well: 160 Horatio, or I do forget myself.
HORATIO	The same, my lord, and your poor servant ever.
HAMLET	Sir, my good friend; I'll change that name with you. And what make you from Wittenberg, Horatio? Marcellus?
MARCELLUS	My good lord,— 165
HAMLET	I am very glad to see you. *[To BERNARDO]* Good even, sir. But what, in faith, make you from Wittenberg?
HORATIO	A truant disposition, good my lord.
HAMLET	I would not hear your enemy say so, 170 Nor shall you do mine ear that violence, To make it truster of your own report Against yourself; I know you are no truant. But what is your affair in Elsinore? We'll teach you to drink deep ere you depart. 175
HORATIO	My lord, I came to see your father's funeral.
HAMLET	I pray thee, do not mock me, fellow-student; I think it was to see my mother's wedding.
HORATIO	Indeed, my lord, it follow'd hard upon.
HAMLET	Thrift, thrift, Horatio! the funeral bak'd meats 180 Did coldly furnish forth the marriage tables. Would I had met my dearest foe in heaven Or ever I had seen that day, Horatio! My father, methinks I see my father.
HORATIO	O! where, my lord?
HAMLET	In my mind's eye, Horatio. 185
HORATIO	I saw him once; he was a goodly king.
HAMLET	He was a man, take him for all in all, I shall not look upon his like again.
HORATIO	My lord, I think I saw him yesternight.

HORATIO	Greetings to the crown prince.
HAMLET	It's good to see you well, Horatio.

HORATIO	I am equally glad to see you. I am always loyal to you.
HAMLET	You are my friend and I am yours. Why have you left Wittenberg, Horatio? You too, Marcellus?

MARCELLUS	My lord—
HAMLET	I am happy to see you, Marcellus. *[To BERNARDO]* Good evening to you, Bernardo. Why have you left Wittenberg?
HORATIO	I am enjoying truancy from school, my lord.
HAMLET	I would not allow anyone to call you a slacker. You assault my ear to speak ill of yourself. I know you are never truant. Why have you come to Elsinore? We'll go out drinking before you leave town.

HORATIO	My lord, I came for your father's funeral.
HAMLET	Don't toy with me, Horatio. I think you came for my mother's wedding.
HORATIO	You're right. The wedding took place quickly after the funeral.
HAMLET	They were saving money, Horatio, by serving leftover meats from the funeral at the wedding reception. I would sooner greet my worst enemy in heaven than to witness these events, Horatio! I can see my father.

HORATIO	Where, my lord?
HAMLET	I see him in my mind, Horatio.
HORATIO	I saw him once. He was a noble monarch.
HAMLET	He was a rare man. I shall never see anyone like him.

HORATIO	My lord, I think I saw him last night.

HAMLET	Saw who?	190
HORATIO	My lord, the king your father.	
HAMLET	The king, my father!	
HORATIO	Season your admiration for a while With an attent ear, till I may deliver, Upon the witness of these gentlemen, This marvel to you.	
HAMLET	For God's love, let me hear.	195
HORATIO	Two nights together had these gentlemen, Marcellus and Bernardo, on their watch, In the dead vast and middle of the night, Been thus encounter'd: a figure like your father, Armed at point exactly, cap-a-pe, Appears before them, and with solemn march Goes slow and stately by them: thrice he walk'd By their oppress'd and fear-surprised eyes, Within his truncheon's length; whilst they, distill'd Almost to jelly with the act of fear, Stand dumb and speak not to him. This to me In dreadful secrecy impart they did, And I with them the third night kept the watch; Where, as they had deliver'd, both in time, Form of the thing, each word made true and good, The apparition comes. I knew your father; These hands are not more like.	200 205 210
HAMLET	But where was this?	
MARCELLUS	My lord, upon the platform where we watch'd.	
HAMLET	Did you not speak to it?	
HORATIO	My lord, I did; But answer made it none; yet once methought It lifted up its head and did address Itself to motion, like as it would speak; But even then the morning cock crew loud, And at the sound it shrunk in haste away And vanish'd from our sight.	215

HAMLET	Saw whom?
HORATIO	My lord, I saw King Hamlet.
HAMLET	My father, the former king!
HORATIO	Hold your questions until I can tell you what I and these two witnesses saw.

HAMLET	For God's sake, tell me.
HORATIO	For two consecutive nights, Marcellus and Bernardo were standing watch late at night when they saw the ghost. A shape like King Hamlet, armed from head to foot, marched solemnly past them. He passed by three times no farther from their eyes than the length of his scepter. Marcellus and Bernardo, turned to jelly by fear, said nothing to him. They told me in secret of their encounter with the ghost. On the third night, I stood watch with them. It happened again, just as they had said. The ghost approached. I knew your father. The apparition looked as much like him as one of my hands looks like the other.

HAMLET	Where did this happen?
MARCELLUS	My lord, at the sentry post where we stood guard.
HAMLET	Didn't you speak to the ghost?
HORATIO	My lord, I did, but the ghost made no reply. At one point, the spirit lifted its head as though it would talk to me. At the crowing of the rooster at morning, the ghost hurried away and vanished.

ACT I

TRANSLATION

HAMLET	'Tis very strange.	220

HORATIO   As I do live, my honour'd lord, 'tis true;
And we did think it writ down in our duty
To let you know of it.

HAMLET   Indeed, indeed, sirs, but this troubles me.
Hold you the watch to-night?

MARCELLUS AND BERNARDO	We do, my lord.	225

HAMLET   Arm'd, say you?

MARCELLUS AND BERNARDO   Arm'd, my lord.

HAMLET   From top to toe?

MARCELLUS AND BERNARDO   My lord, from head to foot.

HAMLET   Then saw you not his face?

HORATIO   O yes! my lord; he wore his beaver up.

HAMLET	What! look'd he frowningly?	230

HORATIO   A countenance more in sorrow than in anger.

HAMLET   Pale or red?

HORATIO   Nay, very pale.

HAMLET   And fix'd his eyes upon you?

HORATIO   Most constantly.

HAMLET   I would I had been there.

HORATIO	It would have much amaz'd you.	235

HAMLET   Very like, very like. Stay'd it long?

HORATIO   While one with moderate haste might tell a hundred.

HAMLET	This is strange news.
HORATIO	As sure as I'm alive, my noble lord, I speak the truth. We thought it was our military duty to report the sighting to you.
HAMLET	Yes, yes, you did the right thing. But I am concerned. Are you standing guard tonight?
MARCELLUS AND BERNARDO	We are, my lord.
HAMLET	Did you say the ghost was armed?
MARCELLUS AND BERNARDO	It was, my lord.
HAMLET	From head to toe?
MARCELLUS AND BERNARDO	My lord, from its head to its feet.
HAMLET	Then you didn't see his face?
HORATIO	Yes, my lord. The ghost had its visor raised.
HAMLET	And you say he frowned?
HORATIO	He looked sad rather than angry.
HAMLET	Pale or red in the face?
HORATIO	Quite pale.
HAMLET	And did he stare at you?
HORATIO	Constantly.
HAMLET	I wish that I had been there.
HORATIO	You would have been amazed.
HAMLET	Very likely. Did it stay long?
HORATIO	About as long as it would take me to count to one hundred.

ACT I

TRANSLATION

MARCELLUS AND BERNARDO	Longer, longer.
HORATIO	Not when I saw it.
HAMLET	His beard was grizzled, no?
HORATIO	It was, as I have seen it in his life, 240 A sable silver'd.
HAMLET	I will watch to-night; Perchance 'twill walk again.
HORATIO	I warrant it will.
HAMLET	If it assume my noble father's person, I'll speak to it, though hell itself should gape And bid me hold my peace. I pray you all, 245 If you have hitherto conceal'd this sight, Let it be tenable in your silence still; And whatsoever else shall hap to-night, Give it an understanding, but no tongue: I will requite your loves. So, fare you well. 250 Upon the platform, 'twixt eleven and twelve, I'll visit you.
ALL	Our duty to your honour.
HAMLET	Your loves, as mine to you. Farewell. *[Exeunt HORATIO, MARCELLUS, and BERNARDO]* My father's spirit (in arms!) all is not well; I doubt some foul play: would the night were come! 255 Till then sit still, my soul: foul deeds will rise, Though all the earth o'erwhelm them, to men's eyes. *[Exit]*

MARCELLUS AND BERNARDO	Even longer than that.
HORATIO	Not when I saw it.
HAMLET	Was his beard gray?
HORATIO	It looked life-like—black and silver.
HAMLET	I will stand guard tonight. Perhaps the ghost will appear again.
HORATIO	I guarantee that it will.
HAMLET	If it is the spirit of my father, I will talk to it, even if hell breaks open and commands me to be silent. I ask that you all keep quiet about what you have told me. Whatever happens tonight, observe, but say nothing. I will repay your loyalty. Farewell until between eleven and twelve o'clock, when I will join you at the sentry post.
ALL	We are faithful to your royal station.
HAMLET	I accept your friendship as you must accept mine. Farewell. *[HORATIO, MARCELLUS, and BERNARDO depart]* My father's ghost in armor! Something is wrong. I suspect a crime. I wish it were already night! Till then, I must be patient. Crimes always surface, even if they are buried under the earth. *[He goes out]*

TRANSLATION

ACT I, SCENE 3

A room in Polonius's house.

[Enter LAERTES and OPHELIA]

LAERTES   My necessaries are embark'd; farewell:
And, sister, as the winds give benefit
And convoy is assistant, do not sleep,
But let me hear from you.

OPHELIA   Do you doubt that?

LAERTES   For Hamlet, and the trifling of his favour,   5
Hold it a fashion and a toy in blood,
A violet in the youth of primy nature,
Forward, not permanent, sweet, not lasting,
The perfume and suppliance of a minute;
No more.

OPHELIA   No more but so?

LAERTES   Think it no more: 10
For nature, crescent, does not grow alone
In thews and bulk; but, as this temple waxes,
The inward service of the mind and soul
Grows wide withal. Perhaps he loves you now,
And now no soil nor cautel doth besmirch   15
The virtue of his will; but you must fear,
His greatness weigh'd, his will is not his own,
For he himself is subject to his birth;
He may not, as unvalu'd persons do,
Carve for himself, for on his choice depends   20
The safety and the health of the whole state;
And therefore must his choice be circumscrib'd
Unto the voice and yielding of that body
Whereof he is the head. Then if he says he loves you,
It fits your wisdom so far to believe it   25
As he in his particular act and place
May give his saying deed; which is no further
Than the main voice of Denmark goes withal.
Then weigh what loss your honour may sustain,
If with too credent ear you list his songs,   30
Or lose your heart, or your chaste treasure open
To his unmaster'd importunity.

ACT I, SCENE 3

A room in Polonius's house.

[Enter LAERTES and OPHELIA]

LAERTES   I have already sent my luggage to the ship. Goodbye. And, Ophelia, as the wind carries my ship away, write to me before you go to bed.

OPHELIA   Do you think I will fail to write to you?

LAERTES   As for Hamlet's flirting, regard it as a trifling pastime, like a violet before it blooms. Such courtship is trivial, sweet, but short-term. It will last no more than the moment.

OPHELIA   Is his flirting no more than that?

LAERTES   Don't take his wooing seriously. When living things grow, they develop more than weight and muscles. As the body grows, the mind and soul mature as well. Perhaps he is infatuated with you without trying to deceive you. But you must be cautious because he is a crown prince and, therefore, may not make choices for himself. Because he is royal, he may not satisfy his own desires the way an ordinary man would do. His choice of a wife influences the welfare of Denmark. His selection of a mate must agree with that of the people he serves. If he declares his love for you, you would be wise to believe him only for the moment, which is no longer than public opinion lasts. Consider your own reputation if you listen too eagerly to his sweet words. Don't give away your heart or your virginity to pressure from an immature boyfriend.

Fear it, Ophelia, fear it, my dear sister;
And keep you in the rear of your affection,
Out of the shot and danger of desire.   35
The chariest maid is prodigal enough
If she unmask her beauty to the moon;
Virtue herself 'scapes not calumnious strokes;
The canker galls the infants of the spring
Too oft before their buttons be disclos'd,   40
And in the morn and liquid dew of youth
Contagious blastments are most imminent.
Be wary then; best safety lies in fear:
Youth to itself rebels, though none else near.

OPHELIA   I shall th' effect of this good lesson keep,   45
As watchman to my heart. But, good my brother,
Do not, as some ungracious pastors do,
Show me the steep and thorny way to heaven,
Whiles, like a puff'd and reckless libertine,
Himself the primrose path of dalliance treads,   50
And recks not his own rede.

LAERTES   O! fear me not.
I stay too long; but here my father comes.
[Enter POLONIUS]
A double blessing is a double grace;
Occasion smiles upon a second leave.

POLONIUS   Yet here, Laertes! aboard, aboard, for shame!   55
The wind sits in the shoulder of your sail,
And you are stay'd for. There, my blessing with thee!
And these few precepts in thy memory
Look thou character. Give thy thoughts no tongue,
Nor any unproportion'd thought his act.   60
Be thou familiar, but by no means vulgar;
The friends thou hast, and their adoption tried,
Grapple them to thy soul with hoops of steel;
But do not dull thy palm with entertainment
Of each new-hatch'd, unfledg'd comrade. Beware   65
Of entrance to a quarrel, but, being in,
Bear 't that th' opposed may beware of thee.
Give every man thine ear, but few thy voice;
Take each man's censure, but reserve thy judgment.

Be careful, Ophelia, my dear sister. Control your heart and keep it safe from his desire. The most modest girl is wasteful enough if she bares her face to the moon. Virginity cannot escape charges of impropriety. Disease destroys spring buds before they can bloom. Young people are most likely to suffer blight. Be careful. You will be safest if you fear deception. Young people often abandon good sense.

OPHELIA   I will obey your warning as though you were guarding my heart. But, my good brother, don't tell me of the difficult path to heaven like a scolding preacher. While, like a wayward despoiler of young women, he courts young maidens and ignores his own advice.

LAERTES   Don't worry about me. I am late, but father is approaching. *[POLONIUS comes in]* A second goodbye is a double blessing. It is good that I can say goodbye again.

POLONIUS   Are you still here, Laertes? Get on board. Shame on you! The crew waits for you while the wind fills their sails. You have my blessing along with this advice: Don't speak all that is in your mind. Don't take action on inappropriate ideas. Be a friend, but don't behave rudely. Keep your true friends, but don't waste your time with every companion who comes along. Don't encourage quarrels, but, if you do argue, be strong in your opinion. Listen to everyone, but speak to only a few. Listen to each person's complaints, but reserve your own views.

TRANSLATION

	Costly thy habit as thy purse can buy, 70
	But not express'd in fancy; rich, not gaudy;
	For the apparel oft proclaims the man,
	And they in France of the best rank and station
	Are most select and generous, chief in that.
	Neither a borrower, nor a lender be; 75
	For loan oft loses both itself and friend,
	And borrowing dulls the edge of husbandry.
	This above all: to thine own self be true,
	And it must follow, as the night the day,
	Thou canst not then be false to any man. 80
	Farewell; my blessing season this in thee!

LAERTES   Most humbly do I take my leave, my lord.

POLONIUS   The time invites you; go, your servants tend.

LAERTES   Farewell, Ophelia; and remember well
What I have said to you.

OPHELIA   'Tis in my memory lock'd,   85
And you yourself shall keep the key of it.

LAERTES   Farewell.
[Exit]

POLONIUS   What is 't, Ophelia, he hath said to you?

OPHELIA   So please you, something touching the Lord Hamlet.

POLONIUS   Marry, well bethought: 90
'Tis told me, he hath very oft of late
Given private time to you; and you yourself
Have of your audience been most free and bounteous.
If it be so,—as so 'tis put on me,
And that in way of caution,—I must tell you,   95
You do not understand yourself so clearly
As it behooves my daughter and your honour.
What is between you? give me up the truth.

OPHELIA   He hath, my lord, of late made many tenders
Of his affection to me.   100

POLONIUS   Affection! pooh! you speak like a green girl,
Unsifted in such perilous circumstance.
Do you believe his tenders, as you call them?

OPHELIA   I do not know, my lord, what I should think.

ORIGINAL

"to be or not to be"

Macbeth

Shakespeare

Julius Caesar

Romeo and Juliet

Hamlet

Hamlet

Shakespeare

Julius
Caesar

Romeo and
Juliet

Macbeth

To be or not to be

Buy quality clothing, but don't follow fads. Look tasteful-
ly dressed rather than showy. Clothing often reveals a
man's character. The French are good at dressing to suit
their social class. Don't borrow or lend. Lending often
results in the loss of a friend and of the loan, and bor-
rowing causes the borrower to be wasteful instead of
thrifty. Most of all, be true to yourself. If you are honest
with yourself, just as night follows day, you can't or
won't want to deceive anyone. Goodbye. Let my blessing
help you mature!

LAERTES   I humbly depart from you, my lord.

POLONIUS   It is time to sail; go, your servants are waiting.

LAERTES   Goodbye, Ophelia. Remember what I told you.

OPHELIA   Your words are locked in my mind and you hold the key.

LAERTES   Goodbye. *[He departs]*

POLONIUS   What did he tell you, Ophelia.

OPHELIA   He discussed my relationship with Hamlet.

POLONIUS   Well, that was timely. I have heard that you spend much
time alone with the prince. You have been generous with
your presence. If this is true, as I have heard, I must warn
you that you are not ready for a courtship that might not
suit my daughter or an honorable woman. What is
between you and Hamlet? Tell me the truth.

OPHELIA   He has been loving to me lately.

POLONIUS   Loving! Pooh, you sound like a gullible child, inexperienced at courtship. Do you believe his tender words?

OPHELIA   I don't know what to think, my lord.

POLONIUS	Marry, I'll teach you: think yourself a baby,	105
	That you have ta'en these tenders for true pay,	
	Which are not sterling. Tender yourself more dearly;	
	Or,—not to crack the wind of the poor phrase,	
	Running it thus,—you'll tender me a fool.	
OPHELIA	My lord, he hath importun'd me with love	110
	In honourable fashion.	
POLONIUS	Ay, fashion you may call it: go to, go to.	
OPHELIA	And hath given countenance to his speech, my lord,	
	With almost all the holy vows of heaven.	
POLONIUS	Ay, springes to catch woodcocks. I do know,	115
	When the blood burns, how prodigal the soul	
	Lends the tongue vows: these blazes, daughter,	
	Giving more light than heat, extinct in both,	
	Even in their promise, as it is a-making,	
	You must not take for fire. From this time	120
	Be somewhat scanter of your maiden presence;	
	Set your entreatments at a higher rate	
	Than a command to parley. For Lord Hamlet,	
	Believe so much in him, that he is young,	
	And with a larger tether may he walk	125
	Than may be given you: in few, Ophelia,	
	Do not believe his vows, for they are brokers,	
	Not of that dye which their investments show,	
	But mere implorators of unholy suits,	
	Breathing like sanctified and pious bonds,	130
	The better to beguile. This is for all:	
	I would not, in plain terms, from this time forth,	
	Have you so slander any moment's leisure,	
	As to give words or talk with the Lord Hamlet	
	Look to 't, I charge you; come your ways.	135
OPHELIA	I shall obey, my lord. *[Exeunt]*	

POLONIUS   I will tell you what to think: You are a child if you fall for his sweet offers, which are worthless. Value yourself more highly. To build on this sentiment, don't offer yourself to him or you will make a fool of yourself.

OPHELIA   My lord, the prince has spoken of love in honorable style.

POLONIUS   Yes, he is stylish. Forget it.

OPHELIA   He has confirmed his words, my lord, with holy pledges.

POLONIUS   Yes, snares to capture birds. I know from experience how extravagant a lover's words may be. His fire, daughter, is more flash than steady flame. It will burn out before it takes hold. You must not take his impetuous words for true love. From now on, don't be too available for meetings with him. Value your conversation more than common chitchat. As for Hamlet, realize that he is young and that he is free to court lots of girls, while you must be more disciplined. In short, Ophelia, don't believe his pledges, for they are temptations. His vows of love fall short of a lifetime investment. He is misdirecting you toward a casual love by pretending to be solemn and respectful. In conclusion, I don't want you to waste your time by talking with Prince Hamlet. See to it. Come along.

OPHELIA   I will obey you, my lord. *[They depart]*

TRANSLATION

ACT I, SCENE 4

The platform.

[Enter HAMLET, HORATIO, and MARCELLUS]

HAMLET	The air bites shrewdly; it is very cold.
HORATIO	It is a nipping and an eager air.
HAMLET	What hour now?
HORATIO	I think it lacks of twelve.
MARCELLUS	No, it is struck.

HORATIO   Indeed? I heard it not: then it draws near the season   5
Wherein the spirit held his wont to walk.
[A flourish of trumpets, and ordnance shot off, within]
What does this mean, my lord?

HAMLET   The king doth wake to-night and takes his rouse,
Keeps wassail and the swaggering up-spring reels;
And, as he drains his draughts of Rhenish down,   10
The kettle-drum and trumpet thus bray out
The triumph of his pledge.

HORATIO   Is it a custom?

HAMLET   Ay, marry, is 't:
But to my mind,—though I am native here
And to the manner born,—it is a custom   15
More honour'd in the breach than the observance.
This heavy-headed revel east and west
Makes us traduc'd and tax'd of other nations;
They clepe us drunkards, and with swinish phrase
Soil our addition; and indeed it takes   20
From our achievements, though perform'd at height,
The pith and marrow of our attribute.
So, oft it chances in particular men,
That for some vicious mole of nature in them,
As, in their birth,—wherein they are not guilty,   25
Since nature cannot choose his origin,—
By the o'ergrowth of some complexion,
Oft breaking down the pales and forts of reason,
Or by some habit that too much o'er-leavens
The form of plausive manners; that these men,   30
Carrying, I say, the stamp of one defect,

ACT I, SCENE 4

The sentry post.

[Enter HAMLET, HORATIO, and MARCELLUS]

HAMLET	The air is biting and cold.
HORATIO	It is a nippy night.
HAMLET	What time is it?
HORATIO	Almost twelve o'clock.
MARCELLUS	The clock has struck twelve already.
HORATIO	Really? I didn't hear it. It is about the time that the ghost walks. *[A trumpet salute and the firing of cannon in the castle]* What is the meaning of this noise, my lord?
HAMLET	King Claudius is up late tonight drinking, toasting, and dancing reels. Every time he drinks a cup of Rhine wine, the timpani and trumpet announce his toast.
HORATIO	Is this customary?
HAMLET	Yes, it is. But, although I grew up with this custom, I think it would be better avoided. This muddle-headed drinking causes nations east and west of us to dishonor and denounce us. Such carousing defames our reputation, even when performed in celebration of our renown. It is often this way with individual people. Some fault in their character like their birth—which they have no control over—may destroy reason or some bad habit may ruin their more agreeable behaviors.

Being nature's livery, or fortune's star,
His virtues else, be they as pure as grace,
As infinite as man may undergo,
Shall in the general censure take corruption   35
From that particular fault: the dram of evil
Doth all the noble substance often doubt,
To his own scandal.
[Enter GHOST]

HORATIO   Look, my lord, it comes.

HAMLET   Angels and ministers of grace defend us!
Be thou a spirit of health or goblin damn'd,   40
Bring with thee airs from heaven or blasts from hell,
Be thy intents wicked or charitable,
Thou com'st in such a questionable shape
That I will speak to thee: I'll call thee Hamlet,
King, father; royal Dane, O! answer me: 45
Let me not burst in ignorance; but tell
Why thy canoniz'd bones, hearsed in death,
Have burst their cerements; why the sepulchre,
Wherein we saw thee quietly inurn'd,
Hath op'd his ponderous and marble jaws,   50
To cast thee up again. What may this mean,
That thou, dead corse, again in complete steel
Revisits thus the glimpses of the moon,
Making night hideous; and we fools of nature
So horridly to shake our disposition   55
With thoughts beyond the reaches of our souls?
Say, why is this, wherefore? what should we do?
[The Ghost beckons HAMLET]

HORATIO   It beckons you to go away with it,
As if it some impartment did desire
To you alone.

MARCELLUS   Look, with what courteous action   60
It waves you to a more removed ground:
But do not go with it.

HORATIO   No, by no means.

HAMLET   It will not speak; then, will I follow it.

HORATIO   Do not, my lord.

ACT 1

Such people, burdened with only one fault, may let that single fault corrupt the strengths of their character. This small defect of character may cause others to think the worst of him. *[Enter GHOST]*

HORATIO	Look, my lord, the spirit is coming.
HAMLET	Angels and guardians preserve us! Are you a good or evil spirit carrying heavenly blessing or hellish curses? Whether you are wicked or good, you come in such a conversational pose that I will speak to you. I see that you are my father, King Hamlet, the Danish monarch. Oh, answer me. Don't leave me to suffer unanswered. Tell me why your blessed skeleton, properly buried, has left the tomb. Why has your grave, where you were peacefully buried, opened its mouth to spit you out again? What does it mean when a lifeless corpse puts on armor and walks each night to terrify. You cause us to tremble with thoughts beyond human understanding. Tell me, why have you left your grave? What do you want from me? *[The GHOST beckons to HAMLET]*
HORATIO	The spirit gestures for you to follow it as though it wants to speak to you alone.
MARCELLUS	Look how politely it summons you to a distant spot. Don't go with it.
HORATIO	No. Don't dare go.
HAMLET	Unless I follow, it will not speak.
HORATIO	Do not, my lord.

TRANSLATION

HAMLET	Why, what should be the fear? I do not set my life at a pin's fee; 65 And for my soul, what can it do to that, Being a thing immortal as itself? It waves me forth again; I'll follow it.
HORATIO	What if it tempt you toward the flood, my lord, Or to the dreadful summit of the cliff 70 That beetles o'er his base into the sea, And there assume some other horrible form, Which might deprive your sovereignty of reason And draw you into madness? think of it; The very place puts toys of desperation, 75 Without more motive, into every brain That looks so many fathoms to the sea And hears it roar beneath.
HAMLET	It waves me still. Go on, I'll follow thee.
MARCELLUS	You shall not go, my lord.
HAMLET	Hold off your hands! 80
HORATIO	Be rul'd; you shall not go.
HAMLET	My fate cries out, And makes each petty artery in this body As hardy as the Nemean lion's nerve. *[Ghost beckons]* Still am I call'd. Unhand me, gentlemen, *[Breaking from them]* By heaven! I'll make a ghost of him that lets me: 85 I say, away! Go on, I'll follow thee. *[Exeunt Ghost and HAMLET]*
HORATIO	He waxes desperate with imagination.
MARCELLUS	Let's follow; 'tis not fit thus to obey him.
HORATIO	Have after. To what issue will this come?
MARCELLUS	Something is rotten in the state of Denmark. 90
HORATIO	Heaven will direct it.
MARCELLUS	Nay, let's follow him. *[Exeunt]*

ORIGINAL

HAMLET   What should I fear of it? I don't value my life as much as a pin. How can a ghost harm my soul, since my spirit is eternal? It gestures for me to come. I will follow it.

HORATIO   What will you do, my lord, if the ghost leads you over a cliff into the sea? What if it takes another shape and drives you mad? Consider the possibilities. A cliff can tease people to lean too far toward the sea below.

HAMLET   It is still gesturing. Lead and I will follow you.

MARCELLUS   Don't go, my lord.

HAMLET   Let go of me!

HORATIO   Listen to us. You shouldn't go.

HAMLET   I am destined to go. My body struggles like the lion of Nemea that Hercules faced. *[GHOST beckons]* It continues to summon me. Let go, friends. *[HAMLET breaks away]* By heaven, I will kill anyone who holds me back. Go away. Continue, spirit. I am following you. *[The GHOST and HAMLET depart]*

HORATIO   His imagination has made him desperate.

MARCELLUS   Let's follow him. It's not right for us to let him venture on alone.

HORATIO   Go after him. What can come of this meeting with a ghost?

MARCELLUS   There is corruption in Denmark.

HORATIO   God will guide us.

MARCELLUS   No. Let's follow Hamlet and the ghost. *[They go out]*

TRANSLATION

ACT I, SCENE 5

Another part of the platform.

[Enter Ghost and HAMLET]

HAMLET   Whither wilt thou lead me? speak; I'll go no further.

GHOST   Mark me.

HAMLET   I will.

GHOST   My hour is almost come,
When I to sulphurous and tormenting flames
Must render up myself.

HAMLET   Alas! poor ghost.

GHOST   Pity me not, but lend thy serious hearing   5
To what I shall unfold.

HAMLET   Speak; I am bound to hear.

GHOST   So art thou to revenge, when thou shalt hear.

HAMLET   What?

ACT I, SCENE 5

Another section of the sentry post.

[Enter GHOST and HAMLET]

HAMLET	Where are you taking me? Speak. I will follow you no farther.
GHOST	Listen to me.
HAMLET	I will.
GHOST	It is almost time for me to enter the flames of hell.
HAMLET	I'm sorry, poor ghost.
GHOST	Don't pity me. Listen to the account I am going to tell you.
HAMLET	Speak. I will hear you.
GHOST	You must take revenge for what you are about to hear.
HAMLET	What?

GHOST	I am thy father's spirit;
	Doom'd for a certain term to walk the night, 10
	And for the day confin'd to fast in fires,
	Till the foul crimes done in my days of nature
	Are burnt and purg'd away. But that I am forbid
	To tell the secrets of my prison-house,
	I could a tale unfold whose lightest word 15
	Would harrow up thy soul, freeze thy young blood,
	Make thy two eyes like stars start from their spheres,
	Thy knotted and combined locks to part,
	And each particular hair to stand on end,
	Like quills upon the fretful porpentine: 20
	But this eternal blazon must not be
	To ears of flesh and blood. List, list, O list!
	If thou didst ever thy dear father love—

HAMLET O God!

GHOST Revenge his foul and most unnatural murder. 25

HAMLET Murder!

GHOST Murder most foul, as in the best it is;
But this most foul, strange, and unnatural.

HAMLET Haste me to know't, that I, with wings as swift
As meditation or the thoughts of love, 30
May sweep to my revenge.

GHOST I find thee apt,
And duller shouldst thou be than the fat weed
That rots itself in ease on Lethe wharf,
Wouldst thou not stir in this. Now, Hamlet, hear:
'Tis given out, that sleeping in mine orchard, 35
A serpent stung me; so the whole ear of Denmark
Is by a forged process of my death
Rankly abus'd; but know, thou noble youth,
The serpent that did sting thy father's life
Now wears his crown.

HAMLET O my prophetic soul! 40
My uncle?

GHOST   I am your father's ghost. I am doomed for a time to walk by night. I must spend each day in fires that cleanse me of my sins. I can't tell you about purgatory, where the sinful are purified. If I could tell you about it, the smallest detail would terrify your soul, freeze your blood, make your two eyes pop out, cause your hair to part, and each hair to stand up like porcupine quills. This talk of eternity is not suited to mortal ears. Listen to me, if you ever loved your father—

HAMLET   Oh, God!

GHOST   Avenge his murder.

HAMLET   Was it murder that killed him?

GHOST   A foul and unusual killing.

HAMLET   Hurry and tell me that I may speed on my way to avenge you.

GHOST   You are attentive. You would be limp as a thick weed on the pier of hell's river of forgetfulness if this story did not stir you to action. Listen, Hamlet. Danes have heard my death explained as the result of a snake bite while I slept in the orchard. This lie is what everyone was led to believe. But you should know that the snake that bit me now wears the crown of Denmark.

HAMLET   Oh, I guessed it! It was my uncle Claudius?

TRANSLATION

GHOST

Ay, that incestuous, that adulterate beast,
With witchcraft of his wit, with traitorous gifts,—
O wicked wit and gifts, that have the power
So to seduce!—won to his shameful lust   45
The will of my most seeming-virtuous queen.
O Hamlet! what a falling-off was there;
From me, whose love was of that dignity
That it went hand in hand even with the vow
I made to her in marriage; and to decline   50
Upon a wretch whose natural gifts were poor
To those of mine!
But virtue, as it never will be mov'd,
Though lewdness court it in a shape of heaven,
So lust, though to a radiant angel link'd,   55
Will sate itself in a celestial bed,
And prey on garbage.
But, soft! methinks I scent the morning air;
Brief let me be. Sleeping within mine orchard,
My custom always of the afternoon,   60
Upon my secure hour thy uncle stole,
With juice of cursed hebona in a vial,
And in the porches of mine ears did pour
The leperous distilment; whose effect
Holds such an enmity with blood of man   65
That swift as quicksilver it courses through
The natural gates and alleys of the body,
And with a sudden vigour it doth posset
And curd, like eager droppings into milk,
The thin and wholesome blood: so did it mine;   70
And a most instant tetter bark'd about,
Most lazar-like, with vile and loathsome crust
All my smooth body.
Thus was I, sleeping, by a brother's hand,
Of life, of crown, of queen, at once dispatch'd;   75
Cut off even in the blossoms of my sin,
Unhousel'd, disappointed, unanel'd,
No reckoning made, but sent to my account
With all my imperfections on my head:
O, horrible! O, horrible! most horrible!   80
If thou hast nature in thee, bear it not;
Let not the royal bed of Denmark be
A couch for luxury and damned incest.
But, howsoever thou pursu'st this act,
Taint not thy mind, nor let thy soul contrive   85
Against thy mother aught; leave her to heaven,
And to those thorns that in her bosom lodge,
To prick and sting her. Fare thee well at once!
The glow-worm shows the matin to be near,
And 'gins to pale his uneffectual fire;   90
Adieu, adieu! Hamlet, remember me. *[Exit]*

ORIGINAL

GHOST Yes, that adulterous villain who used his charm for evil purpose and seduced my widow, who seemed so virtuous before. Oh, Hamlet, what a sin she committed against a husband who kept his marriage vows. She sank to the level of Claudius, who is less worthy of her than I am. But goodness, when courted by a demon in the shape of an angel, gives way to lust. It will grow weary in a heavenly bed and embrace trash. Look, the morning is dawning. I must be brief. While I was taking my afternoon nap in the orchard at the usual hour, your uncle Claudius crept up and poured the juice of a poisonous herb into my ear. The effect is so venomous that it swiftly infected my blood like the curdling of milk. Instantly, a crust formed over my body. Thus, while I slept, my brother robbed me of my life, my crown, and my wife. I died without benefit of confession and holy oil. Without forgiveness, I went to my doom with my sins intact. Oh, horror! If you have any feeling, don't tolerate this crime. Don't let the royal bed be stained with incest and adultery. But, however you avenge this murder, don't accuse or harm your mother. Leave her to God and to the pangs of her conscience. I must say goodbye immediately! The lightning bug indicates that it is almost morning by dimming his glow. God keep you, Hamlet. Remember me. *[The GHOST departs]*

HAMLET	O all you host of heaven ! O earth! What else?
	And shall I couple hell? O fie! Hold, hold, my heart!
	And you, my sinews, grow not instant old,
	But bear me stiffly up! Remember thee! 95
	Ay, thou poor ghost, while memory holds a seat
	In this distracted globe. Remember thee!
	Yea, from the table of my memory
	I'll wipe away all trivial fond records,
	All saws of books, all forms, all pressures past 100
	That youth and observation copied there;
	And thy commandment all alone shall live
	Within the book and volume of my brain,
	Unmix'd with baser matter: yes, by heaven!
	O most pernicious woman! 105
	O villain, villain, smiling, damned villain!
	My tables,—meet it is I set it down,
	That one may smile, and smile, and be a villain;
	At least I'm sure it may be so in Denmark: *[Writing]*
	So, uncle, there you are. Now to my word; 110
	It is 'Adieu, adieu! remember me.'
	I have sworn 't.

HORATIO	*[Within]* My lord, my lord!	
MARCELLUS	*[Within]*	Lord Hamlet!
HORATIO	*[Within]*	Heaven secure him!
MARCELLUS	*[Within]* So be it!	
HORATIO	*[Within]* Illo, ho, ho, my lord! 115	
HAMLET	Hillo, ho, ho, boy! come, bird, come.	
	[Enter HORATIO and MARCELLUS]	
MARCELLUS	How is 't, my noble lord?	
HORATIO		What news, my lord?
HAMLET	O wonderful.	
HORATIO		Good my lord, tell it.
HAMLET	No; you will reveal it.	
HORATIO	Not I, my lord, by heaven!	
MARCELLUS		Nor I, my lord. 120
HAMLET	How say you then, would heart of man once think it?	
	But you'll be secret?	
HORATIO AND MARCELLUS	Ay, by heaven, my lord.	

HAMLET	Oh all you heavenly angels! Oh earth! What will happen now? Shall I become an agent of hell? Oh damn! Be still, my heart! My strength, don't fail me, but help me to stand up. Remember you! Yes, you tormented spirit, so long as my brain holds memories. Remember you! Yes, from my memory I will erase all knowledge, all shapes, all impressions that I have saved from boyhood. Your command will survive alone in my mind, untainted by unimportant things. Yes, by God! O most wicked woman! Oh villain, smiling, accursed criminal. My memory—I should be mindful that a murderer can wear a deceptive smile. At least, it can happen in Denmark. *[HAMLET writes]* So, Uncle Claudius, I have written down your name. Now, as to my pledge: it is "God be with you! Remember me." I have sworn to avenge you.

HORATIO	*[From the castle]* My lord, are you all right?
MARCELLUS	*[From the castle]* Prince Hamlet!
HORATIO	*[From the castle]* Heaven take care of him!
MARCELLUS	*[From the castle]* Amen!
HORATIO	*[From the castle]* Hello, my lord, where are you?
HAMLET	Hello, my friends, I return like a bird to the falconer. *[HORATIO and MARCELLUS enter]*
MARCELLUS	Are you all right, my lord?
HORATIO	What did you learn, my lord?
HAMLET	Oh, wonderful news.
HORATIO	My lord, tell us the news.
HAMLET	No, you will reveal my secret.
HORATIO	By God, I won't, my lord.
MARCELLUS	Neither will I, my lord.
HAMLET	Do you repeat what another knows? Can you keep a secret?
HORATIO AND MARCELLUS	Yes, by God, my lord.

TRANSLATION

HAMLET	There's ne'er a villain dwelling in all Denmark But he's an arrant knave.
HORATIO	There needs no ghost, my lord, come from the grave, 125 To tell us this.
HAMLET	Why, right; you are i' the right; And so without more circumstance at all, I hold it fit that we shake hands and part; You, as your business and desire shall point you,— For every man hath business and desire, 130 Such as it is,—and, for mine own poor part, Look you, I'll go pray.
HORATIO	These are but wild and whirling words, my lord.
HAMLET	I am sorry they offend you, heartily; Yes, faith, heartily.
HORATIO	There's no offence, my lord. 135
HAMLET	Yes, by Saint Patrick, but there is, Horatio, And much offence, too. Touching this vision here, It is an honest ghost, that let me tell you; For your desire to know what is between us, O'ermaster't as you may. And now, good friends, 140 As you are friends, scholars, and soldiers, Give me one poor request.
HORATIO	What is 't, my lord? we will.
HAMLET	Never make known what you have seen to-night.
HORATIO **AND** **MARCELLUS**	My lord, we will not.
HAMLET	Nay, but swear 't.
HORATIO	In faith, 145 My lord, not I.
MARCELLUS	Nor I, my lord, in faith.
HAMLET	Upon my sword.
MARCELLUS	We have sworn, my lord, already.
HAMLET	Indeed, upon my sword, indeed.
GHOST	*[Beneath]* Swear.
HAMLET	Ha, ha, boy! sayst thou so? art thou there, true-penny? 150 Come on,—you hear this fellow in the cellarage,— Consent to swear.

ORIGINAL

HAMLET	There is no villain in Denmark who isn't an outright scoundrel.
HORATIO	We didn't need a ghost from the graveyard to tell us that.
HAMLET	Then you are right. Without delay, let us shake hands and depart. You go about your business as everybody does. As for me, I will go pray.
HORATIO	Your words make no sense, my lord.
HAMLET	I am sorry to insult you, truly. Yes, truly.
HORATIO	You haven't offended us, my lord.
HAMLET	Yes, I have insulted you, Horatio, and greatly. Concerning the ghost, it was a true vision. Control your urge to learn what it said to me. Before I go, my friends, as you are friends, students, and soldiers, allow me one favor.
HORATIO	Whatever it is, my lord, we will.
HAMLET	Tell no one what you have seen tonight.
HORATIO AND MARCELLUS	My lord, we won't.
HAMLET	Swear that you will keep it secret.
HORATIO	On my faith, my lord, I won't tell.
MARCELLUS	Nor I, my lord, on my faith.
HAMLET	Swear on my sword.
MARCELLUS	We have already sworn, my lord.
HAMLET	Swear again on my sword.
GHOST	*[From below]* Swear.
HAMLET	What did you say, old boy? Are you still here, old fellow? Come on, then. You heard the ghost below. Agree to swear.

TRANSLATION

HORATIO	Propose the oath, my lord.
HAMLET	Never to speak of this that you have seen,
	Swear by my sword.
GHOST	*[Beneath]* Swear.

155

HAMLET	*Hic et ubique?* then we'll shift our ground.
	Come hither, gentlemen,
	And lay your hands again upon my sword:
	Never to speak of this that you have heard,
	Swear by my sword.

160

GHOST	*[Beneath]* Swear.
HAMLET	Well said, old mole! canst work i' the earth so fast?
	A worthy pioner! once more remove, good friends.

HORATIO	O day and night, but this is wondrous strange!
HAMLET	And therefore as a stranger give it welcome.

165

There are more things in heaven and earth, Horatio,
Than are dreamt of in your philosophy.
But come;
Here, as before, never, so help you mercy,
How strange or odd soe'er I bear myself,

170

As I perchance hereafter shall think meet
To put an antic disposition on,
That you, at such times seeing me, never shall,
With arms encumber'd thus, or this head-shake,
Or by pronouncing of some doubtful phrase,

175

As, 'Well, well, we know,' or, 'We could, an if we would;'
Or, 'If we list to speak,' or, 'There be, an if they might;'
Or such ambiguous giving out, to note
That you know aught of me: this not to do,
So grace and mercy at your most need help you,

180

Swear.

GHOST	*[Beneath]* Swear. *[They swear]*
HAMLET	Rest, rest, perturbed spirit! So, gentlemen,

With all my love I do commend me to you:
And what so poor a man as Hamlet is

185

May do, to express his love and friending to you
God willing, shall not lack. Let us go in together;
And still your fingers on your lips, I pray.
The time is out of joint; O cursed spite,
That ever I was born to set it right!

190

Nay, come, let's go together.
[Exeunt]

ORIGINAL

HORATIO	State the oath, my lord.
HAMLET	Never tell what you have seen. Swear on my sword.
GHOST	*[From below]* Swear.
HAMLET	Are you here and everywhere? Then we will move. Come over here, friends, and place your hands again on my sword. Don't ever speak of what you have heard. Swear on my sword.
GHOST	*[From below]* Swear.
HAMLET	Thanks for your urging. Can you move under the earth as fast as a mole? You are a good digger. Let's move again, my friends.
HORATIO	By day and night, you are acting very strangely.
HAMLET	As though it were a stranger you were meeting for the first time, welcome this pledge. There are more strange things on earth and in heaven, Horatio, than you could imagine. Listen, on your honor, however oddly I may behave when you next see me, if I seem crazy, don't seem perplexed or dubious of my reason. Promise that you won't say, "We could explain his behavior if we were allowed to." Don't pretend that you know anything about my quirks. Promise not to intervene, if you ever expect mercy and aid. Swear.
GHOST	*[From below]* Swear. *[The men swear]*
HAMLET	Rest yourself, agitated ghost! So, friends, with all my love, whatever I can do for you out of affection and friendship, I will do, God willing. Let us enter the castle together. Don't breathe a word of my secret, I beg. The times are disjointed. Oh cursed evil, that I am destined to punish this crime. Come, let's go in together. *[They depart]*

ACT II, SCENE 1

A room in Polonius's house.

[Enter POLONIUS and REYNALDO]

POLONIUS	Give him this money and these notes, Reynaldo.
REYNALDO	I will, my lord.
POLONIUS	You shall do marvellous wisely, good Reynaldo, Before you visit him, to make inquiry Of his behaviour.
REYNALDO	My lord, I did intend it.

POLONIUS	Marry, well said, very well said. Look you sir, Inquire me first what Danskers are in Paris; And how, and who, what means, and where they keep, What company, at what expense; and finding By this encompassment and drift of question That they do know my son, come you more nearer Than your particular demands will touch it: Take you, as 'twere, some distant knowledge of him; As thus, 'I know his father, and his friends, And, in part, him'; do you mark this, Reynaldo?	10 15

REYNALDO	Ay, very well, my lord.
POLONIUS	'And, in part, him; but,' you may say, 'not well: But if 't be he I mean, he's very wild, Addicted so and so;' and there put on him What forgeries you please; marry, none so rank As may dishonour him; take heed of that; But, sir, such wanton, wild, and usual slips As are companions noted and most known To youth and liberty.
REYNALDO	As gaming, my lord?
POLONIUS	Ay, or drinking, fencing, swearing, quarreling, Drabbing; you may go so far.
REYNALDO	My lord, that would dishonour him.

ACT II, SCENE 1

A room in Polonius's house.

[Enter POLONIUS and REYNALDO]

POLONIUS	Give Laertes this money and these letters, Reynaldo.
REYNALDO	I will, my lord.
POLONIUS	It would be wise, Reynaldo, if you'd investigate Laertes's behavior before you visit him.
REYNALDO	My lord, I already planned to ask about him.
POLONIUS	Good idea, Reynaldo. First learn what Danish people are in Paris. Inquire who they are, why they come there, where they stay, who pays their expenses, and who accompanies them. After you gain this information, ease into the question of whether they know my son. This roundabout method will suit your inquiry. Pretend that you are distantly acquainted with him. Say, "I know his father and friends and, by association, Laertes as well." Do you understand my method, Reynaldo?
REYNALDO	Yes, I understand you well, my lord.
POLONIUS	Say, "I am acquainted with Laertes, but I don't know him well." State that you heard that Laertes is an out-of-control drinker and make up what other comments you need. But, Reynaldo, mention the usual wild behaviors and carousing that young men are known to commit when they have the opportunity.
REYNALDO	Like gambling, my lord?
POLONIUS	Yes, or drinking, dueling, swearing, fighting, consorting with prostitutes. You may go to the limit.
REYNALDO	My lord, those charges would insult Laertes.

ACT II

TRANSLATION

POLONIUS	Faith, no; as you may season it in the charge.
	You must not put another scandal on him,
	That he is open to incontinency; 30
	That's not my meaning; but breathe his faults so quaintly
	That they may seem the taints of liberty,
	The flash and outbreak of a fiery mind,
	A savageness in unreclaimed blood,
	Of general assault.

REYNALDO   But, my good lord,—   35

POLONIUS   Wherefore should you do this?

REYNALDO   Ay, my lord,
I would know that.

POLONIUS   Marry, sir, here's my drift;
And I believe it is a fetch of warrant:
You laying these slight sullies on my son,
As 'twere a thing a little soil'd i' the working,   40
Mark you,
Your party in converse, him you would sound,
Having ever seen in the prenominate crimes
The youth you breathe of guilty, be assur'd,
He closes with you in this consequence;   45
'Good sir,' or so; 'friend,' or 'gentleman,'
According to the phrase or the addition
Of man and country.

REYNALDO   Very good, my lord.

POLONIUS   And then, sir, does he this,—he does,—
What was I about to say? By the mass I was about   50
To say something: where did I leave?

REYNALDO   At 'closes in the consequence.'
At 'friend or so,' and 'gentleman.'

POLONIUS	Indeed, no. You may qualify your charges. Don't scandalize him by saying he is given to sexual overindulgence. I don't mean you should go so far. But imply his weaknesses so skillfully that they may seem like the excesses of freedom from home, the evidence of a vigorous spirit, a misbehavior arising from an untamed character, the usual fault of one so young.
REYNALDO	But, sir. . . .
POLONIUS	Are you asking why I am sending you to spy on Laertes?
REYNALDO	Yes, my lord. I would like to know your reason.
POLONIUS	Indeed, sir, this is my purpose: I think you can learn about him by trickery; by implying these slight faults in my son as though they were only indiscretions. Note that the person you ask will accuse Laertes of these faults if he has evidence of them. He will reply with a polite phrase according to his country's custom.
REYNALDO	Very well, my lord.
POLONIUS	And then, sir, if he . . . , if he . . . . What was I about to say? By the Holy Mass, I was going to say something. Where did I leave off?
REYNALDO	If he has evidence of them, he will reply with a polite phrase according to his country's custom.

ACT II

POLONIUS	At 'closes in the consequence,' ay, marry;
	He closes with you thus: 'I know the gentleman; 55
	I saw him yesterday, or t' other day,
	Or then, or then; with such, or such; and, as you say,
	There was a' gaming; there o'ertook in 's rouse;
	There falling out at tennis'; or perchance,
	'I saw him enter such a house of sale,' 60
	Videlicet, a brothel, or so forth.
	See you now;
	Your bait of falsehood takes this carp of truth;
	And thus do we of wisdom and of reach,
	With windlasses, and with assays of bias, 65
	By indirections find directions out:
	So by my former lecture and advice
	Shall you my son. You have me, have you not?
REYNALDO	My lord, I have.
POLONIUS	God be wi' you; fare you well.
REYNALDO	Good my lord! 70
POLONIUS	Observe his inclination in yourself.
REYNALDO	I shall, my lord.
POLONIUS	And let him ply his music.
REYNALDO	Well, my lord.
POLONIUS	Farewell!
	[Exit REYNALDO. Enter OPHELIA]
	How now, Ophelia! what's the matter?
OPHELIA	O! my lord, my lord, I have been so affrighted! 75
POLONIUS	With what, in the name of God?
OPHELIA	My lord, as I was sewing in my closet,
	Lord Hamlet, with his doublet all unbrac'd;
	No hat upon his head; his stockings foul'd,
	Ungarter'd, and down gyved to his ankle; 80
	Pale as his shirt; his knees knocking each other;
	And with a look so piteous in purport
	As if he had been loosed out of hell
	To speak of horrors, he comes before me.
POLONIUS	Mad for thy love?
OPHELIA	My lord, I do not know; 85
	But truly I do fear it.

POLONIUS	If he has evidence of them, he will reply: "I know Laertes. I saw him yesterday, or recently, or whenever with this or that person. As you imply, there was gambling; he was drunk," or "there was a fight at the tennis match," or perhaps "I saw him enter a bawdy house," which is to say a "bordello," and so forth. This is how you spy on Laertes: By planting lies, you learn the truth. This is how wise and sly men reel in the truth by testing opinions. By indirect questioning, you will learn what I ask. So, as I have explained, will you inquire about Laertes? You understand me, don't you?
REYNALDO	My lord, I do.
POLONIUS	God go with you. Farewell.
REYNALDO	Goodbye, my lord!
POLONIUS	Make your own observations of Laertes's behavior.
REYNALDO	I will, my lord.
POLONIUS	Let him dance to his own tune.
REYNALDO	I will, my lord.
POLONIUS	Farewell! *[REYNALDO leaves; OPHELIA appears]* Ophelia, what is wrong?
OPHELIA	Oh, my lord, my lord! I am so scared!
POLONIUS	Of what, in God's name?
OPHELIA	My lord, while I was sewing in my room, I saw Prince Hamlet, with his vest unbuttoned, hatless, his socks dirty and drooping to his ankle. He came to me, as white as his shirt. His knees knocked and he looked so pitiful as if he had come from hell to describe its horrors.
POLONIUS	Was he mad with passion?
OPHELIA	My lord, I don't know. But I am afraid so.

ACT II

TRANSLATION

POLONIUS   What said he?

OPHELIA   He took me by the wrist and held me hard,
Then goes he to the length of all his arm,
And with his other hand thus o'er his brow,
He falls to such perusal of my face   90
As he would draw it. Long stay'd he so;
At last, a little shaking of mine arm,
And thrice his head thus waving up and down,
He rais'd a sigh so piteous and profound
That it did seem to shatter all his bulk   95
And end his being. That done, he lets me go,
And with his head over his shoulder turn'd,
He seem'd to find his way without his eyes;
For out o' doors he went without their help,
And to the last bended their light on me.   100

POLONIUS   Come, go with me; I will go seek the king.
This is the very ecstasy of love,
Whose violent property fordoes itself
And leads the will to desperate undertakings
As oft as any passion under heaven   105
That does afflict our natures. I am sorry.
What! have you given him any hard words of late?

OPHELIA   No, my good lord; but, as you did command,
I did repel his letters and denied
His access to me.

POLONIUS   That hath made him mad.   110
I am sorry that with better heed and judgment
I had not quoted him; I fear'd he did but trifle,
And meant to wrack thee; but, beshrew my jealousy!
By heaven, it is as proper to our age
To cast beyond ourselves in our opinions   115
As it is common for the younger sort
To lack discretion. Come, go we to the king:
This must be known; which, being kept close, might move
More grief to hide than hate to utter love.
Come. *[Exeunt]*   120

POLONIUS	What did he say?
OPHELIA	He grabbed my wrist and squeezed it. Then he leaned back at arm's length, put his other hand to his forehead, and stared at my face as if he wanted to draw it. He stayed like that a long time. At last, after shaking my arm and shaking his head up and down, he sighed so pitifully and deeply that his emotion seemed to shatter his body and life. After that, he dropped my wrist and looked at me over his shoulder while he walked away as though he didn't need eyes to see the way. He continued staring at me over his shoulder as he went outdoors, until I was out of sight.
POLONIUS	Come with me. I will report this to the king. Hamlet suffers from love sickness. Violent passion destroys itself and forces the mind to desperate deeds. I am sorry for Hamlet. Have you been rude to him recently?
OPHELIA	No, my lord. I did as you told me—I refused his letters and stayed away from him.
POLONIUS	Your refusal has driven him mad. I regret that I did not witness this myself. I was afraid he was merely flirting and that he intended to take advantage of you. Curse my jealousy! It is as common to older people to overreach in our opinions as it is common to young people to be foolish. Come, let's go to the king. He must know about Hamlet's strange behavior. If we don't inform him, Hamlet may grieve his family worse than he would by loving a girl beneath his station. *[They go out]*

ACT II

ACT II, SCENE 2

A room in the castle.

[Enter KING, QUEEN, ROSENCRANTZ, GUILDENSTERN, and Attendants]

KING   Welcome, dear Rosencrantz and Guildenstern!
              Moreover that we much did long to see you,
              The need we have to use you did provoke
              Our hasty sending. Something have you heard
              Of Hamlet's transformation; so call it,   5
              Sith nor the exterior nor the inward man
              Resembles that it was. What it should be
              More than his father's death, that thus hath put him
              So much from the understanding of himself,
              I cannot dream of: I entreat you both,   10
              That, being of so young days brought up with him,
              And sith so neighbour'd to his youth and humour,
              That you vouchsafe your rest here in our court
              Some little time; so by your companies
              To draw him on to pleasures, and to gather,   15
              So much as from occasion you may glean,
              Whe'r aught to us unknown afflicts him thus,
              That open'd lies within our remedy.

QUEEN   Good gentlemen, he hath much talk'd of you;
              And sure I am two men there are not living   20
              To whom he more adheres. If it will please you
              To show us so much gentry and good will
              As to expend your time with us awhile,
              For the supply and profit of our hope,
              Your visitation shall receive such thanks   25
              As fits a king's remembrance.

ROSENCRANTZ   Both your majesties
              Might, by the sovereign power you have of us,
              Put your dread pleasures more into command
              Than to entreaty.

GUILDENSTERN   But we both obey,
              And here give up ourselves in the full bent,   30
              To lay our service freely at your feet,
              To be commanded.

KING   Thanks, Rosencrantz and gentle Guildenstern.

QUEEN   Thanks, Guildenstern and gentle Rosencrantz;
              And I beseech you instantly to visit   35

ACT II, SCENE 2

A room in the castle.

[Enter KING, QUEEN, ROSENCRANTZ, GUILDENSTERN, and Attendants]

KING   Welcome, Rosencrantz and Guildenstern! I wanted to see you. I summoned you in haste because I need your help. You may have heard about the change in Hamlet's behavior. Outwardly and inwardly, he isn't the same man he was. It seems unlikely that grief for his father's death would have changed him so. I beg both of you, who grew up with him and know his ways, that you remain here at the castle for a time. While you spend time with him, learn as much about him as you can. Find out what troubles him that I might help him.

QUEEN   Gentlemen, he speaks often of you. I am sure that he has no closer friends than you. If you would be so kind and willing to stay here a while, you might fulfill our hopes. Your visit will earn the kind of thanks that a king can bestow.

ROSENCRANTZ   Both you and the king may command our help rather than ask for it.

GUILDENSTERN   We will obey you and pour ourselves wholeheartedly into your service, if you command it.

KING   Thanks, Rosencrantz and kind Guildenstern.

QUEEN   Thanks, Guildenstern and kind Rosencrantz. Go immediately to Hamlet, who is too severely changed.

ACT II

TRANSLATION

	My too much changed son. Go, some of you, And bring these gentlemen where Hamlet is.	
GUILDENSTERN	Heavens make our presence and our practices Pleasant and helpful to him!	
QUEEN	Ay, amen! *[Exeunt ROSENCRANTZ, GUILDENSTERN, and some Attendants. Enter POLONIUS]*	
POLONIUS	The ambassadors from Norway, my good lord, Are joyfully return'd.	40
KING	Thou still hast been the father of good news.	
POLONIUS	Have I, my Lord? Assure you, my good liege, I hold my duty, as I hold my soul, Both to my God and to my gracious king; And I do think—or else this brain of mine Hunts not the trail of policy so sure As it hath us'd to do—that I have found The very cause of Hamlet's lunacy.	45
KING	O! speak of that; that do I long to hear.	50
POLONIUS	Give first admittance to the ambassadors; My news shall be the fruit to that great feast.	
KING	Thyself do grace to them, and bring them in. *[Exit POLONIUS]* He tells me, my dear Gertrude, he hath found The head and source of all your son's distemper.	55
QUEEN	I doubt it is no other but the main; His father's death, and our o'erhasty marriage.	
KING	Well, we shall sift him. *[Re-enter POLONIUS, with VOLTIMAND and CORNELIUS]* Welcome, my good friends! Say, Voltimand, what from our brother Norway?	
VOLTIMAND	Most fair return of greetings and desires. Upon our first, he sent out to suppress His nephew's levies, which to him appear'd To be a preparation 'gainst the Polack; But, better look'd into, he truly found It was against your highness: whereat griev'd, That so his sickness, age, and impotence Was falsely borne in hand, sends out arrests On Fortinbras; which he, in brief, obeys, Receives rebuke from Norway, and, in fine, Makes vow before his uncle never more	60 65 70

Some of you courtiers, take these men to Hamlet.

GUILDENSTERN May Heaven allow our visit and our activities to please and soothe him!

QUEEN Yes, so be it! *[ROSENCRANTZ and GUILDENSTERN depart with some servants. POLONIUS enters]*

POLONIUS The ambassadors we sent to Norway are safely returned, my lord.

KING You have been the source of good tidings.

POLONIUS Have I, my lord? I assure you that I value duty as I value my soul, both to God and to my generous king. I think—or else my brain deceives me—that I have found the cause of Hamlet's strange behavior.

KING Oh, tell me. I am eager to hear the cause.

POLONIUS First feast on news from the ambassadors from Norway. Let my news be your dessert.

KING You are courteous to them. Show them in. *[POLONIUS leaves]* Polonius tells me, dear Gertrude, that he has found the cause of Hamlet's depression.

QUEEN I think the main reason for his mental disorder is grief for his father's death and disapproval of our hasty marriage.

KING Well, we will question Polonius. *[POLONIUS returns with VOLTIMAND and CORNELIUS]* Welcome, good friends! Tell me, Voltimand, what have you learned from visiting the king of Norway?

VOLTIMAND He sends you kind greetings and wishes. When we first arrived, he stopped his nephew from raising an army, which the king thought was to raise to wage war against Poland. However, when the king investigated further, he discovered that his nephew wanted to attack Denmark. The king was upset that poor health, old age, and loss of strength had allowed this deception. He had Fortinbras arrested. Fortinbras received a scolding from the king of Norway and promised his uncle that he would never again attack Denmark.

ACT II

TRANSLATION

To give the assay of arms against your majesty.
Whereon old Norway, overcome with joy,
Gives him three thousand crowns in annual fee,
And his commission to employ those soldiers,
So levied as before, against the Polack;   75
With an entreaty, herein further shown, *[Giving a paper]*
That it might please you to give quiet pass
Through your dominions for this enterprise,
On such regards of safety and allowance
As therein are set down.

KING   It likes us well;   80
And at our more consider'd time we'll read,
Answer, and think upon this business:
Meantime we thank you for your well-took labour.
Go to your rest; at night we'll feast together:
Most welcome home.
[Exeunt VOLTIMAND and CORNELIUS]

POLONIUS   This business is well ended.   85
My liege, and madam, to expostulate
What majesty should be, what duty is,
Why day is day, night night, and time is time,
Were nothing but to waste night, day, and time.
Therefore, since brevity is the soul of wit,   90
And tediousness the limbs and outward flourishes,
I will be brief. Your noble son is mad:
Mad call I it; for, to define true madness,
What is 't but to be nothing else but mad?
But let that go.

QUEEN   More matter, with less art.   95

POLONIUS   Madam, I swear I use no art at all.
That he is mad, 'tis true; 'tis true 'tis pity;
And pity 'tis 'tis true; a foolish figure;
But farewell it, for I will use no art.
Mad let us grant him, then; and now remains   100
That we find out the cause of this effect,
Or rather say, the cause of this defect,
For this effect defective comes by cause;
Thus it remains, and the remainder thus.
Perpend.   105
I have a daughter, have while she is mine;
Who, in her duty and obedience, mark,
Hath given me this: now, gather, and surmise.
[Reads the letter]
    'To the celestial, and my soul's idol, the most
    beautified Ophelia—

ORIGINAL

The king of Norway was so heartened that he offered Fortinbras an annual stipend of three thousand crowns and assigned him to muster his soldiers for a war on Poland.The king even wrote a request *[hands the KING a document]* that you allow Fortinbras' soldiers to march peacefully through Denmark toward Poland.

KING   I am pleased. I will read the request, write a reply, and ponder the approach of Fortinbras' army. Meanwhile, thanks for your successful journey. Rest. Tonight we will enjoy a feast. Welcome home. *[CORNELIUS and VOLTIMAND go out]*

POLONIUS   The legation to Norway was successful. My king and queen, to debate the meaning of monarchy and duty or why day is day, night is night, and time is time is a waste. Since brevity suits wisdom and longwindedness wearies the body, I will summarize my message. Hamlet is insane. Call it insanity because that is what it is. Don't debate the diagnosis.

QUEEN   Tell us just the plain facts.

POLONIUS   Madam, I am not embroidering the facts. That he is insane is true. The fact is pitiful. It is a pity that I tell the truth—a meaningless statement. But I abandon it; I don't want to be too wordy. Let us accept the diagnosis of insanity. Now we must find out the reason for his peculiar behavior. That is the truth of the matter. Look at it this way. I have a daughter who, out of obedience to her father, has given me this letter. Now, ponder this love note. *To the beautiful Ophelia, a heavenly and adored woman. . . .*

That's an ill phrase, a vile phrase; 'beautified' is a   110
vile phrase; but you shall hear. Thus:
[Reads] In her excellent white bosom, these, &c.

QUEEN   Came this from Hamlet to her?

POLONIUS   Good madam, stay awhile; I will be faithful.
[Reads]
Doubt thou the stars are fire;   *115*
Doubt that the sun doth move;
Doubt truth to be a liar;
But never doubt I love.
O dear Ophelia! I am ill at these numbers: I have not art
to reckon my groans; but that I love thee best,   *120*
O most best! believe it.
Adieu.
Thine evermore, most dear lady, whilst this
machine is to him,
Hamlet.
This in obedience hath my daughter shown me;   125
And more above, hath his solicitings,
As they fell out by time, by means, and place,
All given to mine ear.

KING   But how hath she
Receiv'd his love?

POLONIUS   What do you think of me?

KING   As of a man faithful and honourable.   130

POLONIUS   I would fain prove so. But what might you think,
When I had seen this hot love on the wing—
As I perceiv'd it (I must tell you that)
Before my daughter told me,—what might you,
Or my dear majesty, your queen here, think,   135
If I had play'd the desk or table-book,
Or given my heart a winking, mute and dumb,
Or look'd upon this love with idle sight;
What might you think? No, I went round to work,
And my young mistress thus I did bespeak: 140
'Lord Hamlet is a prince, out of thy star;
This must not be:' and then I prescripts gave her,
That she should lock herself from his resort,

That's an inappropriate statement, but I will continue reading Hamlet's letter to her. It reads, *In her beautiful white breast, these, etcetera. . . .*

QUEEN   Did Hamlet send this letter to her?

POLONIUS   Dear madam, be patient. I will read it word for word. *[POLONIUS reads] Doubt that the stars are hot. Doubt that the sun moves. Doubt that the truth is really a lie. But never doubt that I love you. O dear Ophelia! I write poor poetry. I have no talent to express my emotions. But you can trust that I love you most of all. Goodbye. I am yours forever, dear lady, while I live in this body. Hamlet.* This note my daughter has revealed to me out of obedience. She also told me of his courtship bit by bit as it took place. All of this she confessed to me.

KING   How does she respond to Hamlet's courtship?

POLONIUS   What is your opinion of me?

KING   You are faithful and honorable.

POLONIUS   I intend to be both faithful and honorable. What would you think of me, when I observed this growing love interest — I suspected it before she confessed it. What would Your Highness and the queen think of me if I had kept their love locked up in my desk, or pretended I didn't notice, or considered the matter of no importance? What would you think of me? No, I took immediate action and spoke with my daughter: "Prince Hamlet is royalty, above your status," I said to her. "This love match must not be." Then I ordered her to stay away from Hamlet, receive no messages, and accept no love gifts.

Admit no messengers, receive no tokens.
Which done, she took the fruits of my advice;   145
And he, repulsed,—a short tale to make,—
Fell into a sadness, then into a fast,
Thence to a watch, thence into a weakness,
Thence to a lightness; and by this declension
Into the madness wherein now he raves,   150
And all we mourn for.

KING   Do you think 'tis this?

QUEEN   It may be, very like.

POLONIUS   Hath there been such a time,—I'd fain know that,—
That I have positively said, ''Tis so,'
When it prov'd otherwise?

KING   Not that I know.   155

POLONIUS   Take this from this, if this be otherwise:
[Pointing to his head and shoulder]
If circumstances lead me, I will find
Where truth is hid, though it were hid indeed
Within the centre.

KING   How may we try it further?

POLONIUS   You know sometimes he walks four hours together   160
Here in the lobby.

QUEEN   So he does indeed.

POLONIUS   At such a time I'll loose my daughter to him;
Be you and I behind an arras then;
Mark the encounter; if he love her not,
And be not from his reason fallen thereon,   165
Let me be no assistant for a state,
But keep a farm, and carters.

KING   We will try it.

QUEEN   But look, where sadly the poor wretch comes reading.

POLONIUS   Away! I do beseech you, both away.
I'll board him presently.
[Exeunt KING, QUEEN, and Attendants.
Enter HAMLET, reading]
                            O! give me leave.   170
How does my good Lord Hamlet?

HAMLET   Well, God a-mercy.

POLONIUS   Do you know me, my lord?

HAMLET   Excellent well; you are a fishmonger.

ORIGINAL

She obeyed my good advice. Hamlet, whom she refused, in short, became depressed. He had no appetite. He stopped sleeping. He grew weak and dizzy. From this decline, he sank into raving madness. We all are sorry for his suffering.

KING	Do you accept this explanation?
QUEEN	It sounds likely.
POLONIUS	Have I ever reached a conclusion that proved untrue?

KING	Not that I know of.
POLONIUS	*[Points to his head and shoulder]* If I am wrong, cut my head from my shoulder. I always deduce truth from evidence, even if it is buried in the center of the earth.

KING	How can we test your theory?
POLONIUS	You know that Hamlet sometimes paces the foyer for four hours.
QUEEN	That is true.
POLONIUS	While he is pacing, I will send Ophelia to him. You and I will hide behind the drape and eavesdrop. If we discover that he does not love her and is not insane with passion, I will resign my job as court adviser and become a farmer.

KING	We will test your theory.
QUEEN	Look. Here comes my miserable son reading a book.
POLONIUS	Please go, both of you. I will engage him in conversation. *[The KING, QUEEN, and servants depart. HAMLET enters, reading a book]* Excuse me, Hamlet. How are you?

HAMLET	I am well, thank God.
POLONIUS	Do you recognize me, my lord?
HAMLET	Certainly. You sell fish.

TRANSLATION

POLONIUS	Not I, my lord.	175
HAMLET	Then I would you were so honest a man.	
POLONIUS	Honest, my lord!	
HAMLET	Ay, sir; to be honest, as this world goes, is to be one man picked out of ten thousand.	
POLONIUS	That's very true, my lord.	180
HAMLET	For if the sun breed maggots in a dead dog, being a good kissing carrion,—Have you a daughter?	
POLONIUS	I have, my lord.	
HAMLET	Let her not walk i' the sun: conception is a blessing; but as your daughter may conceive, friend, look to 't.	185
POLONIUS	*[Aside]* How say you by that? Still harping on my daughter: yet he knew me not at first; he said I was a fishmonger: he is far gone, far gone: and truly in my youth I suffered much extremity for love; very near this. I'll speak to him again. What do you read, my lord?	190
HAMLET	Words, words, words.	
POLONIUS	What is the matter, my lord?	
HAMLET	Between who?	195
POLONIUS	I mean the matter that you read, my lord.	
HAMLET	Slanders, sir: for the satirical rogue says here that old men have grey beards, that their faces are wrinkled, their eyes purging thick amber and plumtree gum, and that they have a plentiful lack of wit, together with most weak hams: all which, sir, though I most powerfully and potently believe, yet I hold it not honesty to have it thus set down; for yourself, sir, shall grow old as I am, if, like a crab, you could go backward.	200 205
POLONIUS	*[Aside]* Though this be madness, yet there is method in 't. Will you walk out of the air, my lord?	
HAMLET	Into my grave?	
POLONIUS	Indeed, that is out o' the air. *[Aside]* How pregnant sometimes his replies are! a happiness that often madness hits on, which reason and	210

ORIGINAL

POLONIUS	No I don't, my lord.
HAMLET	I wish you were as honest as a fish seller.
POLONIUS	What do you mean by honest, my lord!
HAMLET	Sir, in this world, only one man in ten thousand is honest.
POLONIUS	That is true, my lord.
HAMLET	If sunshine causes maggots to reproduce in a dead dog, then the sun god kisses rotten flesh. Do you have a daughter?
POLONIUS	Yes, I do, my lord.
HAMLET	Keep her out of the sun. It is a blessing to conceive, but you don't want your daughter to be pregnant.
POLONIUS	*[To himself]* What do you think of that? He is obsessed with Ophelia. Yet he did not recognize me. He thought I was a fish seller. He is seriously disturbed. When I was young, I also suffered from extreme passion. Almost as much as Hamlet suffers. I'll converse with him again. What are you reading, my lord?
HAMLET	Just words.
POLONIUS	On what subject, my lord?
HAMLET	Between what people?
POLONIUS	I mean the topic that you read about, my lord.
HAMLET	I read slanders, sir. The satirist says that old men have gray beards, that their skin is wrinkled, their eyes pour yellow, gummy fluid, and that they make no sense. They also have weak legs. Even though I believe what I read, I think it was falsely written. You, sir, would return to my age if, like a crab, you could go backward.
POLONIUS	*[To himself]* Though this is insane, he makes sense. Will you walk indoors, my lord?
HAMLET	To my grave?
POLONIUS	Certainly, a grave is indoors. *[To himself]* How meaningful his answers seem! He speaks the kind of truth that often comes to madmen.

ACT II

TRANSLATION

| | sanity could not so prosperously be delivered of. I will leave him, and suddenly contrive the means of meeting between him and my daughter. My honourable lord, I will most humbly take my leave of you. | 215 |

HAMLET   You cannot, sir, take from me anything that
I will more willingly part withal; except my life,
except my life, except my life.

POLONIUS   Fare you well, my lord. *[Going]*   220

HAMLET   These tedious old fools!
[Enter ROSENCRANTZ and GUILDENSTERN]

POLONIUS   You go to seek the Lord Hamlet; there he is.

ROSENCRANTZ   *[To POLONIUS]* God save you, sir!
[Exit POLONIUS]

GUILDENSTERN   Mine honoured lord!

ROSENCRANTZ   My most dear lord!   225

HAMLET   My excellent good friends! How dost thou,
Guildenstern? Ah, Rosencrantz! Good lads, how do
ye both?

ROSENCRANTZ   As the indifferent children of the earth.

GUILDENSTERN   Happy in that we are not over-happy;   230
On Fortune's cap we are not the very button.

HAMLET   Nor the soles of her shoe?

ROSENCRANTZ   Neither, my lord.

HAMLET   Then you live about her waist, or in the
middle of her favours?   235

GUILDENSTERN   Faith, her privates we.

HAMLET   In the secret parts of Fortune? O! most true;
she is a strumpet. What news?

ROSENCRANTZ   None, my lord, but that the world's
grown honest.   240

HAMLET   Then is doomsday near; but your news is
not true. Let me question more in particular: what
have you, my good friends, deserved at the hands of
Fortune, that she sends you to prison hither?

GUILDENSTERN   Prison, my lord!   245

HAMLET   Denmark's a prison.

ROSENCRANTZ   Then is the world one.

ORIGINAL

I will depart and think up a way for Hamlet to encounter Ophelia. My lord, I will take my leave.

HAMLET   You can't take anything that I would part with more willingly. Except my life.

POLONIUS   Farewell, my lord. *[He leaves]*

HAMLET   These boring old fools! *[ROSENCRANTZ and GUILDEN-STERN come in]*

POLONIUS   If you are looking for Hamlet, there he is.

ROSENCRANTZ   *[To POLONIUS]* God save you, sir! *[POLONIUS goes out]*

GUILDENSTERN   My honorable lord!

ROSENCRANTZ   My dear lord!

HAMLET   My old friends! How are you, Guildenstern? Ah, Rosencrantz! Good fellows, how are you both?

ROSENCRANTZ   Not bad.

GUILDENSTERN   We are glad to be only so-so. We wouldn't want to be the very tiptop of good luck.

HAMLET   Nor the bottoms of Fortune's feet?

ROSENCRANTZ   Neither extreme, my lord.

HAMLET   Then you live at her middle or in the midst of her charms?

GUILDENSTERN   Truly, we are intimate friends of Fortune.

HAMLET   Close to her private parts? She is certainly a prostitute. What news do you bring?

ROSENCRANTZ   Nothing special, my lord. I think the world's become honest.

HAMLET   It must be near the end of time. But your remark is false. Let me pursue this statement in detail: What have you done to deserve a prison sentence?

GUILDENSTERN   Prison, my lord!

HAMLET   Denmark has become a prison.

ROSENCRANTZ   The whole world is a prison.

TRANSLATION

ACT II

HAMLET	A goodly one; in which there are many confines, wards, and dungeons, Denmark being one o' the worst. 250
ROSENCRANTZ	We think not so, my lord.
HAMLET	Why then, 'tis none to you; for there is nothing either good or bad, but thinking makes it so: to me it is a prison.
ROSENCRANTZ	Why, then your ambition makes it one; 255 'tis too narrow for your mind.
HAMLET	O God! I could be bounded in a nutshell, and count myself a king of infinite space, were it not that I have bad dreams.
GUILDENSTERN	Which dreams, indeed, are ambition, for 260 the very substance of the ambitious is merely the shadow of a dream.
HAMLET	A dream itself is but a shadow.
ROSENCRANTZ	Truly, and I hold ambition of so airy and light a quality that it is but a shadow's shadow. 265
HAMLET	Then are our beggars bodies, and our monarchs and outstretched heroes the beggars' shadows. Shall we to the court? for, by my fay, I cannot reason.
ROSENCRANTZ AND GUILDENSTERN	We'll wait upon you.
HAMLET	No such matter; I will not sort you with the 270 rest of my servants, for, to speak to you like an honest man, I am most dreadfully attended. But, in beaten way of friendship, what make you at Elsinore?
ROSENCRANTZ	To visit you, my lord; no other occasion.
HAMLET	Beggar that I am, I am even poor in thanks; 275 but I thank you: and sure, dear friends, my thanks are too dear a halfpenny. Were you not sent for? Is it your own inclining? Is it a free visitation? Come, come, deal justly with me: come, come; nay, speak.
GUILDENSTERN	What should we say, my lord? 280
HAMLET	Why anything, but to the purpose. You were sent for; and there is a kind of confession in your looks which your modesties have not craft enough to colour: I know the good king and queen have sent for you.

ORIGINAL

HAMLET	It certainly is. In the world's prison there are cells, cell blocks, and dungeons. Denmark is one of the worst of the world's dungeons.
ROSENCRANTZ	We don't agree, my lord.
HAMLET	Maybe not for you. There is nothing either good or bad that can't become a prison in the mind. To me, Denmark is a prison.
ROSENCRANTZ	Ambition makes you feel caged. Denmark is too small for your ambition.
HAMLET	Oh God, I could fit in a nutshell and have plenty of room if I didn't suffer from nightmares.
GUILDENSTERN	The cause of your bad dreams is ambition, for the successes of ambitious men are less real than dreams.
HAMLET	A dream is only a shadow.
ROSENCRANTZ	Yes. I think ambition is so unreal and filmy a quality that it is only a shadow of a shadow.
HAMLET	Then it is beggars who are solid flesh, and kings and overblown heroes are merely the shadows of beggars. Shall we proceed to the main hall? In faith, I can't talk sense.
ROSENCRANTZ AND GUILDENSTERN	We will follow you.
HAMLET	No. I will not class you among my servants. To be truthful, I am poorly served by them. Tell me, friends, why have you come to Elsinore castle?
ROSENCRANTZ	Only to visit you, my lord.
HAMLET	I am so poor that I give poor thanks. But I am glad you are here. Indeed, my friends, my gratitude is not worth half a cent. Didn't someone summon you? Did you come of your own free will? Is this a casual visit? Please, be fair with me. Tell me.
GUILDENSTERN	I don't know what to say, my lord.
HAMLET	Tell me anything, but the real answer. You were summoned. I see the truth in your faces, which you can't conceal. I know the king and queen asked you to visit me.

ACT II

ROSENCRANTZ	To what end, my lord?	285
HAMLET	That you must teach me. But let me conjure you, by the rights of our fellowship, by the consonancy of our youth, by the obligation of our ever-preserved love, and by what more dear a better proposer could charge you withal, be even and direct with me, whether you were sent for or no!	290
ROSENCRANTZ	*[Aside to GUILDENSTERN]* What say you?	
HAMLET	*[Aside]* Nay, then, I have an eye of you. If you love me, hold not off.	295
GUILDENSTERN	My lord, we were sent for.	
HAMLET	I will tell you why; so shall my anticipation prevent your discovery, and your secrecy to the king and queen moult no feather. I have of late,—but wherefore I know not,—lost all my mirth, forgone all custom of exercises; and indeed it goes so heavily with my disposition that this goodly frame, the earth, seems to me a sterile promontory; this most excellent canopy, the air, look you, this brave o'erhanging firmament, this majestical roof fretted with golden fire, why, it appears no other thing to me but a foul and pestilent congregation of vapours. What a piece of work is a man! How noble in reason! how infinite in faculty! in form, in moving, how express and admirable! in action how like an angel! in apprehension how like a god! the beauty of the world! the paragon of animals! And yet, to me, what is this quintessence of dust? man delights not me; no, nor woman neither, though, by your smiling, you seem to say so.	300 305 310
ROSENCRANTZ	My lord, there was no such stuff in my thoughts.	315
HAMLET	Why did you laugh then, when I said, 'man delights not me?'	
ROSENCRANTZ	To think, my lord, if you delight not in man, what lenten entertainment the players shall receive from you: we coted them on the way; and hither are they coming, to offer you service.	320
HAMLET	He that plays the King shall be welcome; his majesty shall have tribute of me; the adventurous Knight shall use his foil and target; the Lover shall not sigh gratis; the Humorous Man shall end his part	325

ROSENCRANTZ	Why would they do that, my lord?
HAMLET	You must explain the reason. For whatever purpose you were summoned, I urge you, by the friendship we enjoyed in boyhood, by our ongoing brotherhood, or for whatever reason, tell me the truth.
ROSENCRANTZ	*[Secretly to GUILDENSTERN]* Should we do as he asks?
HAMLET	*[Privately]* Don't whisper. If you are real friends, tell me the truth.
GUILDENSTERN	My lord, we were summoned to Elsinore.
HAMLET	I will explain the summons. I want to spare you being charged with revealing a secret. Lately, for some unknown reason, I have been depressed and lost interest in my usual activities. My spirits are so low that the earth seems like a lifeless spit of land. The clean air above and sunshine seem like diseased gases. Human life is so wonderful, so filled with logic and talent. The body deserves admiration for its movement. People seem like angels and perceive truth like gods. Humanity is most beautiful, the height of the animal kingdom. However, to me, why should I admire humanity, which was molded from dust? I admire neither men nor women. Your smiles suggest that you disagree.
ROSENCRANTZ	My lord, I was not disagreeing with your thought.
HAMLET	Why did you laugh when I said that I don't admire men?
ROSENCRANTZ	I am amused that, if you don't admire men, the actors will receive meager welcome. We passed the troupe on our way here. They are coming to Elsinore to perform for you.
HAMLET	The actor who plays a king is welcome. I will praise his fake majesty. The actor who plays the lover shall not perform his emotions free of charge. The character actor will perform without interference.

ACT II

TRANSLATION

in peace; the Clown shall make those laugh whose
lungs are tickle o' the sere; and the Lady shall say her
mind freely, or the blank verse shall halt for't. What
players are they?   330

ROSENCRANTZ   Even those you were wont to take
delight in, the tragedians of the city.

HAMLET   How chances it they travel? their residence,
both in reputation and profit, was better both ways.

ROSENCRANTZ   I think their inhibition comes by the   335
means of the late innovation.

HAMLET   Do they hold the same estimation they did
when I was in the city? Are they so followed?

ROSENCRANTZ   No, indeed they are not.

HAMLET   How comes it? Do they grow rusty?   340

ROSENCRANTZ   Nay, their endeavour keeps in the
wonted pace: but there is, sir, an aery of children,
little eyases, that cry out on the top of question, and
are most tyrannically clapped for 't: these are now the
fashion, and so berattle the common stages,—so they   345
call them,—that many wearing rapiers are afraid of
goose-quills, and dare scarce come thither.

HAMLET   What! are they children? who maintains 'em?
how are they escoted? Will they pursue the
quality no longer than they can sing? will they not say   350
afterwards, if they should grow themselves to common
players,—as it is most like, if their means are not
better,—their writers do them wrong, to make them
exclaim against their own succession?

ROSENCRANTZ   Faith, there has been much to-do on   355
both sides: and the nation holds it no sin to tarre them
to controversy: there was, for a while, no money bid for
argument, unless the Poet and the Player went to cuffs
in the question.

HAMLET   Is it possible?   360

GUILDENSTERN   O! there has been much throwing about
of brains.

HAMLET   Do the boys carry it away?

ROSENCRANTZ   Ay, that they do, my lord; Hercules and
his load too.   365

The comedian will entertain those who laugh easily. The female impersonator will speak freely or the line of verse will limp along. What troupe is coming this way?

ROSENCRANTZ   Those that you like from the city.

HAMLET   Why are they touring? They would profit from staying in the city.

ROSENCRANTZ   They are suffering from recent competition.

HAMLET   Are they still popular in the city? Do they have fans?

ROSENCRANTZ   No, they are no longer popular.

HAMLET   Why? Have they stopped rehearsing?

ROSENCRANTZ   No, they work hard at their art. Competing against them are nests of child actors who demand audience attention and receive applause. Child troupes are fashionable. They so unnerve people associated with standard theaters that adult actors fear the taunts of playwrights.

HAMLET   These are troupes made up of children? Who manages them? Who pays them? Will they remain actors only until their voices change? If these child actors continue on stage until they grow up, don't the playwrights wrong them by condemning adult players?

ROSENCRANTZ   There are opinions on both sides of the argument. The public thinks it proper to prolong the argument. At one time, no one profited from arguments unless the playwright and actor pursued debate on stage.

HAMLET   Is this controversy possible?

GUILDENSTERN   Oh, both sides toss their opinions about.

HAMLET   Do the child actors steal adult arguments?

ROSENCRANTZ   Yes, they do, my lord. The children carry as much as Hercules and all his burdens.

ACT II

HAMLET	It is not very strange; for my uncle is King of Denmark, and those that would make mows at him while my father lived, give twenty, forty, fifty, a hundred ducats a-piece for his picture in little. 'Sblood, there is something in this more than natural, if philosophy could find it out. 370 *[Flourish of trumpets within]*
GUILDENSTERN	There are the players.
HAMLET	Gentlemen, you are welcome to Elsinore. Your hands, come then; the appurtenance of welcome is fashion and ceremony: let me comply with you in this 375 garb, lest my extent to the players—which, I tell you, must show fairly outward—should more appear like entertainment than yours. You are welcome; but my uncle-father and aunt-mother are deceived.
GUILDENSTERN	In what, my dear lord? 380
HAMLET	I am but mad north-north-west: when the wind is southerly I know a hawk from a handsaw. *[Enter POLONIUS]*
POLONIUS	Well be with you, gentlemen!
HAMLET	Hark you, Guildenstern; and you too; at each ear a hearer: that great baby you see there is 385 not yet out of his swaddling-clouts.
ROSENCRANTZ	Happily he's the second time come to them; for they say an old man is twice a child.
HAMLET	I will prophesy he comes to tell me of the players; mark it. You say right, sir; o' Monday 390 morning; 'twas so indeed.
POLONIUS	My lord, I have news to tell you.
HAMLET	My lord, I have news to tell you. When Roscius was an actor in Rome,—
POLONIUS	The actors are come hither, my lord. 395
HAMLET	Buz, buz!
POLONIUS	Upon my honour,—
HAMLET	Then came each actor on his ass,—

HAMLET	Isn't it strange that, while Claudius is king of Denmark, those who mocked him while my father was king, now pay twenty, forty, fifty, . . . up to one hundred ducats each for his portrait in miniature? God's blood, there is power in acting, if I can figure out how to use it. *[A burst of trumpet calls in the castle]*
GUILDENSTERN	The troupe has arrived.
HAMLET	Friends, I welcome you to Elsinore. Let's shake hands. Ritual and courtesy should accompany welcome. Let me greet you formally lest my welcome to the troupe should seem warmer. I welcome you. But my uncle/father and aunt/mother are fooled if they think you will spy on me.
GUILDENSTERN	How are they tricked?
HAMLET	I am crazy only in one direction. When the wind blows the opposite way, I know an ax from a saw. *[POLONIUS comes in]*
POLONIUS	Greetings, gentlemen!
HAMLET	Notice, Guildenstern, and you too, Rosencrantz, what you say among other listeners. That oversized ninny you see has not outgrown babyhood.
ROSENCRANTZ	Perhaps he is in a second childhood. Old people often return to infancy.
HAMLET	I predict that he will report on the arrival of the acting troupe. Observe him. *[Pretends to carry on a conversation]* You are correct, it was Monday morning.
POLONIUS	My lord, I bring news.
HAMLET	And I have news for you. When Roscius was a stage actor in Rome . . . .
POLONIUS	The theatrical troupe has arrived, my lord.
HAMLET	I already know about them.
POLONIUS	Upon my honor . . . .
HAMLET	Each actor rode here on his ass . . . .

ACT II

TRANSLATION

POLONIUS   The best actors in the world, either for
              tragedy, comedy, history, pastoral, pastoral-comical,   400
              historical-pastoral, tragical-historical, tragical-comical-
              historical-pastoral, scene individable, or poem unlim-
              ited: Seneca cannot be too heavy, nor Plautus too
              light. For the law of writ and the liberty, these are
              the only men.   405

HAMLET   O Jephthah, judge of Israel, what a treasure
              hadst thou!

POLONIUS   What a treasure had he, my lord?

HAMLET   Why,
              One fair daughter and no more,   410
              The which he loved passing well.

POLONIUS   *[Aside]* Still on my daughter.

HAMLET   Am I not i' the right, old Jephthah?

POLONIUS   If you call me Jephthah, my lord, I have a
              daughter that I love passing well.   415

HAMLET   Nay, that follows not.

POLONIUS   What follows, then, my lord?

HAMLET   Why,
              As by lot, God wot.
              And then, you know,   420
              It came to pass, as most like it was.
              The first row of the pious chanson will show you
              more; for look where my abridgment comes.
              [Enter four or five Players]
              You are welcome, masters; welcome, all. I am glad to
              see thee well: welcome, good friends. O, my old friend!   425
              Why, thy face is valanced since I saw thee last: comest
              thou to beard me in Denmark? What! my young
              lady and mistress! By 'r lady, your ladyship is nearer
              heaven than when I saw you last, by the altitude of a
              chopine. Pray God, your voice, like a piece of uncurrent 430
              gold, be not cracked within the ring. Masters,
              you are all welcome. We'll e'en to 't like French
              falconers, fly at anything we see: we'll have a speech
              straight. Come, give us a taste of your quality; come,
              a passionate speech.   435

POLONIUS	They are world famous for tragedy, comedy, history, rustic-dramatic, rustic-humorous, historical-rustic, tragic-historical, tragic-humorous-historical-rustic, complete scenes, and verse that doesn't follow the rules of drama. The Roman tragedian Seneca is not too serious nor the comic Roman playwright Plautus too silly. For classic and modern drama, these are the only actors who can play all types.
HAMLET	Oh Jephthah, Israel's judge, what a treasure you had!
POLONIUS	What was his treasure, my lord?
HAMLET	Why, *his beautiful daughter, whom he loved.*
POLONIUS	*[To himself]* Hamlet is still obsessed with my daughter.
HAMLET	Am I not correct, old Jephthah?
POLONIUS	If I am Jephthah, my lord, then I, too, have a daughter whom I love.
HAMLET	No. That makes no sense.
POLONIUS	What does make sense, my lord?
HAMLET	Why, *By chance, God knows.* Then, you must know, *It happened as it should have.* The first line of the godly ballad will explain more to you. Look, here comes someone who will interrupt my comments. *[Four or five Players enter]* Master actors, welcome. You all are welcome. I am glad to see you in good health. Welcome, good friends. Ah, my old friend! Why, you have grown whiskers since I last saw you. Did you come to chafe me in Denmark? What, my young boy player! By Our Lady, your female performance is closer to heaven than when I last saw you. You have on high heels. I hope that your voice has not changed to a man's voice. Master players, I welcome you all. We'll go at it like French falconers and pounce on anything we see. We'll have you do a speech right away. Give me a sample of your art. Deliver an emotional speech.

ACT II

FIRST PLAYER   What speech, my good lord?

HAMLET   I heard thee speak me a speech once, but it
was never acted; or, if it was, not above once; for
the play, I remember, pleased not the million; 'twas
caviare to the general: but it was—as I received it,   440
and others, whose judgments in such matters cried in
the top of mine—an excellent play, well digested in
the scenes, set down with as much modesty as cunning.
I remember one said there were no sallets in the
lines to make the matter savoury, nor no matter in the   445
phrase that might indict the author of affectation; but
called it an honest method, as wholesome as sweet,
and by very much more handsome than fine. One
speech in it I chiefly loved; 'twas Aeneas' tale to Dido
and thereabout of it especially, where he speaks of   450
Priam's slaughter. If it live in your memory, begin
at this line: let me see, let me see:—
The rugged Pyrrhus, like the Hyrcanian beast,—
'tis not so, it begins with Pyrrhus:—
The rugged Pyrrhus, he, whose sable arm,   455
Black as his purpose, did the night resemble
When he lay couched in the ominous horse,
Hath now this dread and black complexion smear'd
With heraldry more dismal; head to foot
Now is he total gules, horridly trick'd   460
With blood of fathers, mothers, daughters, sons,
Bak'd and impasted with the parching streets,
That lend a tyrannous and damned light
To their vile murders: roasted in wrath and fire,
And thus o'er-sized with coagulated gore,   465
With eyes like carbuncles, the hellish Pyrrhus
Old grandsire Priam seeks.—
So proceed you.

POLONIUS   'Fore God, my lord, well spoken; with
good accent and good discretion.

FIRST PLAYER	Which speech would you like, my lord?
HAMLET	Once, I heard you deliver an oration that was never given as part of a staged play. If it was, it was no more than once. I recall that the play was not very popular. Performing it was like serving caviar to ordinary people. The work—as I heard it and others who share my judgment agreed—was an excellent play. The parts suited the whole. It was written simply, but craftily. One reviewer said that there were no tasty bits in the text to make it spicy and no topic in the dialogue that seemed overdone. The play was straightforward, wholesome, charming, and more elegant than subtle. One speech I liked above all others. It was Aeneas's comment to Queen Dido on the subject of the murder of Priam, king of Troy. If you still know the speech, begin with this line. Let's see, *The graceless Pyrrhus, like a tiger*—No, that's not right. It starts with Pyrrhus . . . . *The graceless Pyrrhus had a black arm as dark as his plot while he hid in the Trojan horse. Pyrrhus seemed more dire and evil with his dismal insignia. From head to foot, he wears red—the blood of fathers, mothers, daughters, sons, baked to a paste on the burning streets of Troy. The fire blazes with a doomed glow on the Greek slaughter of Trojans. Heated with anger and vengeance and grown massive from bloody gobs, with eyes like rubies, the hellish Pyrrhus tracked poor old Priam . . . .* Continue on from there.

ACT II

POLONIUS	By God, my lord, you are a good actor. You display both enunciation and interpretation.

TRANSLATION

FIRST PLAYER	Anon, he finds him 470

Striking too short at Greeks; his antique sword,
Rebellious to his arm, lies where it falls,
Repugnant to command. Unequal match'd,
Pyrrhus at Priam drives; in rage strikes wide;
But with the whiff and wind of his fell sword   475
The unnerved father falls. Then senseless Ilium,
Seeming to feel this blow, with flaming top
Stoops to his base, and with a hideous crash
Takes prisoner Pyrrhus' ear: for lo! his sword,
Which was declining on the milky head   480
Of reverend Priam, seem'd i' the air to stick:
So, as a painted tyrant, Pyrrhus stood,
And like a neutral to his will and matter,
Did nothing.
But, as we often see, against some storm,   485
A silence in the heavens, the rack stand still,
The bold winds speechless and the orb below
As hush as death, anon the dreadful thunder
Doth rend the region; so, after Pyrrhus' pause,
Aroused vengeance sets him new a-work;   490
And never did the Cyclops' hammer fall
On Mars's armour, forg'd for proof eterne,
With less remorse than Pyrrhus' bleeding sword
Now falls on Priam.
Out, out, thou strumpet, Fortune! All you gods,   495
In general synod, take away her power;
Break all the spokes and fellies from her wheel,
And bowl the round nave down the hill of heaven,
As low as to the fiends!

POLONIUS	This is too long.	500

HAMLET	It shall to the barber's with your beard.

Prithee, say on: he's for a jig or a tale of bawdry,
or he sleeps. Say on; come to Hecuba.

FIRST PLAYER	But who, O! who had seen the mobled queen—

HAMLET	'The mobled queen?'—	505

POLONIUS	That's good; 'mobled queen' is good.

FIRST PLAYER	Soon, Pyrrhus finds Priam lashing ineffectually at the Greek enemy. His traditional sword, unsuited to his arm, falls to the ground because the king is too old and weak to wield it. In this unequal match, Pyrrhus lunges at Priam. Pyrrhus is so angry that he misses. But the old man collapses from the sweep of the deadly weapon. Then Troy seems to feel the attack on its king. From burning walls crashing down to the ground, the destruction stuns Pyrrhus. Pyrrhus's sword, which he raised over the white hair of old Priam, pauses in midair. Like a painting, Pyrrhus halted in mid-strike. As though undecided about striking Priam, he took no action. Just as a thunderstorm may suddenly fall silent and the winds die down. The Earth becomes totally quiet. Then a new peal of thunder shatters the area. Similarly, after Pyrrhus stopped in the act of striking Priam, a new surge of vengeance animates him again. Cyclops's hammer never struck Mars's eternal armor with less pity than Pyrrhus's bloody blade fell on Priam. Away, Fortune, you deceiver! The whole family of gods should strip her of power. Break the spokes and rim of her wheel and roll the hub down heaven's slope all the way to the demons in hell!

POLONIUS	This is too long a speech.
HAMLET	Send it to the barber with your beard. Please, continue the speech. Polonius prefers a frolic or a vulgar tale, or else he falls asleep in the theater. Continue. Come to the part about Hecuba.
FIRST PLAYER	But who has seen the muffled queen . . . .
HAMLET	The muffled Queen? . . . .
POLONIUS	I like that part. "Muffled queen" is good.

TRANSLATION

FIRST PLAYER	Run barefoot up and down, threat'ning the flames
	With bisson rheum; a clout upon that head
	Where late the diadem stood; and, for a robe,
	About her lank and all o'er-teemed loins, 510
	A blanket, in the alarm of fear caught up;
	Who this had seen, with tongue in venom steep'd,
	'Gainst Fortune's state would treason have pronounc'd:
	But if the gods themselves did see her then,
	When she saw Pyrrhus make malicious sport 515
	In mincing with his sword her husband's limbs,
	The instant burst of clamour that she made—
	Unless things mortal move them not at all—
	Would have made milch the burning eyes of heaven,
	And passion in the gods. 520

POLONIUS Look! wh'er he has not turned his colour
and has tears in 's eyes. Prithee, no more.

HAMLET 'Tis well; I'll have thee speak out the rest
soon. Good my lord, will you see the players well
bestowed? Do you hear, let them be well used; for 525
they are the abstracts and brief chronicles of the time:
after your death you were better have a bad epitaph
than their ill report while you live.

POLONIUS My lord, I will use them according to their
desert. 530

HAMLET God's bodikins, man, much better; use every
man after his desert, and who shall 'scape whipping?
Use them after your own honour and dignity:
the less they deserve, the more merit is in your
bounty. Take them in. 535

POLONIUS Come, sirs.

HAMLET Follow him, friends: we'll hear a play
to-morrow.
    [Exit POLONIUS, with all the Players but the First]
Dost thou hear me, old friend; can you play The
Murder of Gonzago? 540

FIRST PLAYER Ay, my lord.

ORIGINAL

FIRST PLAYER	*She runs in bare feet up and down Troy, threatening the fire with her tears. Because of the suddenness of the alarm, she wears a scarf on her head rather than her crown. For a robe, about her birth-ravaged body and legs, she clutches a blanket. Anyone who saw Hecuba's actions, with toxic words, would have charged luck with treason. If the gods had looked down on her as she watched Pyrrhus enjoy chopping her husband's limbs with a sword, the outcry that she raised—unless nothing human moves the gods—would have moistened the burning eyes of the sky and aroused emotion in them.*

POLONIUS	Look! The actor has changed color and is weeping. Please, no more of this speech.
HAMLET	Good work! I will have you finish the speech later. Polonius, will you provide for the troupe? Listen to me. Treat them well, for actors condense the history of our time. After you die, you are better off having a bad epitaph on your tombstone than a bad reputation while you were alive.
POLONIUS	My lord, I will treat them well, as they deserve.
HAMLET	God's body, Polonius, treat them better than they deserve. If you gave men what they deserved, we would all merit a whipping. Treat them with honor and dignity. The more you award them, the more you earn for your generosity. Escort them into the castle.
POLONIUS	Come in, sirs.
HAMLET	Follow him, friends. We will enjoy a play tomorrow. *[POLONIUS departs with all the troupe except one]* Tell me, old friend, can you perform *The Murder of Gonzago?*
FIRST PLAYER	Yes, my lord.

HAMLET	We'll ha't tomorrow night. You could, for a need, study a speech of some dozen or sixteen lines, which I would set down and insert in 't, could you not?

545

FIRST PLAYER	Ay, my lord.
HAMLET	Very well. Follow that lord; and look you mock him not. *[Exit First Player. To ROSENCRANTZ and GUILDENSTERN]* My good friends, I'll leave you till night; you are welcome to Elsinore.

550

ROSENCRANTZ	Good my lord! *[Exeunt ROSENCRANTZ and GUILDENSTERN]*
HAMLET	Ay, so, God be wi' ye! Now I am alone. O! what a rogue and peasant slave am I: Is it not monstrous that this player here, But in a fiction, in a dream of passion, Could force his soul so to his own conceit That from her working all his visage wann'd, Tears in his eyes, distraction in 's aspect, A broken voice, and his whole function suiting With forms to his conceit? and all for nothing! For Hecuba! What's Hecuba to him or he to Hecuba That he should weep for her? What would he do Had he the motive and the cue for passion That I have? He would drown the stage with tears, And cleave the general ear with horrid speech, Make mad the guilty and appal the free, Confound the ignorant, and maze indeed The very faculties of eyes and ears. Yet I, A dull and muddy-mettled rascal, peak, Like John-a-dreams, unpregnant of my cause, And can say nothing; no, not for a king, Upon whose property and most dear life A damn'd defeat was made. Am I a coward? Who calls me villain? breaks my pate across? Plucks off my beard and blows it in my face? Tweaks me by the nose? gives me the lie i' the throat, As deep as to the lungs? Who does me this, ha? 'Swonds, I should take it, for it cannot be But I am pigeon-liver'd, and lack gall To make oppression bitter, or ere this I should have fatted all the region kites With this slave's offal. Bloody, bawdy villian!

555

560

565

570

575

580

ORIGINAL

HAMLET	Perform it tomorrow night. Could you learn a speech of twelve or sixteen lines that I will compose and add to the text?
FIRST PLAYER	Yes, my lord.
HAMLET	Excellent. Follow Polonius, but don't ridicule him. *[The First Player departs. To ROSENCRANTZ and GUILDEN-STERN]* My good friends, I leave you to yourselves until tonight. I welcome you to Elsinore castle.
ROSENCRANTZ	My lord. *[ROSENCRANTZ and GUILDENSTERN go out]*
HAMLET	Yes, God be with you! Now that I am alone, I feel like a rascal and slave. Is it not grotesque that an actor can pretend emotion and cause his imagination to summon a white face and weeping eyes? He pretended to be frenzied, his voice cracked; even his body language conveyed emotion. It was all pretense! For the Trojan queen Hecuba! Why should an actor weep for Hecuba, queen of the ancient Trojans? How would he behave if he had my reason for grief and anger? He would flood the stage with tears and split the audience's ears with terrifying speech. He would drive the guilty to madness and appall the innocent. He would astound the ignorant and amaze their sight and hearing. Yet, I, a spiritless dullard, mope about like an aimless dreamer. And I can say nothing. I make no charge in defense of a king whose realm and life were smashed. Am I a coward? Who calls me a criminal, smacks me on the head, pulls my beard and blows the hair in my face, tweaks my nose, and calls me a liar from throat to lungs? Why am I such a weakling? God's wounds, I should take ridicule for I am a chicken-livered sissy who lacks the spirit to inflict bitter retribution. Otherwise, I would have fattened up the kingdom's vultures with Claudius's guts. Blood-thirsty, adulterous criminal!

ACT II

Remorseless, treacherous, lecherous, kindless villain! 585
O! vengeance!
Why, what an ass am I! This is most brave
That I, the son of a dear father murder'd,
Prompted to my revenge by heaven and hell,
Must, like a whore, unpack my heart with words, 590
And fall a-cursing, like a very drab,
A scullion! Fie upon 't foh!
About, my brain; hum, I have heard,
That guilty creatures sitting at a play
Have by the very cunning of the scene 595
Been struck so to the soul that presently
They have proclaim'd their malefactions;
For murder, though it have no tongue, will speak
With most miraculous organ. I'll have these players
Play something like the murder of my father 600
Before mine uncle; I'll observe his looks;
I'll tent him to the quick: if he but blench
I know my course. The spirit that I have seen
May be the devil: and the devil hath power
To assume a pleasing shape; yea, and perhaps 605
Out of my weakness and my melancholy—
As he is very potent with such spirits—
Abuses me to damn me. I'll have grounds
More relative than this: the play's the thing
Wherein I'll catch the conscience of the king. *[Exit]* 610

Oh, revenge, why am I such a fool? This is not brave of me. I, the son of a dear wronged father, pushed to avenge him by heaven and hell, I must, like a whore, act out my heart's desire only with words and fall swearing, like a slut, a kitchen slave! Shame on me! Get to work, my brain. I have heard that guilty people in an audience have been so moved by a play that they confess their crimes. For murderers, who conceal their crimes, will confess through unusual circumstances. I will have this troupe act out a copy of my father's murder for the entertainment of my uncle Claudius. I will observe his reaction. I'll probe him to the soul. If he flinches, I will know what to do. The spirit that I saw on the battlements may be Satan. Satan has the power to transform himself into pleasant shapes. Perhaps, because of my weakness and grief, the devil, a powerful manipulator, forces me to damnation. I will have evidence more real than the appearance of a ghost. The play will reveal King Claudius's conscience. *[HAMLET goes out]*

ACT II

ACT III, SCENE 1

A room in the castle.

[Enter KING, QUEEN, POLONIUS, OPHELIA, ROSENCRANTZ, and GUILDENSTERN]

KING	And can you, by no drift of conference,	
	Get from him why he puts on this confusion,	
	Grating so harshly all his days of quiet	
	With turbulent and dangerous lunacy?	
ROSENCRANTZ	He does confess he feels himself distracted;	5
	But from what cause he will by no means speak.	
GUILDENSTERN	Nor do we find him forward to be sounded,	
	But, with a crafty madness, keeps aloof,	
	When we would bring him on to some confession	
	Of his true state.	
QUEEN	Did he receive you well?	10
ROSENCRANTZ	Most like a gentleman.	
GUILDENSTERN	But with much forcing of his disposition.	
ROSENCRANTZ	Niggard of question, but of our demands	
	Most free in his reply.	
QUEEN	Did you assay him	
	To any pastime?	15
ROSENCRANTZ	Madam, it so fell out that certain players	
	We o'er-raught on the way; of these we told him,	
	And there did seem in him a kind of joy	
	To hear of it: they are here about the court,	
	And, as I think, they have already order	20
	This night to play before him.	
POLONIUS	'Tis most true;	
	And he beseech'd me to entreat your majesties	
	To hear and see the matter.	
KING	With all my heart; and it doth much content me	
	To hear him so inclin'd.	25
	Good gentlemen, give him a further edge,	
	And drive his purpose on to these delights.	
ROSENCRANTZ	We shall, my lord.	
	[Exeunt ROSENCRANTZ and GUILDENSTERN]	

ACT III, SCENE 1

A room in the castle.

[Enter KING, QUEEN, POLONIUS, OPHELIA, ROSENCRANTZ, and GUILDENSTERN]

KING   Can you find out by some roundabout means why he acts so confused, destroying his past sense with turbulent and disturbing madness?

ROSENCRANTZ   He admits that he is distracted, but he won't say why.

GUILDENSTERN   He was not eager to answer questions. With subtle madness, he remains distant when we try to discuss his current state.

QUEEN   Did he welcome you?

ROSENCRANTZ   He was as courteous as a gentleman.

GUILDENSTERN   But he had to make himself be polite.

ROSENCRANTZ   He avoided asking us questions, but replied freely when we pressed him.

QUEEN   Did you try to engage him in any activity?

ROSENCRANTZ   Madam, it happened that we passed an acting troupe on our way here. When we informed him of its approach, he seemed delighted at the news. The actors have arrived at court and are under orders to perform for Hamlet tonight.

POLONIUS   This is true. And Hamlet has asked me to invite your royal highnesses to attend the play.

KING   Truly, I am pleased to hear that he wants to see a play. Gentlemen, encourage him to take pleasure in drama.

ROSENCRANTZ   We will, my lord. *[ROSENCRANTZ and GUILDENSTERN depart]*

TRANSLATION

KING	Sweet Gertrude, leave us too;
	For we have closely sent for Hamlet hither,
	That he, as 'twere by accident, may here 30
	Affront Ophelia.
	Her father and myself, lawful espials,
	Will so bestow ourselves, that, seeing, unseen,
	We may of their encounter frankly judge,
	And gather by him, as he is behav'd, 35
	If 't be the affliction of his love or no
	That thus he suffers for.
QUEEN	I shall obey you.
	And for your part, Ophelia, I do wish
	That your good beauties be the happy cause
	Of Hamlet's wildness; so shall I hope your virtues 40
	Will bring him to his wonted way again,
	To both your honours.
OPHELIA	Madam, I wish it may.
	[Exit QUEEN]
POLONIUS	Ophelia, walk you here. Gracious, so please you,
	We will bestow ourselves. *[To OPHELIA]* Read
	on this book;
	That show of such an exercise may colour 45
	Your loneliness. We are oft to blame in this,
	'Tis too much prov'd, that with devotion's visage
	And pious action we do sugar o'er
	The devil himself.
KING	*[Aside]* O! 'tis too true;
	How smart a lash that speech doth give my conscience! 50
	The harlot's cheek, beautied with plastering art,
	Is not more ugly to the thing that helps it
	Than is my deed to my most painted word:
	O heavy burden!
POLONIUS	I hear him coming; let's withdraw my lord. 55
	[Exeunt KING and POLONIUS. Enter HAMLET]

KING	Sweet Gertrude, leave me with Polonius. We have sent for Hamlet so he may encounter Ophelia as though by coincidence. Polonius and I will hide and eavesdrop to determine by his behavior if he is lovesick or not.
QUEEN	I will do as you ask. And, Ophelia, I hope that your good qualities are the source of Hamlet's unpredictable behavior. I hope that your merits will make him sane again, to the honor of you both.
OPHELIA	Madam, I wish the same as you. *[The QUEEN goes out]*
POLONIUS	Ophelia, walk here. If you please, we will hide. *[To OPHELIA]* Read this book to give the appearance of being lonely. People are often blamed, and rightly so, for using the appearance of religious devotion to coat evil intent.
KING	*[To himself]* Oh, this is true. How sharp a lash Polonius's speech has assaulted my conscience! The slut's cheek, coated in makeup, is no more ugly to her face powder than is my crime to my lying words. I bear a heavy burden.
POLONIUS	I hear Hamlet approaching. Let's hide, my lord. *[The KING and POLONIUS depart. HAMLET enters]*

ACT III

HAMLET	To be, or not to be: that is the question:	
	Whether 'tis nobler in the mind to suffer	
	The slings and arrows of outrageous fortune,	
	Or to take arms against a sea of troubles,	
	And by opposing end them? To die: to sleep;	60
	No more; and, by a sleep to say we end	
	The heart-ache and the thousand natural shocks	
	That flesh is heir to, 'tis a consummation	
	Devoutly to be wish'd. To die, to sleep;	
	To sleep: perchance to dream: ay, there's the rub;	65
	For in that sleep of death what dreams may come	
	When we have shuffled off this mortal coil,	
	Must give us pause. There's the respect	
	That makes calamity of so long life;	
	For who would bear the whips and scorns of time,	70
	The oppressor's wrong, the proud man's contumely,	
	The pangs of dispriz'd love, the law's delay,	
	The insolence of office, and the spurns	
	That patient merit of the unworthy takes,	
	When he himself might his quietus make	75
	With a bare bodkin? who would fardels bear,	
	To grunt and sweat under a weary life,	
	But that the dread of something after death,	
	The undiscover'd country from whose bourn	
	No traveller returns, puzzles the will,	80
	And makes us rather bear those ills we have	
	Than fly to others that we know not of?	
	Thus conscience does make cowards of us all;	
	And thus the native hue of resolution	
	Is sicklied o'er with the pale cast of thought,	85
	And enterprises of great pitch and moment	
	With this regard their currents turn awry,	
	And lose the name of action. Soft you now!	
	The fair Ophelia! Nymph, in thy orisons	
	Be all my sins remember'd.	

OPHELIA   Good my lord,   90
How does your honour for this many a day?

HAMLET   I humbly thank you; well, well, well.

OPHELIA   My lord, I have remembrances of yours,
That I have longed long to re-deliver;
pray you, now receive them.

HAMLET   No, not I;   95
I never gave you aught.

ORIGINAL

HAMLET	I debate whether to be or not to be an avenger. Is it more honorable to endure the effects of fate or to arm myself against a host of crimes and end them? To die, to sleep forever. . . . To live no more. . . : Dying would end my heartache and the thousand other pains that assault people. I devoutly wish my life would end. To die, to sleep forever. . . . Sleeping may bring me dreams, that's the fearful possibility. After I die, the dreams that assault me when I have departed my body are a point worth considering. That's the aspect that turns a long life into a catastrophe. Who would knowingly seek a life of pain and oppression, insults, the hurt of rejected love, delayed justice, arrogant officials, and the snubs belonging to the unworthy when a stab of the knife could end all suffering? Who would shoulder burdens, and grunt and sweat with weariness, were it not for the dread of the afterlife, that mysterious realm that no one returns from? Who would continue puzzling and bearing pain except that the alternative is to embrace the unknown? Thus, we concentrate so long on the unknown that we lose our nerve. And actions of great height and importance go wrong and lose momentum. Hush! The beautiful Ophelia! Lovely sprite, remember my sins in your prayers.

OPHELIA	My lord, how have you been?
HAMLET	Thank you, I am well.
OPHELIA	My lord, I have some keepsakes that I wanted to return. Please, accept them now.
HAMLET	No. I never gave you anything.

TRANSLATION

OPHELIA	My honour'd lord, you know right well you did; And, with them, words of so sweet breath compos'd As made the things more rich: their perfume lost, Take these again; for to the noble mind Rich gifts wax poor when givers prove unkind. There, my lord.	100
HAMLET	Ha, ha! are you honest?	
OPHELIA	My lord!	
HAMLET	Are you fair?	105
OPHELIA	What means your lordship?	
HAMLET	That if you be honest and fair, your honesty should admit no discourse to your beauty.	
OPHELIA	Could beauty, my lord, have better commerce than with honesty?	110
HAMLET	Ay, truly; for the power of beauty will sooner transform honesty from what it is to a bawd than the force of honesty can translate beauty into his likeness: this was sometime a paradox, but the time gives it proof. I did love you once.	115
OPHELIA	Indeed, my lord, you made me believe so.	
HAMLET	You should not have believed me; for virtue cannot so inoculate our old stock but we shall relish of it: I loved you not.	
OPHELIA	I was the more deceived.	120
HAMLET	Get thee to a nunnery: why wouldst thou be a breeder of sinners? I am myself indifferent honest; but yet I could accuse me of such things that it were better my mother had not borne me. I am very proud, revengeful, ambitious; with more offences at my beck than I have thoughts to put them in, imagination to give them shape, or time to act them in. What should such fellows as I do crawling between heaven and earth? We are arrant knaves, all; believe none of us. Go thy ways to a nunnery. Where's your father?	125 130
OPHELIA	At home, my lord.	
HAMLET	Let the doors be shut upon him, that he may play the fool nowhere but in's own house. Farewell.	
OPHELIA	O! help him, you sweet heavens!	135

OPHELIA	My lord, you know that you did. And with the gifts, you offered sweet words to enrich the items. Now that the sweetness of your words is gone, I want to return these. To a noble person, expensive gifts seem cheap when the giver proves unkind. There, my lord.
HAMLET	Aha, are you pure?
OPHELIA	My lord!
HAMLET	Are you fair?
OPHELIA	What do you mean?
HAMLET	To be honest and fair, your purity should have nothing to do with your looks.
OPHELIA	Could beauty have a better associate than honesty, my lord?
HAMLET	Yes, truly. Beauty's strength will turn purity to bawdiness before honesty can turn beauty into chastity. This statement appears to contradict itself, but time will prove it true. I did love you.
OPHELIA	Indeed, my lord, I once believed your vow of love.
HAMLET	You should have doubted me. For goodness cannot upgrade human weakness. Otherwise, we would long for goodness. I didn't love you.
OPHELIA	You tricked me.
HAMLET	Go to a convent. Why would you want to give birth to sinful offspring? I am moderately good. Yet I could accuse myself of such wrongs that it would be better that I had not been born. I am proud, vengeful, and ambitious. I have more sins to confess than I have thoughts to contain them, imagination to engineer them, or time to commit them. Why should so sinful a man as I live on earth? All men are wandering evildoers. Don't trust any of us. Go to a convent. Where is Polonius?
OPHELIA	At home, my lord.
HAMLET	Let him stay there lest he act the fool anywhere but at home. Farewell.
OPHELIA	Oh, heaven, cure Hamlet!

ACT III

TRANSLATION

HAMLET	If thou dost marry, I'll give thee this plague
	for thy dowry: be thou as chaste as ice, as pure as
	snow, thou shalt not escape calumny. Get thee to a
	nunnery, go; farewell. Or, if thou wilt needs marry,
	marry a fool; for wise men know well enough what　140
	monsters you make of them. To a nunnery, go; and
	quickly too. Farewell.

OPHELIA　　O heavenly powers, restore him!

HAMLET　　I have heard of your paintings too, well
enough; God hath given you one face, and you make　145
yourselves another: you jig, you amble, and you lisp,
and nickname God's creatures, and make your wantonness
your ignorance. Go to, I'll no more on 't: it
hath made me mad. I say, we will have no more
marriages; those that are married already, all but one,　150
shall live; the rest shall keep as they are. To a
nunnery, go. *[Exit]*

OPHELIA　　O! what a noble mind is here o'erthrown:
The courtier's, soldier's, scholar's, eye, tongue, sword;
The expectancy and rose of the fair state,　155
The glass of fashion and the mould of form,
The observ'd of all observers, quite, quite down!
And I, of ladies most deject and wretched,
That suck'd the honey of his music vows,
Now see that noble and most sovereign reason,　160
Like sweet bells jangled, out of tune and harsh;
That unmatch'd form and feature of blown youth
Blasted with ecstasy: O! woe is me,
To have seen what I have seen, see what I see!
[Re-enter KING and POLONIUS]

KING　　Love! his affections do not that way tend;　165
Nor what he spake, though it lack'd form a little,
Was not like madness. There's something in his soul
O'er which his melancholy sits on brood;
And, I do doubt, the hatch and the disclose
Will be some danger; which for to prevent,　170
I have in quick determination
Thus set it down: he shall with speed to England,
For the demand of our neglected tribute:
Haply the seas and countries different
With variable objects shall expel　175
This something-settled matter in his heart,
Whereon his brains still beating puts him thus
From fashion of himself. What think you on 't?

ORIGINAL

HAMLET	If you marry, I offer this curse for a dowry—if you be as pure as ice, as untouched as snow, you will still not avoid slander. Go to a convent, go. Farewell. Or if you choose to marry, wed a fool. Wise men anticipate that wives will turn them into monsters. Go to a convent quickly. Farewell.
OPHELIA	Oh heavenly powers, restore his sanity!
HAMLET	I have learned that you wear makeup. God gives you women faces that you turn into something else. You sway, you slink, and you lisp like a coquette. And you make up names for God's creatures. In your misbehavior, you pretend to be unaware of wrongdoing. Stop, I want no more of your flirtation. It has made me crazy. I declare that I will endure no more weddings. Those that are already wed—all but one—shall survive. The rest shall remain celibate. Go to a convent. *[He departs]*
OPHELIA	Oh, what a noble intelligence is destroyed. He was a courtier, soldier, scholar—handsome, smart, and bold. The hope of Denmark, a stylish man, well built to draw the observer's eye. He is struck down! And I, the most dejected and sad of women, who once tasted the sweetness of his musical words, I now see his mind jangling like untuned bells. That matchless shape and youthful face overcome with madness. Oh, I miss what used to be. *[The KING and POLONIUS appear]*
KING	Hamlet is not in love. And what he spoke, though it wandered, it was not the raving of a madman. There is something troubling his spirit. When he eventually reveals his trouble, he might be dangerous to himself and others. To prevent this danger, I have formulated a plan. He will demand that England pay an overdue tax to Denmark. Perhaps by enjoying the sea air and ocean travel, he may dislodge the trouble from his heart to keep his mind from brooding and altering his usual behavior. What do you think of my plan?

ACT III

TRANSLATION

POLONIUS	It shall do well: but yet do I believe
	The origin and commencement of his grief 180
	Sprung from neglected love. How now, Ophelia!
	You need not tell us what Lord Hamlet said;
	We heard it all. My lord, do as you please;
	But, if you hold it fit, after the play,
	Let his queen mother all alone entreat him 185
	To show his grief: let her be round with him;
	And I'll be plac'd, so please you, in the ear
	Of all their conference. If she find him not,
	To England send him, or confine him where
	Your wisdom best shall think. 190
KING	It shall be so:
	Madness in great ones must not unwatch'd go.
	[Exeunt]

POLONIUS   It should work. But I still think his sorrow comes from rejected love. Ophelia, you don't need to summarize what Hamlet said. We overhead all of it. My lord, do as you have decided. If you think it fitting, after the play, let Gertrude speak with Hamlet alone to learn his sorrow. Let her speak openly with him. I will hide, if you don't mind, and overhear their discussion. If she fails to discover his trouble, then send him to England or keep him where you think best.

KING   That is a good plan. Madness in important people should not thrive unwatched. *[They depart]*

ACT III, SCENE 2

A hall in the castle.

[Enter HAMLET and certain Players]

HAMLET Speak the speech, I pray you, as I pronounced
it to you, trippingly on the tongue; but if you
mouth it, as many of your players do, I had as lief the
town-crier spoke my lines. Nor do not saw the air too
much with your hand, thus; but use all gently: for   5
in the very torrent, tempest, and—as I may say—
whirlwind of passion, you must acquire and beget
a temperance, that may give it smoothness. O! it
offends me to the soul to hear a robustious periwig-
pated fellow tear a passion to tatters, to very rags, to   10
split the ears of the groundlings, who for the most part
are capable of nothing but inexplicable dumb-shows
and noise: I would have such a fellow whipped for
o'er-doing Termagant; it out-herods Herod: pray you,
avoid it.   15

FIRST PLAYER I warrant your honour.

HAMLET Be not too tame neither, but let your own
discretion be your tutor: suit the action to the word,
the word to the action; with this special observance,
that you o'erstep not the modesty of nature; for any-   20
thing so overdone is from the purpose of playing, whose
end, both at the first and now, was and is, to hold, as
'twere, the mirror up to nature; to show virtue her
own feature, scorn her own image, and the very age and
body of the time his form and pressure. Now, this   25
overdone, or come tardy off, though it make the
unskilful laugh, cannot but make the judicious grieve;
the censure of which one must in your allowance o'er-
weigh a whole theatre of others. O! there be players
that I have seen play, and heard others praise, and   30
that highly, not to speak it profanely, that, neither
having the accent of Christians nor the gait of Christian,
pagan, nor man, have so strutted and bellowed
that I have thought some of nature's journeymen
had made men and not made them well, they   35
imitated humanity so abominably.

ORIGINAL

ACT III, SCENE 2

A hall in the castle.

[Enter HAMLET and certain Players]

HAMLET
Perform your speech the way I said it, easily on the tongue. If you exaggerate the speech, as many of your actors do, I would rather have the town crier speak my lines. And don't gesture too much with your hands, like this; but move about gently. In the raging and passion of words, you must control the speech and make it smooth. I am offended when I hear a bewigged player rend a speech to rags and split the ears of the poor, uneducated members of the audience standing in the pit below the stage, who are usually incapable of enjoying anything but pantomime. I would have a ham actor punished for overacting. Such displays overdo the tyranny of Herod. Please, avoid overacting.

FIRST PLAYER
I guarantee that I will obey you.

HAMLET
But don't be too tame. Let your gut instinct be your guide. Suit the action to the text and fit your speeches to the action. I urge you not to overdo normal behavior. Overacting retreats from the purpose of drama, which is to mimic reality. Good acting displays goodness just as it is. If you overact or miss your cue, even if the crude audience laughs, the true critic will dislike it. You must value the true critic over all the other listeners. There are actors who earn praise even though they lack the appearance and speech of their parts. Such hams have so strutted and yelled that they seemed like amateurish copies of real people.

ACT III

TRANSLATION

FIRST PLAYER	I hope we have reformed that indifferently with us.
HAMLET	O! reform it altogether. And let those that play your clowns speak no more than is set down 40 for them; for there be of them that will themselves laugh, to set on some quantity of barren spectators to laugh too, though in the mean time some necessary question of the play be then to be considered; that's villainous, and shows a most pitiful ambition in the 45 fool that uses it. Go, make you ready. *[Exit Players]* *[Enter POLONIUS, ROSENCRANTZ, and GUILDENSTERN]* How now, my lord! will the king hear this piece of work?
POLONIUS	And the queen too, and that presently.
HAMLET	Bid the players make haste. 50 *[Exit POLONIUS]* Will you two help to hasten them?
GUILDENSTERN AND ROSENCRANTZ	We will, my lord. *[Exeunt ROSENCRANTZ and GUILDENSTERN]*
HAMLET	What, ho! Horatio! *[Enter HORATIO]*
HORATIO	Here, sweet lord, at your service.
HAMLET	Horatio, thou art e'en as just a man 55 As e'er my conversation cop'd withal.
HORATIO	O! my dear lord,—

FIRST PLAYER	I hope we have rid ourselves nearly completely of these errors.
HAMLET	Oh, expunge overacting altogether. And let your comics speak only their lines, nothing more. Some comedians, to get a laugh out of the audience, forget the true purpose of the play. Such behavior is criminal and proves the fool eager to pad his part. Go and get ready to perform. *[The PLAYERS go out. POLONIUS, ROSENCRANTZ, and GUILDENSTERN come in]* Greetings, Polonius. Will Claudius attend this performance?
POLONIUS	And the queen as well and soon.
HAMLET	Tell the players to hurry. *[POLONIUS goes out]* Will you two help the players hurry?
GUILDENSTERN AND ROSENCRANTZ	We will, my lord. *[ROSENCRANTZ and GUILDENSTERN depart]*
HAMLET	Horatio! Where are you? *[HORATIO comes in]*
HORATIO	Here I am, lord, at your service.
HAMLET	Horatio, you are as honorable a man as any I have talked to.
HORATIO	Oh, my lord . . . .

ACT III

TRANSLATION

HAMLET	Nay, do not think I flatter;

For what advancement may I hope from thee,
That no revenue hast but thy good spirits
To feed and clothe thee? Why should the poor be flattered? 60
No; let the candied tongue lick absurd pomp,
And crook the pregnant hinges of the knee
Where thrift may follow fawning. Dost thou hear?
Since my dear soul was mistress of her choice
And could of men distinguish, her election 65
Hath seal'd thee for herself; for thou hast been
As one, in suffering all, that suffers nothing,
A man that fortune's buffets and rewards
Hast ta'en with equal thanks; and bless'd are those
Whose blood and judgment are so well co-mingled 70
That they are not a pipe for fortune's finger
To sound what stop she please. Give me that man
That is not passion's slave, and I will wear him
In my heart's core, ay, in my heart of heart,
As I do thee. Something too much of this. 75
There is a play to-night before the king;
One scene of it comes near the circumstance
Which I have told thee of my father's death:
I prithee, when thou seest that act afoot,
Even with the very comment of thy soul 80
Observe mine uncle; if his occulted guilt
Do not itself unkennel in one speech,
It is a damned ghost that we have seen
And my imaginations are as foul
As Vulcan's stithy. Give him heedful note; 85
For I mine eyes will rivet to his face,
And after we will both our judgments join
In censure of his seeming.

HORATIO	Well, my lord:

If he steal aught the whilst this play is playing,
And 'scape detecting, I will pay the theft. 90

HAMLET They are coming to the play; I must be idle:
Get you a place.
*[Danish march. A Flourish. Enter KING, QUEEN, POLONIUS,
OPHELIA, ROSENCRANTZ, GUILDENSTERN, and Others]*

KING How fares our cousin Hamlet?

HAMLET Excellent, i' faith; of the chameleon's dish:
I eat the air, promise-crammed; you cannot feed 95
capons so.

ORIGINAL

HAMLET	Don't think that I am merely flattering you. What promotion could you give me? You have no money, only a cheerful outlook. No, let the sugary hypocrite posture and kneel while fawning on a great person in the hopes of gain. Do you understand? For as long as I could choose worthy people, I have preferred you. You remain the same, whether you receive punishments or rewards. You accept all equally. Those people are blessed who are so even-tempered that they care nothing for the tune of fortune. Give me a friend who is not a slave to extremes and I will clutch him to my heart, in the core of my being, as I admire you. I don't want to overstate my feelings. The troupe will perform a play for the king tonight. One scene describes the circumstances of my father's murder. Please, when the performance reaches that point, look carefully at my uncle Claudius. If this speech doesn't disclose Claudius's hidden guilt, then I have seen a damned demon that has turned my thoughts as black as Vulcan's forge. Look carefully at Claudius. I also will glue my eyes to his face. And after the play, we will compare notes on his behavior.
HORATIO	Good idea, my lord. If he conceals anything during the play and escapes detection, I will pay for his thievery.
HAMLET	The actors are coming on stage. I must look uninvolved. Get a good seat. [*A Danish march plays with drum rolls. The KING, QUEEN, POLONIUS, OPHELIA, ROSENCRANTZ, GUILDENSTERN, and Others come in*]
KING	How do you feel, Hamlet?
HAMLET	Excellent. I eat air from the chameleon's plate. The food is full of empty promises. You can't fatten capons on air.

ACT III

TRANSLATION

KING	I have nothing with this answer, Hamlet; these words are not mine.
HAMLET	No, nor mine now. *[To POLONIUS]* My lord, you played once i' the university, you say? 100
POLONIUS	That did I, my lord, and was accounted a good actor.
HAMLET	And what did you enact?
POLONIUS	I did enact Julius Caesar: I was killed i' the Capitol; Brutus killed me. 105
HAMLET	It was a brute part of him to kill so capital a calf there. Be the players ready?
ROSENCRANTZ	Ay, my lord; they stay upon your patience.
QUEEN	Come hither, my good Hamlet, sit by me. 110
HAMLET	No, good mother, here's metal more attractive.
POLONIUS	*[To the KING]* O ho! do you mark that?
HAMLET	Lady, shall I lie in your lap? *[Lying down at OPHELIA's feet]*
OPHELIA	No, my lord. 115
HAMLET	I mean, my head upon your lap?
OPHELIA	Ay, my lord.
HAMLET	Do you think I meant country matters?
OPHELIA	I think nothing, my lord.
HAMLET	That's a fair thought to lie between maid's legs. 120
OPHELIA	What is, my lord?
HAMLET	Nothing.
OPHELIA	You are merry, my lord.
HAMLET	Who, I? 125
OPHELIA	Ay, my lord.
HAMLET	O God, your only jig-maker. What should a man do but be merry? for, look you, how cheerfully my mother looks, and my father died within's two hours. 130

ORIGINAL

KING	I can make no sense of your answer, Hamlet. These words are foreign to me.
HAMLET	They are foreign to me, too. Polonius, you acted in university productions, didn't you?
POLONIUS	Yes, my lord, and was judged a good actor.
HAMLET	In what plays did you perform.
POLONIUS	I played Julius Caesar. Brutus stabbed me in the Capitol.
HAMLET	It was savage of him to murder so good a player. Is the troupe ready?
ROSENCRANTZ	Yes, my lord. They wait for your cue.
QUEEN	Come here, Hamlet, and sit by me.
HAMLET	No, mother, this is a more attractive offer.
POLONIUS	*[To the KING]* Did you hear that?
HAMLET	Lady, may I recline on your lap? *[Lies down at OPHELIA's feet]*
OPHELIA	No, my lord.
HAMLET	I mean, may I put my head in your lap?
OPHELIA	Yes, my lord.
HAMLET	Did you think I meant something coarse?
OPHELIA	I thought nothing of it, my lord.
HAMLET	It's a pleasant thought to lie between a girl's legs.
OPHELIA	What did you say, my lord?
HAMLET	Nothing.
OPHELIA	You are teasing me, my lord.
HAMLET	Me?
OPHELIA	Yes, my lord.
HAMLET	Oh God, I am the only jester. What should a person do but be jolly? Look, how cheerful my mother looks when my father died only two hours ago.

ACT III

TRANSLATION

OPHELIA	Nay, 'tis twice two months, my lord.
HAMLET	So long? Nay, then, let the devil wear black, for I'll have a suit of sables. O heavens! die two months ago, and not forgotten yet? Then there's hope a great man's memory may outlive his life half a year; 135 but, by'r lady, he must build churches then, or else shall he suffer not thinking on, with the hobby-horse, whose epitaph is, 'For, O! for, O! the hobby-horse is forgot.'

[Hautboys play. The dumb-show enters]
[Enter a King and a Queen, very lovingly; the Queen embracing him, and he her. She kneels, and makes show of protestation unto him. He takes her up, and declines his head upon her neck; lays him down upon a bank of flowers: she, seeing him asleep, leaves him. Anon comes in a fellow, takes off his crown, kisses it, and pours poison in the King's ears, and exits. The Queen returns, finds the King dead, and makes passionate action. The Poisoner, with some two or three Mutes, comes in again, seeming to lament with her. The dead body is carried away. The Poisoner wooes the Queen with gifts; she seems loath and unwilling awhile but in the end accepts his love. Exeunt]

OPHELIA	What means this, my lord? 140
HAMLET	Marry, this is miching mallecho; it means mischief.
OPHELIA	Belike this show imports the argument of the play.

[Enter Prologue]

HAMLET	We shall know by this fellow: the players 145 cannot keep counsel; they'll tell all.
OPHELIA	Will he tell us what this show meant?
HAMLET	Ay, or any show that you'll show him; be not you ashamed to show, he'll not shame to tell you what it means. 150
OPHELIA	You are naught, you are naught. I'll mark the play.
PROLOGUE	For us and for our tragedy, Here stooping to your clemency, We beg your hearing patiently. 155

ORIGINAL

OPHELIA	No, it was two months ago, my lord.
HAMLET	Was it that long ago? Then let Satan wear black, for I want a suit of black fur. Heavens, dead only two months and not yet forgotten. Then maybe a great man's memory may last six months. But, by the Virgin Mary, he should be a builder of churches or else he will be forgotten, like the toy horse, whose epitaph is "Oh, no one remembers the toy horse." *[Oboes sound. A pantomime begins. A King and Queen enter, embracing each other. She kneels and behaves lovingly. He lifts her and leans his head on her neck. He then lies down in a flower bed. She leaves him to take a nap. A man enters, takes the King's crown, kisses it, and pours poison in the King's ears, then goes out. The Queen returns, discovers that the King is dead, and becomes emotional. The murderer, in company with two or three silent attendants, enters and consoles her. The King's corpse is carried out. The murderer courts the Queen with presents. She seems unwilling at first, but finally accepts his courtship. They go out]*

ACT III

OPHELIA	What does this scene mean, my lord?
HAMLET	Truly, this is a sneaky crime. It intends mischief.
OPHELIA	Perhaps this pantomime describes the theme of the play. *[Prologue takes the stage]*
HAMLET	We shall learn from the actor presenting the prologue. Actors can't keep secrets. They tell all.
OPHELIA	Will he inform us of the play's meaning?
HAMLET	Yes, or any scene you show him. Don't be ashamed to show him. He'll gladly interpret the meaning.
OPHELIA	You are naughty. I want to watch the play.
PROLOGUE	For the troupe and for our tragedy, here awaiting your acceptance, we ask you to listen.

TRANSLATION

HAMLET	Is this a prologue, or the posy of a ring?
OPHELIA	'Tis brief, my lord.
HAMLET	As woman's love.

[Enter two Players, King and Queen]

PLAYER KING Full thirty times hath Phoebus' cart gone
round Neptune's salt wash and Tellus' orbed ground, 160
And thirty dozen moons with borrow'd sheen
About the world have times twelve thirties been,
Since love our hearts and Hymen did our hands
Unite commutual in most sacred bands.

PLAYER QUEEN So many journeys may the sun and moon 165
Makes us again count o'er ere love be done!
But, woe is me! you are so sick of late,
So far from cheer and from your former state,
That I distrust you. Yet, though I distrust,
Discomfort you, my lord, it nothing must; 170
For women's fear and love holds quantity,
In neither aught, or in extremity.
Now, what my love is, proof hath made you know;
And as my love is siz'd, my fear is so.
Where love is great, the littlest doubts are fear; 175
Where little fears grow great, great love grows there.

PLAYER KING Faith, I must leave thee, love, and shortly too;
My operant powers their functions leave to do:
And thou shalt live in this fair world behind,
Honour'd, belov'd; and haply one as kind 180
For husband shalt thou—

PLAYER QUEEN   O! confound the rest;
Such love must needs be treason in my breast:
In second husband let me be accurst;
None wed the second but who kill'd the first.

HAMLET *[Aside]* Wormwood, wormwood. 185

PLAYER QUEEN The instances that second marriage move,
Are base respects of thrift, but none of love;
A second time I kill my husband dead,
When second husband kisses me in bed.

HAMLET	Is this an introduction or a flower in a ring?
OPHELIA	It was brief, my lord.
HAMLET	Like a woman's love. *[Two actors enter to play the parts of King and Queen]*
PLAYER KING	Thirty times has the sun gone around the sea and earth. And thirty dozen moons reflected light on the world twelve times thirty times since our hearts and marriage united at the altar.
PLAYER QUEEN	So many days may we count until our love ends! But I am sad that you are so ill lately and so cheerless and unlike your normal self. I worry about you. Yet, though I am anxious, I don't want to trouble you, my lord; women's fear is equal to their love. It never recedes to nothing or expands to an excess. I have shown you how much I love you. Where there is much love, small doubts become fears. When small fears enlarge, love grows stronger.
PLAYER KING	I must soon leave you, my love. My strength is leaving me. I leave you behind—honored, loved. And perhaps another husband you will . . . .
PLAYER QUEEN	Oh, don't mention other men. I would betray you if I remarried. Let me be cursed if I remarry. The only ones who remarry are those who killed their first mates.
HAMLET	*[To himself]* This is like bitter wormwood.
PLAYER QUEEN	Second marriages are based on money, but not on love. I would kill my dead husband a second time if a second husband embraced me in bed.

ACT III

TRANSLATION

PLAYER KING   I do believe you think what now you speak;   190
But what we do determine oft we break.
Purpose is but the slave to memory,
Of violent birth, but poor validity;
Which now, like fruit unripe, sticks on the tree,
But fall unshaken when they mellow be.   195
Most necessary 'tis that we forget
To pay ourselves what to ourselves is debt;
What to ourselves in passion we propose,
The passion ending, doth the purpose lose.
The violence of either grief or joy   200
Their own enactures with themselves destroy;
Where joy most revels grief doth most lament,
Grief joys, joy grieves, on slender accident.
This world is not for aye, nor 'tis not strange,
That even our love should with our fortunes change;   205
For 'tis a question left us yet to prove
Whe'r love lead fortune or else fortune love.
The great man down, you mark his favourite flies;
The poor advanc'd makes friends of enemies.
And hitherto doth love on fortune tend,   210
For who not needs shall never lack a friend;
And who in want a hollow friend doth try
Directly seasons him his enemy.
But, orderly to end where I begun,
Our wills and fates do so contrary run   215
That our devices still are overthrown,
Our thoughts are ours, their ends none of our own:
So think thou wilt no second husband wed;
But die thy thoughts when thy first lord is dead.

PLAYER QUEEN   Nor earth to me give food, nor heaven light!   220
Sport and repose lock from me day and night!
To desperation turn my trust and hope!
An anchor's cheer in prison be my scope!
Each opposite that blanks the face of joy
Meet what I would have well, and it destroy!   225
But here and hence pursue me lasting strife,
If, once a widow, ever I be wife!

HAMLET   If she should break it now!

PLAYER KING   'Tis deeply sworn. Sweet, leave me here awhile;
My spirits grow dull, and fain I would beguile   230
The tedious day with sleep. *[Sleeps]*

ORIGINAL

PLAYER KING   I think you speak sincerely. But people often violate their intent. People don't remember their original purpose because their intent is strong at the beginning, but quick to weaken. Like green fruit, it remains on the tree limb, but will fall when it ripens. We must reward ourselves what we are owed. What we declare during periods of emotion loses its powers over us when the emotion ebbs. Whether grief or joy, emotion wears itself out. When people are joyous, they can't feel sorrow. Whatever happens to them will allow grief or gladness to control the moment. Nothing lasts forever. It is normal that love alters when we experience a shift of luck. Nobody knows whether love leads to luck or luck leads to love. When a great man dies, his companion departs from loyalty to him. When the poor improve their fortune, they befriend old enemies. Thus, love depends on luck, for a fortunate person always has friends. And when an unfortunate person seeks help from a so-called friend, the so-called friend turns into an enemy. To end my speech, I say that our intent and luck run in opposite directions. Our plans are always overturned, our thoughts are ours, but the outcomes we can't control. You intend not to remarry, but you will change your mind when your first husband dies.

ACT III

PLAYER QUEEN   I hope that I enjoy neither food nor sunlight if you speak the truth! May I have neither amusement nor rest! May my trust and hope turn to despair! May I live like a hermit in a cell! May the opposite of joy rid me of all pleasure! May I encounter constant trouble if I give up widowhood to become a wife!

HAMLET   I wish the Queen would show some understanding of this speech.

PLAYER KING   You make a solemn vow. Sweetheart, let me rest alone. I am drowsy and would like to take a nap. *[He sleeps]*

TRANSLATION

PLAYER QUEEN	Sleep rock thy brain; And never come mischance between us twain! *[Exit]*
HAMLET	Madam, how like you this play?
QUEEN	The lady doth protest too much methinks.
HAMLET	O! but she'll keep her word.
KING	Have you heard the argument? Is there no offence in 't?
HAMLET	No, no, they do but jest, poison in jest; no offence i' the world.
KING	What do you call the play?
HAMLET	The Mouse-trap. Marry, how? Tropically. This play is the image of a murder done in Vienna: Gonzago is the duke's name; his wife, Baptista. You shall see anon; 'tis a knavish piece of work: but what of that? your majesty and we that have free souls, it touches us not: let the galled jade wince, our withers are unwrung. *[Enter Player as Lucianus]* This is one Lucianus, nephew to the king.
OPHELIA	You are a good chorus, my lord.
HAMLET	I could interpret between you and your love, if I could see the puppets dallying.
OPHELIA	You are keen, my lord, you are keen.
HAMLET	It would cost you a groaning to take off my edge.
OPHELIA	Still better, and worse.
HAMLET	So you mistake your husbands. Begin, murderer; pox, leave thy damnable faces, and begin. Come; the croaking raven doth bellow for revenge.
LUCIANUS	Thoughts black, hands apt, drugs fit, and time agreeing; Confederate season, else no creature seeing; Thou mixture rank, of midnight weeds collected, With Hecate's ban thrice blasted, thrice infected, Thy natural magic and dire property, On wholesome life usurp immediately. *[Pours the poison into the Sleeper's ears]*

235

240

245

250

255

260

ORIGINAL

PLAYER QUEEN	May sleep soothe your mind. I hope no bad fortune ever separates us. *[She goes out]*
HAMLET	Madam, are you enjoying the play?
QUEEN	I think the Player Queen makes too lengthy an argument for her loyalty to the Player King.
HAMLET	She will keep her promise.
KING	Do you know the play? Is it offensive?
HAMLET	No, they are playacting. They pretend to poison. There is no harm in the pretense.
KING	What is the title of the play?
HAMLET	It is called "The Mouse Trap," a figure of speech. The story is based on a murder committed in Vienna, Austria. The duke's name is Gonzago; his wife is Baptista. You will soon see. It is about crime, but it should not offend us. The story is not about you or other innocent people. Let the guilty flinch. We won't feel a twinge of conscience. *[Enter Player as Lucianus]* The next actor plays Lucianus, Gonzago's nephew.
OPHELIA	You are a good commentator, my lord.
HAMLET	I could interpret your affection for your lover if I could see the story played on a puppet stage.
OPHELIA	You are sharp-edged, my lord.
HAMLET	You would suffer if you tried to dull my wit.
OPHELIA	You are even wittier and sharper-tongued.
HAMLET	You would betray your husbands. Let the murderer come on stage. A plague on you, stop making up your faces and continue the play. Continue. The blackbird caws for revenge.
LUCIANUS	I am ready—it's the right time, my hands are steady and the poison suited to the crime. It's a good opportunity to commit murder while there is no one else about. A poison blended of deadly herbs three times cursed by the queen of witches to give it triple power. An herbal concoction capable of killing will immediately extinguish life. *[Pours the poison into the Sleeper's ears]*

ACT III

HAMLET	He poisons him i' the garden for 's estate.	265
	His name's Gonzago; the story is extant, and writ in	
	very choice Italian. You shall see anon how the	
	murderer gets the love of Gonzago's wife.	
OPHELIA	The king rises.	
HAMLET	What! frighted with false fire?	270
QUEEN	How fares my lord?	
POLONIUS	Give o'er the play.	
KING	Give me some light: away!	
ALL	Lights, lights, lights!	
	[Exeunt all except HAMLET and HORATIO]	
HAMLET	Why, let the striken deer go weep,	275
	The hart ungalled play;	
	For some must watch, while some must sleep:	
	So runs the world away.	
	Would not this, sir, and a forest of feathers, if the	
	rest of my fortunes turn Turk with me, with two	280
	Provincial roses on my razed shoes, get me a fellowship	
	in a cry of players, sir?	
HORATIO	Half a share.	
HAMLET	A whole one, I.	
	For thou dost know, O Damon dear,	285
	This realm dismantled was	
	Of Jove himself; and now reigns here	
	A very, very—pajock.	
HORATIO	You might have rhymed.	
HAMLET	O good Horatio! I'll take the ghost's word for	290
	a thousand pound. Didst perceive?	
HORATIO	Very well, my lord.	
HAMLET	Upon the talk of the poisoning?	
HORATIO	I did very well note him.	
	[Re-enter ROSENCRANTZ and GUILDENSTERN]	
HAMLET	Ah, ha! Come, some music! come, the	295
	recorders!	
	For if the king like not the comedy,	
	Why then, belike he likes it not, perdy.	
	Come, some music!	

ORIGINAL

HAMLET	Lucianus poisons Gonzago in the garden to claim Gonzago's estate. The Duke's name is Gonzago. The story survives in the original Italian. You will soon see how Lucianus seduces Gonzago's wife.
OPHELIA	The king has left his seat.
HAMLET	Does he fear the pretended violence of the play?
QUEEN	Are you all right, my lord?
POLONIUS	Stop the play.
KING	Light the room. Everyone leave!
ALL	Bring lights! *[Everyone departs except HAMLET and HORATIO]*
HAMLET	Let the guilty weep and the innocent play. Someone must keep watch while others sleep. That's the way of the world. Even if my luck sours, wouldn't I get a job with the troupe along with feathers for my hat and rosettes on my shoes?
HORATIO	You would get half a share in the company.
HAMLET	I should get a whole share. You must know, dear friend, that Jupiter himself upset the Danish kingdom. And now rules like a peacock.
HORATIO	You could have rhymed that statement.
HAMLET	Oh good Horatio! I'll accept the ghost's word for one thousand pounds. Did you see what you were looking for?
HORATIO	I saw it well, my lord.
HAMLET	Just as the players spoke of poisoning?
HORATIO	I did observe Claudius at that point. *[ROSENCRANTZ and GUILDENSTERN come in]*
HAMLET	Aha, let's enjoy music. Bring on the flutes. For if Claudius doesn't like comedy, then he must be in a negative mood, by God. Come, play music!

ACT III

GUILDENSTERN	Good my lord, vouchsafe me a word	300
	with you.	
HAMLET	Sir, a whole history.	
GUILDENSTERN	The king, sir,—	
HAMLET	Ay, sir, what of him?	
GUILDENSTERN	Is in his retirement marvellous distempered.	305
HAMLET	With drink, sir?	
GUILDENSTERN	No, my lord, rather with choler.	
HAMLET	Your wisdom should show itself more richer	
	to signify this to his doctor; for, for me to put him to	310
	his purgation would perhaps plunge him into far more	
	choler.	
GUILDENSTERN	Good my lord, put your discourse into	
	some frame, and start not so wildly from my affair.	
HAMLET	I am tame, sir; pronounce.	315
GUILDENSTERN	The queen, your mother, in most great	
	affliction of spirit, hath sent me to you.	
HAMLET	You are welcome.	
GUILDENSTERN	Nay, good my lord, this courtesy is not	
	of the right breed. If it shall please you to make	320
	me a wholesome answer, I will do your mother's	
	commandment; if not, your pardon and my return shall	
	be the end of my business.	
HAMLET	Sir, I cannot.	
GUILDENSTERN	What, my lord?	325
HAMLET	Make you a wholesome answer; my wit's	
	diseased; but, sir, such answer as I can make, you shall	
	command; or, rather, as you say, my mother:	
	therefore no more, but to the matter: my mother,	
	you say,—	330
ROSENCRANTZ	Then, thus she says: your behaviour hath	
	struck her into amazement and admiration.	
HAMLET	O wonderful son, that can so astonish a	
	mother! But is there no sequel at the heels of this	
	mother's admiration? Impart.	335

GUILDENSTERN	My lord, allow me a word with you.
HAMLET	You may have a whole history of words.
GUILDENSTERN	King Claudius, sir . . . .
HAMLET	Yes, what about him?
GUILDENSTERN	He left terribly upset.
HAMLET	From drinking too much?
GUILDENSTERN	No, my lord, from anger.
HAMLET	You should tell his doctor, not me. If I were to cleanse him of illness, I would make him angrier.
GUILDENSTERN	My lord, state your words clearly and stick to the subject.
HAMLET	I am calm, sir. Continue.
GUILDENSTERN	Queen Gertrude is greatly troubled. She sent me to get you.
HAMLET	You are welcome here.
GUILDENSTERN	No, my lord. Your remark is unsuited to the request. If you will give me an appropriate answer, I will fulfill your mother's request. If you won't answer sensibly, I beg your pardon to complete my errand.
HAMLET	Sir, I can't.
GUILDENSTERN	Can't what, my lord?
HAMLET	I can't give you an appropriate answer. I am not sane, but, I will answer as best I can. As you indicate, I will answer my mother. Enough of this quibbling. You said my mother summons me?
ROSENCRANTZ	That is what she said: she is dumbfounded at your behavior.
HAMLET	I'm a wonder worker if I can astonish my mother. Did my mother say anything else? Tell me.

ACT III

ROSENCRANTZ	She desires to speak with you in her closet ere you go to bed.
HAMLET	We shall obey, were she ten times our mother. Have you any further trade with us?
ROSENCRANTZ	My lord, you once did love me. 340
HAMLET	So I do still, by these pickers and stealers.
ROSENCRANTZ	Good my lord, what is your cause of distemper? you do surely bar the door upon your own liberty, if you deny your griefs to your friend.
HAMLET	Sir, I lack advancement. 345
ROSENCRANTZ	How can that be when you have the voice of the king himself for your succession in Denmark?
HAMLET	Ay, sir, but 'While the grass grows,'—the proverb is something musty. *[Enter Players, with recorders]* O! the recorders: let me see one. To withdraw with 350 you: why do you go about to recover the wind of me, as if you would drive me into a toil?
GUILDENSTERN	O! my lord, if my duty be too bold, my love is too unmannerly.
HAMLET	I do not well understand that. Will you play 355 upon this pipe?
GUILDENSTERN	My lord, I cannot.
HAMLET	I pray you.
GUILDENSTERN	Believe me, I cannot.
HAMLET	I do beseech you. 360
GUILDENSTERN	I know no touch of it, my lord.
HAMLET	'Tis as easy as lying; govern these ventages with your finger and thumb, give it breath with your mouth, and it will discourse most eloquent music. Look you, these are the stops. 365

ROSENCRANTZ	She wants to talk to you in her room before you go to bed.
HAMLET	I will obey her, even if she had the power of ten mothers. Is there anything else?
ROSENCRANTZ	My lord, you were once my friend.
HAMLET	I swear by my hands that I am still your friend.
ROSENCRANTZ	My lord, tell me what is wrong with you. You abandon freedom if you don't confess your problems to a friend.
HAMLET	I want to achieve my ambition.
ROSENCRANTZ	How can you lack a future when you are the crown prince of Denmark?
HAMLET	Yes, according to an old proverb, "While the grass grows, the horse starves." *[The Players enter with flutes]* Oh, flutes. Let me see one. Getting back to your question, why do you move behind me as though you are forcing me into a trap?
GUILDENSTERN	My lord, if my task is too daring, I would be discourteous.
HAMLET	I don't understand you. Do you play the flute?
GUILDENSTERN	No, my lord.
HAMLET	Please, try it.
GUILDENSTERN	Believe me, I can't play the flute.
HAMLET	I beg you.
GUILDENSTERN	I don't know how, my lord.
HAMLET	It is as easy as telling a lie. Cover these holes with your finger and thumb, blow into the flute, and you will make music. Look here, these are the stops.

ACT III

GUILDENSTERN	But these cannot I command to any utterance of harmony; I have not the skill.
HAMLET	Why, look you now, how unworthy a thing you make of me. You would play upon me; you would seem to know my stops; you would pluck out the heart 370 of my mystery; you would sound me from my lowest note to the top of my compass; and there is much music, excellent voice, in this little organ, yet cannot you make it speak. 'Sblood, do you think I am easier to be played on than a pipe? Call me what instrument 375 you will, though you can fret me, you cannot play upon me. *[Enter POLONIUS]* God bless you, sir!
POLONIUS	My lord, the queen would speak with you, and presently. 380
HAMLET	Do you see yonder cloud that's almost in shape of a camel?
POLONIUS	By the mass, and 'tis like a camel, indeed.
HAMLET	Methinks it is like a weasel.
POLONIUS	It is backed like a weasel. 385
HAMLET	Or like a whale?
POLONIUS	Very like a whale.
HAMLET	Then I will come to my mother by and by. *[Aside]* They fool me to the top of my bent. *[Aloud]* I will come by and by. 390
POLONIUS	I will say so. *[Exit]*
HAMLET	'By and by' is easily said. Leave me, friends. *[Exeunt all but HAMLET]* 'Tis now the very witching time of night, When churchyards yawn and hell itself breathes out Contagion to this world: now could I drink hot blood, 395 And do such bitter business as the day Would quake to look on. Soft! now to my mother. O heart! lose not thy nature; let not ever The soul of Nero enter this firm bosom; Let me be cruel, not unnatural; 400 I will speak daggers to her, but use none; My tongue and soul in this be hyprocrites; How in my words soever she be shent, To give them seals never, my soul, consent! *[Exit]*

GUILDENSTERN	But I can't play a melody. I have no training.
HAMLET	In the same way, you treat me unworthily. You would manipulate me. You want to know my stops. You want to get to the heart of my behavior. You would play all my notes, from the lowest to the highest. This flute can make excellent music, but you can't play it. God's blood, do you think you are any better at playing me? Whatever instrument you make of me, even if you try, you can't make music out of me. *[POLONIUS comes in]* God bless you, sir!
POLONIUS	My lord, the queen wants to speak to you now.
HAMLET	Do you see that cloud that is shaped like a camel?
POLONIUS	By the Holy Mass, it does look like a camel.
HAMLET	I think it resembles a weasel.
POLONIUS	It has a back like a weasel.
HAMLET	Or like a whale?
POLONIUS	Very much like a whale.
HAMLET	I will go to my mother eventually. *[To himself]* They toy with me only so long as I allow it. *[To the group]* I will go to my mother eventually.
POLONIUS	I will tell her. *[He departs]*
HAMLET	"Eventually" is easy to say. Leave me alone, friends. *[They leave. HAMLET remains alone]* It is the dark of night, when graveyards open and hell spreads evil over the world. At this hour, I could drink fresh blood and perform such a bitter task that I would never do in daylight. Quiet! I am going to my mother. Don't let me become a mother-killer like Nero, the emperor of Rome. Let me be firm, but not vicious. I will hurl words like daggers, but I won't stab her. My tongue shall betray what I feel in my heart. However she scolds me, my soul, I will not kill her. *[He goes out]*

TRANSLATION

ACT III, SCENE 3

A room in the castle.

[Enter KING, ROSENCRANTZ, and GUILDENSTERN]

KING	I like him not, nor stands it safe with us
	To let his madness range. Therefore prepare you;
	I your commission will forthwith dispatch,
	And he to England shall along with you.
	The terms of our estate may not endure 5
	Hazard so dangerous as doth hourly grow
	Out of his lunacies.
GUILDENSTERN	We will ourselves provide.
	Most holy and religious fear it is
	To keep those many many bodies safe
	That live and feed upon your majesty. 10
ROSENCRANTZ	The single and peculiar life is bound
	With all the strength and armour of the mind
	To keep itself from noyance; but much more
	That spirit upon whose weal depend and rest
	The lives of many. The cease of majesty 15
	Dies not alone, but, like a gulf doth draw
	What's near it with it; it is a massy wheel,
	Fix'd on the summit of the highest mount,
	To whose huge spokes ten thousand lesser things
	Are mortis'd and adjoin'd; which, when it falls, 20
	Each small annexment, petty consequence,
	Attends the boisterous ruin. Never alone
	Did the king sigh, but with a general groan.
KING	Arm you, I pray you, to this speedy voyage;
	For we will fetters put upon this fear, 25
	Which now goes too free-footed.
ROSENCRANTZ AND GUILDENSTERN	We will haste us.
	[Exeunt ROSENCRANTZ and GUILDENSTERN. Enter POLONIUS]
POLONIUS	My lord, he's going to his mother's closet:
	Behind the arras I'll convey myself
	To hear the process; I'll warrant she'll tax him home; 30
	And, as you said, and wisely was it said,
	'Tis meet that some more audience than a mother,
	Since nature makes them partial, should o'erhear
	The speech, of vantage. Fare you well, my liege:
	I'll call upon you ere you go to bed 35
	And tell you what I know.

ORIGINAL

ACT III, SCENE 3

A room in the castle.

[Enter KING, ROSENCRANTZ, and GUILDENSTERN]

KING   I dislike Hamlet. My rule is not secure if he wanders like a madman. Therefore, get ready. I am sending him to England with you. My kingdom is in danger while he becomes more insane by the hour.

       •

GUILDENSTERN   We will pack for the trip. It is a sacred job to keep safe the Danish people who rely on you as their king.

ROSENCRANTZ   The individual must try to keep from harm. But it is more important to protect the person who influences so many lives. A king does not die alone. Like a whirlpool, the death of a monarch pulls down those closest to him. Like a huge wheel at the top of a mountain, kingship is firmly joined to ten thousand less important people. If the king dies, everything attached to his rule collapses into ruin. When the king sighs, the people groan.

KING   Ready yourselves for this quick trip. I will control the fear that races too freely through Denmark.

ROSENCRANTZ AND GUILDENSTERN   We will hurry. *[ROSENCRANTZ and GUILDENSTERN depart. POLONIUS enters]*

POLONIUS   My lord, Hamlet is going to his mother's room. I will hide behind the drape to eavesdrop. I guarantee that she will scold him. As you so wisely said, it is fitting that a less fond person hear their conversation. Mothers are too biased toward their children. Farewell, my king. I will report their conversation to you before you retire for the night.

TRANSLATION

KING   Thanks, dear my lord.
    [Exit POLONIUS]
    O! my offence is rank, it smells to heaven;
    It hath the primal eldest curse upon 't;
    A brother's murder! Pray can I not,
    Though inclination be as sharp as will: 40
    My stronger guilt defeats my strong intent;
    And like a man to double business bound,
    I stand in pause where I shall first begin,
    And both neglect. What if this cursed hand
    Were thicker than itself with brother's blood,   45
    Is there not rain enough in the sweet heavens
    To wash it white as snow? Whereto serves mercy
    But to confront the visage of offence?
    And what's in prayer but this two-fold force,
    To be forestalled, ere we come to fall,   50
    Or pardon'd, being down? Then, I'll look up;
    My fault is past. But, O! what form of prayer
    Can serve my turn? 'Forgive me my foul murder?'
    That cannot be since I am still possess'd
    Of those effects for which I did the murder,   55
    My crown, mine own ambition, and my queen.
    May one be pardon'd and retain the offence?
    In the corrupted currents of this world
    Offence's gilded hand may shove by justice,
    And oft 'tis seen the wicked prize itself   60
    Buys out the law; but 'tis not so above;
    There is no shuffling, there the action lies
    In his true nature, and we ourselves compell'd
    Even to the teeth and forehead of our faults
    To give in evidence. What then? what rests?   65
    Try what repentance can: what can it not?
    Yet what can it, when one can not repent?
    O wretched state! O bosom black as death!
    O limed soul, that struggling to be free
    Art more engaged! Help, angels! make assay;   70
    Bow, stubborn knees; and heart with strings of steel
    Be soft as sinews of the new-born babe.
    All may be well. *[Retires and kneels. Enter HAMLET]*

KING Thanks, dear lord. *[POLONIUS goes out]* My crime is foul. It smells to the skies. It resembles the murder of a brother in the book of Genesis, for which Cain was cursed. I killed my brother! I can no longer pray, even though I need to. My guilt is too strong to allow it. I'm like a man carrying out two tasks. I ponder the two and complete neither one. If my hand were coated with enough blood to make it twice as thick, is there not enough rain in the sky to wash it clean? Would it not be a mercy if I could face my crime directly? What is the purpose of prayer but to hinder us from sin and pardon us when we have failed? I will be cheerful. My crime is in the past. But what kind of prayer will help me? "Forgive me, God, for murdering my brother"? That won't work because I still enjoy the profits of Hamlet's murder. I have his crown and his wife. Can I seek forgiveness and keep my rewards? In this sinful world, criminals push justice aside. Often, criminals pay their way out of punishment. But that is not true in heaven. There is no escaping punishment. Before God, the crime is evident and criminals must explain their actions. What shall I do? What remains for me to accomplish? I can repent, but it will not free me of guilt. But why is this so? Is there ever a time when a sinner can't repent? Oh miserable guilt! My heart is as black as death! My soul, like a bird trapped on sticky paper, becomes more trapped the more it struggles. Help me, angels! I must try to repent. I must bend my stubborn knees. May my hard heart be as soft as a baby's muscles. I may succeed yet. *[He goes to his room and kneels. HAMLET enters]*

ACT III

TRANSLATION

HAMLET	Now might I do it pat, now he is praying;
	And now I'll do 't: and so he goes to heaven; 75
	And so am I reveng'd. That would be scann'd:
	A villain kills my father; and for that,
	I, his sole son, do this same villain send
	To heaven.
	Why, this is hire and salary, not revenge. 80
	He took my father grossly, full of bread,
	With all his crimes broad blown, as flush as May;
	And how his audit stands who knows save heaven?
	But in our circumstance and course of thought
	'Tis heavy with him. And am I then reveng'd, 85
	To take him in the purging of his soul,
	When he is fit and season'd for his passage?
	No.
	Up, sword, and know thou a more horrid hent;
	When he is drunk asleep, or in his rage, 90
	Or in the incestuous pleasure of his bed,
	At gaming, swearing, or about some act
	That has no relish of salvation in 't;
	Then trip him, that his heels may kick at heaven,
	And that his soul may be as damn'd and black 95
	As hell, whereto it goes. My mother stays:
	This physic but prolongs thy sickly days.
	[Exit. The KING rises and advances]
KING	My words fly up, my thoughts remain below:
	Words without thoughts never to heaven go. *[Exit]*

HAMLET   I can easily kill him now while he is praying. If I do it now, he will go to heaven and I will have my revenge. Let me think this over. A criminal murdered my father. In revenge, I, his only son, kill the murderer and send him to heaven. This is what a hired killer would do, not an avenger. He slew my father, who was burdened with sins as fresh as spring. And how pure he was in heaven's eyes only God knows. The way people look at such crimes as Claudius committed, he is burdened with sin. Would I get my revenge if I killed him while he confesses his sins to God and when he is ready to go to heaven? No. Put up my sword and wait until a more suitable time. I will choose a time when he is drunk, angry, or enjoying adultery with Gertrude or gambling, swearing, or committing some other sinful act. I will catch him so his soul may be damned to hell and his heels kick heaven. My mother is waiting for me. Claudius's prayer allows him to live a little longer. *[HAMLET leaves. The KING rises and advances]*

ACT III

KING   I send my words to heaven, but my earthly troubles remain. Empty words can't reach heaven. *[He goes out]*

TRANSLATION

ACT III, SCENE 4

The queen's apartment.

[Enter QUEEN and POLONIUS]

POLONIUS   He will come straight. Look you lay home to him;
Tell him his pranks have been too broad to bear with,
And that your Grace hath screen'd and stood between
Much heat and him. I'll silence me e'en here.
Pray you, be round with him.   5

HAMLET   *[Within]* Mother, mother, mother!

QUEEN   I'll warrant you;
Fear me not. Withdraw, I hear him coming.
[POLONIUS hides behind the arras. Enter HAMLET]

HAMLET   Now, mother, what's the matter?

QUEEN   Hamlet, thou hast thy father much offended.

HAMLET   Mother, you have my father much offended.   10

QUEEN   Come, come, you answer with an idle tongue.

HAMLET   Go, go, you question with a wicked tongue.

QUEEN   Why, how now, Hamlet!

HAMLET   What's the matter now?

QUEEN   Have you forgot me?

HAMLET   No, by the rood, not so:
You are the queen, your husband's brother's wife;   15
And,—would it were not so!—you are my mother.

QUEEN   Nay then, I'll set those to you that can speak.

HAMLET   Come, come, and sit you down; you shall not budge;
You go not, till I set up a glass
Where you may see the inmost part of you.   20

QUEEN   What wilt thou do? thou wilt not murder me?
Help, help, ho!

POLONIUS   *[Behind]*   What, ho! help! help! help!

HAMLET   *[Draws]* How now! a rat? Dead, for a ducat, dead!
[Makes a pass through the arras]

ORIGINAL

ACT III, SCENE 4

The queen's apartment.

[Enter QUEEN and POLONIUS]

POLONIUS   Hamlet is on the way here. Make it clear to him. Tell him
that you can't tolerate his peculiar behavior. Tell him that
he is pressing the limit of your tolerance. I will hide here.
Please, speak directly to him.

HAMLET   [Outside] Mother!

QUEEN   I will do as you say. Don't worry. Hide, I hear him coming.
[POLONIUS hides behind the drape. HAMLET enters]

HAMLET   Well mother, what do you want?

QUEEN   Hamlet, you have insulted your stepfather.

HAMLET   Mother, you have wronged my real father.

QUEEN   Please, your answer is foolish.

HAMLET   And your answer is evil.

QUEEN   What do you mean, Hamlet!

HAMLET   What do you want?

QUEEN   Have you forgotten that I am your mother?

HAMLET   No, by the holy cross, you are a queen who has married
her brother-in-law. You are my mother, but I wish you
weren't.

QUEEN   Well, I will have you disciplined.

HAMLET   Sit down. Don't budge. Don't move until I can find a
mirror that reflects your heart.

QUEEN   What are you doing? Do you want to kill me? Help me!

POLONIUS   [Behind the drape] What is happening? Help!

HAMLET   [Draws his weapon] Is there a rat behind the drape? I'll
bet a ducat that I can kill it! [Sticks his blade through the
drape]

ACT III

TRANSLATION

POLONIUS	*[Behind]* O! I am slain.
QUEEN	O me! what hast thou done?
HAMLET	Nay, I know not: is it the king?
QUEEN	O! what a rash and bloody deed is this!
HAMLET	A bloody deed! almost as bad, good mother,
	As kill a king, and marry with his brother.
QUEEN	As kill a king!

HAMLET   Ay, lady, 'twas my word. 30
[Lifts up the arras and discovers POLONIUS]
[To POLONIUS] Thou wretched, rash, intruding fool,
farewell!
I took thee for thy better; take thy fortune;
Thou find'st to be too busy in some danger.
Leave wringing of your hands: peace! sit you down,
And let me wring your heart; for so I shall 35
If it be made of penetrable stuff,
If damned custom have not brass'd it so
That it is proof and bulwark against sense.

QUEEN What have I done that thou dar'st wag thy tongue
In noise so rude against me?

HAMLET   Such an act 40
That blurs the grace and blush of modesty,
Calls virtue hypocrite, takes off the rose
From the fair forehead of an innocent love
And sets a blister there, make marriage vows
As false as dicers' oaths; O! such a deed 45
As from the body of contraction plucks
The very soul, and sweet religion makes
A rhapsody of words; heaven's face doth glow,
Yea, this solidity and compound mass,
With tristful visage, as against the doom, 50
Is thought-sick at the act.

QUEEN Ay me! what act,
That roars so loud and thunders in the index?

ORIGINAL

POLONIUS	*[Behind the drape]* Oh, I am dying.
QUEEN	Oh, what have you done?
HAMLET	I don't know. Is Claudius hiding behind there?
QUEEN	You have committed a hasty, bloody crime.
HAMLET	A crime? It is almost as criminal, mother, as to murder a king and marry a brother-in-law.
QUEEN	Murder a king!
HAMLET	Yes, ma'am. That's what I said. *[He lifts the drape and reveals POLONIUS] [To POLONIUS]* You miserable, thoughtless snoop. Farewell! I thought the noise came from the king. Too bad that you intruded in a dangerous situation. Stop wringing your hands. Hush! Sit down and let me wring your heart. That is what I intend to do, if your heart is not so tough and your actions not so bold as to prohibit you from listening to sense.
QUEEN	What have I done to deserve your rude accusations?
HAMLET	You have breached modesty and grace. Your actions have betrayed your goodness. You have stripped the blush from innocent love and left a blister. You make marriage vows as falsely as gamblers swear. Such a crime violates the soul of the marriage contract and turns religious faith into a jumble of words. Heaven sickens at an act that makes the earth sad.
QUEEN	What crime, which you describe so loudly and forcefully?

ACT III

TRANSLATION

HAMLET	Look here, upon this picture, and on this;
	The counterfeit presentment of two brothers.
	See, what a grace was seated on this brow;

HAMLET Look here, upon this picture, and on this;
The counterfeit presentment of two brothers.
See, what a grace was seated on this brow;   55
Hyperion's curls, the front of Jove himself,
An eye like Mars to threaten and command,
A station like the herald Mercury
New-lighted on a heaven-kissing hill,
A combination and a form indeed,   60
Where every god did seem to set his seal,
To give the world assurance of a man.
This was your husband: look you now, what follows.
Here is your husband; like a mildew'd ear,
Blasting his wholesome brother. Have you eyes?   65
Could you on this fair mountain leave to feed,
And batten on this moor? Ha! have you eyes?
You cannot call it love, for at your age
The hey-day in the blood is tame, it's humble,
And waits upon the judgment; and what judgment   70
Would step from this to this? Sense, sure, you have,
Else could you not have motion; but sure, that sense
Is apoplex'd; for madness would not err.
Nor sense to ecstasy was ne'er so thrall'd
But it reserv'd some quantity of choice,   75
To serve in such a difference. What devil was't
That thus hath cozen'd you at hoodman-blind?
Eyes without feeling, feeling without sight,
Ears without hands or eyes, smelling sans all,
Or but a sickly part of one true sense   80
Could not so mope.
O shame! where is thy blush? Rebellious hell,
If thou canst mutine in a matron's bones,
To flaming youth let virtue be as wax,
And melt in her own fire: proclaim no shame   85
When the compulsive ardour gives the charge,
Since frost itself as actively doth burn,
And reason panders will.

QUEEN   O Hamlet! speak no more;
Thou turn'st mine eyes into my very soul;
And there I see such black and grained spots   90
As will not leave their tinct.

HAMLET   Nay, but to live
In the rank sweat of an enseam'd bed,
Stew'd in corruption, honeying and making love
Over the nasty sty,—

ORIGINAL

HAMLET	Look at these pictures, portraits of two brothers. See how gracious one looks. He bears the curls of the sun god and the resemblance of Jupiter himself. The eye looks like Mars, the war god. His posture like winged Mercury perched on a high hill. The combined qualities and posture like a man that the gods would approve of. This was King Hamlet. Look at his successor, your second husband. Claudius is like blighted corn that poisons his brother. Can't you see? Would you desert the upright husband to choose the lesser man? Don't you see? You can't say you love Claudius, for you are too old for passion. Your mature emotions rely on sense. How could you sink from a good husband to Claudius? Of course, you have intellect. Otherwise, you could not move. But your logic must be paralyzed to have made so insane a choice. Your good sense is a slave of your passion, but logic must have influenced your choice of so different a second husband. What demon tricked you at blindman's bluff? Your senses—seeing, feeling, hearing, smelling—could not be so false to logic. Why don't you blush for shame? Evil can invade a woman's bones and turn her into a flaming youth, destroying her in the process. Admit no shame while a passionate obsession takes hold of you. Even frost can catch fire and logic give in to willfulness.

ACT III

QUEEN	Oh, Hamlet! Stop talking. You make me see my soul. I recognize such evil that can't be whitened.
HAMLET	But you continue living in adultery, committing bedroom impropriety, making love over a pig sty. . . .

TRANSLATION

QUEEN	O! speak to me no more;
	These words like daggers enter in mine ears; 95
	No more, sweet Hamlet!

HAMLET   A murderer, and a villain;
A slave that is not twentieth part the tithe
Of your precedent lord; a vice of kings;
A cut-purse of the empire and the rule,
That from a shelf the precious diadem stole,   100
And put it in his pocket!

QUEEN   No more!

HAMLET   A king of shreds and patches,—
[Enter GHOST]
Save me and hover o'er me with your wings,
You heavenly guards! What would your gracious figure?

QUEEN   Alas! he's mad!   105

HAMLET   Do you not come your tardy son to chide,
That, laps'd in time and passion, lets go by
The important acting of your dread command?
O! say.

GHOST   Do not forget: this visitation
Is but to whet thy almost blunted purpose.   110
But, look! amazement on thy mother sits;
O! step between her and her fighting soul;
Conceit in weakest bodies strongest works:
Speak to her, Hamlet.

HAMLET   How is it with you, lady?

QUEEN   Alas! how is't with you,   115
That you do bend your eye on vacancy
And with the incorporal air do hold discourse?
Forth at your eyes your spirits wildly peep;
And, as the sleeping soldiers in the alarm,
Your bedded hair, like life in excrements,   120
Starts up and stands an end. O gentle son!
Upon the heat and flame of thy distemper
Sprinkle cool patience. Whereon do you look?

HAMLET   On him, on him! Look you, how pale he glares!
His form and cause conjoin'd, preaching to stones,   125
Would make them capable. Do not look upon me;
Lest with this piteous action you convert
My stern effects: then what I have to do
Will want true colour; tears perchance for blood.

QUEEN	Say no more. Your words pierce me like daggers. Say no more, sweet Hamlet!
HAMLET	Claudius is a killer, a criminal, a slave not worth one-twentieth of King Hamlet. An impostor king. Claudius has picked the pocket of Denmark and the throne. He snatched the king's crown off the shelf and stuffed it into his pocket.
QUEEN	Say no more!
HAMLET	A hobo king. . . . *[The GHOST enters]* Preserve me, Ghost; wrap me in your wings, heavenly guardians. What do you want, spirit?
QUEEN	Alas! He's insane!
HAMLET	Have you come to scold your inefficient son? Have I lost opportunity and purpose rather than obey your command? Oh, tell me.
GHOST	Don't forget your promise. I am here to remind you of your task. Look, your mother is terrified. Stop debating with your conscience and speak to her. Imagination is strongest in weak people. Comfort her, Hamlet.
HAMLET	Are you all right, lady?
QUEEN	What is wrong with you that you stare at nothing and talk to the air? Your eyes are wild. Like soldiers awakened by an alarm, your hair stands on end. Sweet son! Restore your sense from your raving. What are you looking at?
HAMLET	At him! See, how he glares at me! His shape and message together would move stones. Don't look at me, spirit, lest you alter my serious intent and rob me of intensity. Your tears you trade for blood.

ACT III

TRANSLATION

QUEEN	To whom do you speak this?
HAMLET	Do you see nothing there? 130
QUEEN	Nothing at all; yet all that is I see.
HAMLET	Nor did you nothing hear?
QUEEN	No, nothing but ourselves.
HAMLET	Why, look you there! look, how it steals away;
	My father, in his habit as he liv'd;
	Look! where he goes, even now, out at the portal. 135
	[Exit GHOST]
QUEEN	This is the very coinage of your brain:
	This bodiless creation ecstasy
	Is very cunning in.
HAMLET	Ecstasy!
	My pulse, as yours, doth temperately keep time, 140
	And makes as healthful music. It is not madness
	That I have utter'd: bring me to the test,
	And I the matter will re-word, which madness
	Would gambol from. Mother, for love of grace,
	Lay not that flattering unction to your soul, 145
	That not your trespass but my madness speaks;
	It will but skin and film the ulcerous place,
	Whiles rank corruption, mining all within,
	Infects unseen. Confess yourself to heaven;
	Repent what's past; avoid what is to come; 150
	And do not spread the compost on the weeds
	To make them ranker. Forgive me this my virtue:
	For in the fatness of these pursy times
	Virtue itself of vice must pardon beg,
	Yea, curb and woo for leave to do him good. 155
QUEEN	O Hamlet! thou hast cleft my heart in twain.

ORIGINAL

QUEEN	Who are you talking to?
HAMLET	Don't you see it?
QUEEN	I see everything but the thing you are talking to.
HAMLET	Didn't you hear anything?
QUEEN	No, only our conversation.
HAMLET	Look there, where my father's ghost, dressed in his customary clothes, moves away. See, he goes out the door. *[The GHOST departs]*
QUEEN	Your mind is deceiving you. Your mental illness has created a ghost.
HAMLET	Madness! My pulse, like yours, is normal and steady. It is not madness that I have talked to a ghost. Test me and I will repeat what I said. If I were insane, I would stray from the words. Mother, for your love of goodness, don't try to cleanse your soul of sin by claiming that I'm crazy. Your rejection of my charge will only smooth over your foul crime and let it continue to fester. Confess your crime to God. Repent what you've done. Avoid punishment in the future. Don't fertilize weeds to increase their odor. Forgive me my good intent. In the grossness of this adulterous time, goodness takes second place to crime. Please, stop sinning and beg to be good.
QUEEN	Oh, Hamlet! You have broken my heart.

ACT III

HAMLET	O! throw away the worser part of it,
	And live the purer with the other half.
	Good night; but go not to mine uncle's bed;
	Assume a virtue, if you have it not. 160
	That monster, custom, who all sense doth eat,
	Of habits devil, is angel yet in this,
	That to the use of actions fair and good
	He likewise gives a frock or livery,
	That aptly is put on. Refrain to-night; 165
	And that shall lend a kind of easiness
	To the next abstinence: the next more easy;
	For use almost can change the stamp of nature,
	And exorcise the devil or throw him out
	With wondrous potency. Once more, good-night: 170
	And when you are desirous to be bless'd,
	I'll blessing beg of you. For this same lord,
	[Pointing to POLONIUS]
	I do repent: but heaven hath pleas'd it so,
	To punish me with this, and this with me,
	That I must be their scourge and minister. 175
	I will bestow him, and will answer well
	The death I gave him. So, again, good-night.
	I must be cruel only to be kind:
	Thus bad begins and worse remains behind.
	One word more, good lady.
QUEEN	What shall I do? 180
HAMLET	Not this, by no means, that I bid you do:
	Let the bloat king tempt you again to bed;
	Pinch wanton on your cheek; call you his mouse;
	And let him, for a pair of reechy kisses,
	Or paddling in your neck with his damn'd fingers, 185
	Make you to ravel all this matter out,
	That I essentially am not in madness,
	But mad in craft. 'Twere good you let him know;
	For who that's but a queen, fair, sober, wise,
	Would from a paddock, from a bat, a gib, 190
	Such dear concernings hide? who would do so?
	No, in despite of sense and secrecy,
	Unpeg the basket on the house's top,
	Let the birds fly, and, like the famous ape,
	To try conclusions, in the basket creep, 195
	And break your own neck down.
QUEEN	Be thou assur'd, if words be made of breath,
	And breath of life, I have no life to breathe
	What thou hast said to me.

ORIGINAL

HAMLET	Then toss out the evil part and live righteously with the good half. Good night. Avoid my uncle's bed. Seem like a good person, even if you have to pretend. Habit, which wears down good sense, may work for good. By behaving well, you appear good. Stay away from Claudius tonight. Once you abstain from adultery, goodness will come more easily to you. With practice, you can alter bad habits and, with admirable strength, overcome the urge to sin. Again, good night. And when you are ready for a blessing, I will ask your blessing for myself. *[He points to POLONIUS]* I am sorry that I killed Polonius. But the deed pleased God, who punishes me with a crime. I must serve God as a warrior against evil. I will remove the body and will atone for murdering him. Again, good night. I must be tough to help you. And so I begin with a bad deed and face worse ones to come. One more word, good lady.

ACT III

QUEEN	What shall I do to help you?
HAMLET	I don't want you to commit murder. Let the pompous Claudius summon you to his bed. Let him pinch your flirty cheek and call you "mouse." Let him pay you with foul kisses or stroke your neck while you ponder this crime. I am not insane. Only crafty. It is good that you inform him. Who but a queen—beautiful, serious, wise—would hide such serious matters? Who would conceal sin? No one would overthrow sense, take down a nest from the roof, and let the birds fly away. Then hide in the nest and break your neck.
QUEEN	Be certain that I won't reveal your secret.

TRANSLATION

HAMLET	I must to England; you know that?

QUEEN   Alack!   200
I had forgot: 'tis so concluded on.

HAMLET   There's letters seal'd; and my two schoolfellows,
Whom I will trust as I will adders fang'd,
They bear the mandate; they must sweep my way,
And marshal me to knavery. Let it work;   205
For 'tis the sport to have the enginer
Hoist with his own petard: and 't shall go hard
But I will delve one yard below their mines,
And blow them at the moon. O! 'tis most sweet,
When in one line two crafts directly meet.   210
This man shall set me packing;
I'll lug the guts into the neighbour room.
Mother, good-night. Indeed this counsellor
Is now most still, most secret, and most grave,
Who was in life a foolish prating knave.   215
Come, sir, to draw toward an end with you.
Good-night, mother.
[Exeunt severally; HAMLET tugging in POLONIUS]

HAMLET	You know that Claudius has sent me to England?
QUEEN	I had forgotten. That was his plan.
HAMLET	He gave me sealed letters and charged my old friends, whom I trust like poisonous snakes. They must prepare the way for Claudius's plot to kill me. Let the plan go into action. I want to catch Claudius on the tip of his own spear. It won't be easy, but I will outdistance them and foil their plot. It is good that two plots—mine and Claudius's—merge. Claudius has sent me from Denmark. I'll drag Polonius into the next room. Good night, mother. Polonius, who was a talkative fool, shall be silent, crafty, and serious. Come, sir, I will put an end to you. Good night, mother. *[They depart in different directions. HAMLET drags POLONIUS away]*

ACT III

ACT IV, SCENE 1

A room in the castle.

[Enter KING, QUEEN, ROSENCRANTZ, and GUILDENSTERN]

KING   There's matter in these sighs, these profound heaves:
      You must translate; 'tis fit we understand them.
      Where is your son?

QUEEN   *[To ROSENCRANTZ and GUILDENSTERN]*
      Bestow this place on us a little while.
      [Exeunt ROSENCRANTZ and GUILDENSTERN]
      Ah! my good lord, what have I seen to-night.   5

KING   What, Gertrude? How does Hamlet?

QUEEN   Mad as the sea and wind, when both contend
      Which is the mightier. In his lawless fit,
      Behind the arras hearing something stir,
      Whips out his rapier, cries, 'A rat! a rat!'   10
      And, in his brainish apprehension, kills
      The unseen good old man.

KING   O heavy deed!
      It had been so with us had we been there.
      His liberty is full of threats to all;
      To you yourself, to us, to every one.   15
      Alas! how shall this bloody deed be answer'd?
      It will be laid to us, whose providence
      Should have kept short, restrain'd, and out of haunt,
      This mad young man: but so much was our love,
      We would not understand what was most fit,   20
      But, like the owner of a foul disease,
      To keep it from divulging, let it feed
      Even on the pith of life. Where is he gone?

QUEEN   To draw apart the body he hath kill'd;
      O'er whom his very madness, like some ore   25
      Among a mineral of metals base,
      Shows itself pure: he weeps for what is done.

ACT IV, SCENE 1

A room in the castle.

[Enter KING, QUEEN, ROSENCRANTZ, and GUILDENSTERN]

KING   There's a reason for your sighing. Explain yourself. I want to know the reason. Where is Hamlet?

QUEEN   *[To ROSENCRANTZ and GUILDENSTERN]* Leave us in privacy. *[ROSENCRANTZ and GUILDENSTERN depart]* Oh, my lord, what have I seen tonight?

KING   What is it, Gertrude? How is Hamlet?

QUEEN   In his uncontrolled state, he heard a noise behind the drape. He pulled out his sword, yelling, "A rat! a rat!" And in his frenzy, stabbed Polonius.

KING   If we let Hamlet wander freely, he could injure anybody—you, me, anybody. How shall I punish this murder? People will blame me for letting a madman go free instead of having the foresight to keep him locked up. I loved him so much that I did not see what must be done. I concealed his illness and let it harm others. Where is he now?

QUEEN   Hiding the body that he murdered. Shining through his frenzy is a pure streak of sorrow for what he did.

ACT IV

TRANSLATION

KING   O Gertrude! come away.
The sun no sooner shall the mountains touch
But we will ship him hence; and this vile deed   30
We must, with all our majesty and skill,
Both countenance and excuse. Ho! Guildenstern!
[Re-enter ROSENCRANTZ and GUILDENSTERN]
Friends both, go join you with some further aid:
Hamlet in madness hath Polonius slain,
And from his mother's closet hath he dragg'd him: 35
Go seek him out; speak fair, and bring the body
Into the chapel. I pray you, haste in this.
[Exeunt ROSENCRANTZ and GUILDENSTERN]
Come, Gertrude, we'll call up our wisest friends;
And let them know both what we mean to do,
And what's untimely done: so, haply, slander,   40
Whose whisper o'er the world's diameter,
As level as the cannon to his blank
Transports his poison'd shot, may miss our name,
And hit the woundless air. O! come away;
My soul is full of discord and dismay. *[Exeunt]*   45

KING   Gertrude, stay away from him. Before the sun rises to the mountain top, I will send him to England by ship. I must explain and account for this murder. Come, Guildenstern! *[Re-enter ROSENCRANTZ and GUILDENSTERN]* Friends, I must ask you both to do something else for me. In a frenzy, Hamlet stabbed Polonius and has dragged the corpse from his mother's room. *[ROSENCRANTZ and GUILDENSTERN go out]* Gertrude, let's summon our wisest friends and tell them what Hamlet has done and what we intend to do about it. Come with me. I am disturbed and dismayed. *[They depart]*

ACT IV

ACT IV, SCENE 2

Another room in the same.

[Enter HAMLET]

HAMLET   Safely stowed.

ROSENCRANTZ AND GUILDENSTERN   *[Within]* Hamlet! Lord Hamlet!

HAMLET   What noise? who calls on Hamlet?
O! here they come.
[Enter ROSENCRANTZ and GUILDENSTERN]

ROSENCRANTZ   What have you done, my lord, with the dead body?   5

HAMLET   Compounded it with dust, whereto 'tis kin.

ROSENCRANTZ   Tell us where 'tis, that we may take it thence
And bear it to the chapel.

HAMLET   Do not believe it.

ROSENCRANTZ   Believe what?   10

HAMLET   That I can keep your counsel and not mine
own. Besides, to be demanded of a sponge! what
replication should be made by the son of a king?

ROSENCRANTZ   Take you me for a sponge, my lord?

HAMLET   Ay, sir, that soaks up the king's countenance,   15
his rewards, his authorities. But such officers
do the king best service in the end: he keeps them,
like an ape, in the corner of his jaw; first mouthed,
to be last swallowed: when he needs what you have
gleaned, it is but squeezing you, and, sponge, you   20
shall be dry again.

ROSENCRANTZ   I understand you not, my lord.

ACT IV, SCENE 2

Another room in the castle.

[Enter HAMLET]

HAMLET	Safely hidden.
ROSENCRANTZ AND GUILDENSTERN	*[Within]* Hamlet! Prince Hamlet!
HAMLET	What was that? Who is calling me? Here come Rosencrantz and Guildenstern. *[Enter ROSENCRANTZ and GUILDENSTERN]*
ROSENCRANTZ	Where did you put the corpse, my lord?
HAMLET	I mixed it with dust, from which people are made.
ROSENCRANTZ	Tell us where it is so we can carry it to the chapel.
HAMLET	Don't believe it.
ROSENCRANTZ	Believe what?
HAMLET	That I can keep your secret but I can't keep my own secret. Why should I let a sponge question my actions! What should a royal prince reply?
ROSENCRANTZ	Do you compare me to a sponge, my lord?
HAMLET	Yes. You soak up the king's favor, rewards, and powers. But such toadies serve the king best. He stores them in his jaw like an ape hides nuts. The first he conceals is the last he swallows. When he needs your information, he will squeeze you dry like a sponge.
ROSENCRANTZ	I don't understand, my lord.

HAMLET	I am glad of it: a knavish speech sleeps in a foolish ear.
ROSENCRANTZ	My lord, you must tell us where the body is, and go with us to the king.
HAMLET	The body is with the king, but the king is not with the body. The king is a thing—
GUILDENSTERN	A thing, my lord!
HAMLET	Of nothing: bring me to him. Hide fox, and all after. *[Exeunt]*

HAMLET	I am glad you don't. A wicked speech doesn't convince a fool.
ROSENCRANTZ	My lord, you must tell us where you put the body. We must escort you to the king.
HAMLET	Polonius's body is with King Hamlet, but King Claudius is not with Polonius's body. The king is an object.
GUILDENSTERN	A thing, my lord!
HAMLET	Nothing. Take me to him. Let's play hide and seek. *[They go out]*

ACT IV

ACT IV, SCENE 3

Another room in the same.

[Enter KING, attended]

KING	I have sent to seek him, and to find the body.
	How dangerous is it that this man goes loose!
	Yet must not we put the strong law on him:
	He's lov'd of the distracted multitude,
	Who like not in their judgment, but their eyes; 5
	And where 'tis so, the offender's scourge is weigh'd,
	But never the offence. To bear all smooth and even,
	This sudden sending him away must seem
	Deliberate pause: diseases desperate grown
	By desperate appliance are reliev'd, 10
	Or not at all.
	[Enter ROSENCRANTZ]
	How now! what hath befall'n?
ROSENCRANTZ	Where the dead body is bestow'd, my lord,
	We cannot get from him.
KING	But where is he?
ROSENCRANTZ	Without, my lord; guarded, to know your pleasure.
KING	Bring him before us. 15
ROSENCRANTZ	Ho, Guildenstern! bring in my lord.
	[Enter HAMLET and GUILDENSTERN]
KING	Now, Hamlet, where's Polonius?
HAMLET	At supper.
KING	At supper! Where?
HAMLET	Not where he eats, but where he is eaten: a 20
	certain convocation of politic worms are e'en at him.
	Your worm is your only emperor for diet: we fat all
	creatures else to fat us, and we fat ourselves for
	maggots: your fat king and your lean beggar is but
	variable service; two dishes, but to one table: that's 25
	the end.

ACT IV, SCENE 3

Another room in the castle.

[Enter KING, attended]

KING
I have sent someone to find Hamlet and to locate Polonius's corpse. It is dangerous for Hamlet to go loose! But I must not condemn him under the law. The Danish people love him for his appearance. When people admire a criminal, they ponder his punishment, but not his crime. To smooth over this difficult situation, I must seem to send Hamlet away on purpose. Extreme illness requires extreme remedies. *[Enter ROSENCRANTZ]* What is happening?

ROSENCRANTZ
My lord, we can't learn from Hamlet where he put Polonius's body.

KING
Where is Hamlet?

ROSENCRANTZ
He is outside, my lord, and under guard until you decide what to do with him.

KING
Bring him in.

ROSENCRANTZ
Guildenstern, bring Hamlet here. *[Enter HAMLET and GUILDENSTERN]*

KING
Hamlet, where is Polonius?

HAMLET
Eating dinner.

KING
Eating dinner! Where?

HAMLET
Not where he dines, but where worms dine on him. Worms are all powerful. All creatures grow fat so maggots can eat them. A fat king and a skinny beggar are two examples of the same thing. Both turn up on the worm's table. That's the way of it.

ACT IV

KING	Alas, alas!
HAMLET	A man may fish with the worm that hath eat of a king, and eat of the fish that hath fed of that worm.
KING	What dost thou mean by this?
HAMLET	Nothing, but to show you how a king may go a progress through the guts of a beggar.
KING	Where is Polonius?
HAMLET	In heaven; send thither to see: if your messenger find him not there, seek him i' the other place yourself. But, indeed, if you find him not within this month, you shall nose him as you go up the stairs into the lobby.
KING	*[To some Attendants]* Go seek him there.
HAMLET	He will stay till you come. *[Exeunt Attendants]*
KING	Hamlet, this deed, for thine especial safety, Which we do tender, as we dearly grieve For that which thou hast done, must send thee hence With fiery quickness: therefore prepare thyself; The bark is ready, and the wind at help. The associates tend, and every thing is bent For England.
HAMLET	For England!
KING	Ay, Hamlet.
HAMLET	Good.
KING	So is it, if thou knew'st our purposes.
HAMLET	I see a cherub that sees them. But, come; for England! Farewell, dear mother.
KING	Thy loving father, Hamlet.

30

35

40

45

50

KING	Oh, no!
HAMLET	A person can bait a hook with a worm that ate a king. Then the person can eat the fish that ate the worm.
KING	What are you talking about?
HAMLET	Nothing. Just an example of how a king may proceed through a beggar's intestines.
KING	Where is Polonius?
HAMLET	If your messenger can't find Polonius in heaven, you can look for him in hell yourself. Indeed, if you don't find the body this month, you will smell it as you climb the steps in the foyer.
KING	*[To some Attendants]* Go look for him in the foyer.
HAMLET	He will stay until you get there. *[Attendants depart]*
KING	Hamlet, for the crime you have committed, we must send you away quickly to assure your safety. So, pack for the trip. Your companions wait for you. Everything is ready for the voyage to England.
HAMLET	England!
KING	Yes, Hamlet.
HAMLET	Good.
KING	It is good, if you understand my purpose.
HAMLET	I see an angel that understands your purpose. I'm leaving for England. Goodbye, dear mother.
KING	I am your loving father, Hamlet.

ACT IV

HAMLET   My mother: father and mother is man and
            wife, man and wife is one flesh, and so, my mother.
            Come, for England! *[Exit]*   55

KING   Follow him at foot; tempt him with speed aboard:
            Delay it not, I'll have him hence to-night.
            Away! for every thing is seal'd and done
            That else leans on the affair: pray you, make haste.
            [Exeunt ROSENCRANTZ and GUILDENSTERN]
            And, England, if my love thou hold'st at aught,—   60
            As my great power thereof may give these sense,
            Since yet thy cicatrice looks raw and red
            After the Danish sword, and thy free awe
            Pays homage to us,—thou mayst not coldly set
            Our sovereign process, which imports at full,   65
            By letters congruing to that effect
            The present death of Hamlet. Do it, England;
            For like the hectic in my blood he rages,
            And thou must cure me. Till I know 'tis done,
            Howe'er my haps, my joys were ne'er begun. *[Exit]*   70

ORIGINAL

HAMLET	My mother. A father and mother are man and wife. If man and wife form one flesh, therefore, my parent is my mother. I leave for England. *[He goes out]*
KING	Follow him closely. Urge him to board quickly. Don't delay. I want him gone by tonight. Go. Everything is arranged. Before anything can go wrong, please, hurry. *[ROSENCRANTZ and GUILDENSTERN depart]* Oh King of England, if you care about pleasing me, if my royal power influences you, since your scar from the Danish war is still red and inflamed, if you revere me after the Danish army departed, you can't ignore my royal plan. By letter, I order you to kill Hamlet. Kill him when he arrives in England. He disturbs me like frenzied blood. England must rid me of him. Until I learn of his death, whatever happens to me, I can't be happy. *[He goes out]*

ACT IV

ACT IV, SCENE 4

A plain in Denmark.

[Enter FORTINBRAS, a Captain, and Soldiers, marching]

FORTINBRAS	Go, captain, from me greet the Danish king;
	Tell him that, by his licence, Fortinbras
	Claims the conveyance of a promis'd march
	Over his kingdom. You know the rendezvous.
	If that his majesty would aught with us,
	We shall express our duty in his eye,
	And let him know so.

5

CAPTAIN	I will do't, my lord.

FORTINBRAS	Go softly on.

[Exeunt FORTINBRAS and Soldiers]
[Enter HAMLET, ROSENCRANTZ, GUILDENSTERN, and Others]

HAMLET	Good sir, whose powers are these?

CAPTAIN	They are of Norway, sir.

10

HAMLET	How purpos'd, sir, I pray you?

CAPTAIN	Against some part of Poland.

HAMLET	Who commands them, sir?

CAPTAIN	The nephew to old Norway, Fortinbras.

HAMLET	Goes it against the main of Poland, sir,
	Or for some frontier?

15

CAPTAIN	Truly to speak, and with no addition,
	We go to gain a little patch of ground
	That hath in it no profit but the name.
	To pay five ducats, five, I would not farm it;
	Nor will it yield to Norway or the Pole
	A ranker rate, should it be sold in fee.

20

HAMLET	Why, then the Polack never will defend it.

CAPTAIN	Yes, 'tis already garrison'd.

HAMLET	Two thousand souls and twenty thousand ducats
	Will not debate the question of this straw:
	This is the imposthume of much wealth and peace,
	That inward breaks, and shows no cause without
	Why the man dies. I humbly thank you, sir.

25

ACT IV, SCENE 4

A plain in Denmark.

[Enter FORTINBRAS, a Captain, and Soldiers, marching]

FORTINBRAS   Captain, take my greetings to King Claudius. Report that, as he has allowed, Fortinbras will march his troops through Denmark. You know the meeting place. If Claudius wants to see me personally, tell him where to meet me.

CAPTAIN   I will, my lord.

FORTINBRAS   March peacefully on. *[FORTINBRAS and his soldiers depart] [Enter HAMLET, ROSENCRANTZ, GUILDENSTERN, and Others]*

HAMLET   Captain, whose troops are these?

CAPTAIN   They come from Norway, sir.

HAMLET   Where are they marching, sir?

CAPTAIN   To Poland.

HAMLET   Who is their leader, sir?

CAPTAIN   Fortinbras, the nephew of the old king of Norway.

HAMLET   Is Fortinbras attacking all of Poland, sir, or just the border?

CAPTAIN   We intend to seize a parcel of land for political reasons. I wouldn't pay five ducats to farm it. It wouldn't profit Norway or Poland a greater amount if it were sold.

HAMLET   Then Poland will not defend it.

CAPTAIN   Yes. The Polish army has already set up a defense.

HAMLET   Two thousand men and twenty thousand ducats will not settle the international dispute over a straw. This is the rot arising from wealth and inaction. Such a war is not worth the death of a soldier. Thanks, Captain.

ACT IV

TRANSLATION

CAPTAIN	God be wi' you, sir. *[Exit]*	30
ROSENCRANTZ	Will't please you go, my lord?	
HAMLET	I'll be with you straight. Go a little before.	

               [Exeunt all except HAMLET]
How all occasions do inform against me,
And spur my dull revenge! What is a man,
If his chief good and market of his time
Be but to sleep and feed? a beast, no more.   35
Sure he that made us with such large discourse,
Looking before and after, gave us not
That capability and god-like reason
To fust in us unus'd. Now, whe'r it be
Bestial oblivion, or some craven scruple   40
Of thinking too precisely on the event,
A thought, which, quarter'd, hath but one part wisdom,
And ever three parts coward, I do not know
Why yet I live to say 'This thing's to do';
Sith I have cause and will and strength and means   45
To do 't. Examples gross as earth exhort me:
Witness this army of such mass and charge
Led by a delicate and tender prince,
Whose spirit with divine ambition puff'd
Makes mouths at the invisible event,   50
Exposing what is mortal and unsure
To all that fortune, death and danger dare,
Even for an egg-shell. Rightly to be great
Is not to stir without great argument,
But greatly to find quarrel in a straw   55
When honour's at the stake. How stand I then,
That have a father kill'd, a mother stain'd,
Excitements of my reason and my blood,
And let all sleep, while, to my shame, I see
The imminent death of twenty thousand men,   60
That, for a fantasy and trick of fame,
Go to their graves like beds, fight for a plot
Whereon the numbers cannot try the cause,
Which is not tomb enough and continent
To hide the slain? O! from this time forth,   65
My thoughts be bloody, or be nothing worth! *[Exit]*

CAPTAIN	God go with you, sir. *[He departs]*
ROSENCRANTZ	Are you ready to go, my lord?
HAMLET	I will follow immediately. Precede me. *[They all depart except HAMLET]* Now all events accuse me and arouse my vengeance! What is human worth if a person's value lies only in sleeping and eating? He's an animal, no more than that. God made us with powers of reason to look at the past and into the future. Reason has no value if it rusts from disuse. Whether it be the empty-headedness of an animal or some crafty plot that requires too much thinking, I don't know whether my idea is one part wisdom and three parts cowardice. But I acknowledge that I must seek vengeance. So long as I have purpose, willingness, strength, and the opportunity to kill Claudius. Look at the Norwegian army being led by a young and inexperienced prince, who allows his ambition to ignore the consequences. He risks his men and the outcome of the battle, where death and danger threaten, just to grasp an eggshell. It is right to abstain from war without good cause, but Fortinbras fights over a straw in the name of honor. Look at how I do nothing to avenge a murdered father and scandal-ridden mother. Although my mind and courage tingle, I do nothing. To my shame, I observe twenty thousand Norwegians marching into a deadly situation. These men sink into their graves like going to bed, all in the name of Norway's reputation. These men fight for a bit of land that they can't stand on. There is not enough ground to bury them all or to conceal the wasted lives. From now on, I will foster bloody thoughts or else consider myself worthless! *[He goes out]*

ACT IV

ACT IV, SCENE 5

Elsinore. A room in the castle.

[Enter QUEEN, HORATIO, and a Gentleman]

QUEEN   I will not speak with her.

GENTLEMAN   She is importunate, indeed distract:
Her mood will needs be pitied.

QUEEN   What would she have?

GENTLEMAN   She speaks much of her father; says she hears
There's tricks i' the world; and hems, and beats her heart;   5
Spurns enviously at straws; speaks things in doubt,
That carry but half sense: her speech is nothing,
Yet the unshaped use of it doth move
The hearers to collection; they aim at it,
And botch the words up fit to their own thoughts;   10
Which, as her winks, and nods, and gestures yield them,
Indeed would make one think there might be thought,
Though nothing sure, yet much unhappily.

HORATIO   'Twere good she were spoken with, for she may strew
Dangerous conjectures in ill-breeding minds.   15

QUEEN   Let her come in. *[Exit Gentleman]*
To my sick soul, as sin's true nature is,
Each toy seems prologue to some great amiss:
So full of artless jealousy is guilt,
It spills itself in fearing to be spilt.   20
[Re-enter Gentleman, with OPHELIA]

OPHELIA   Where is the beauteous majesty of Denmark?

QUEEN   How now, Ophelia!

OPHELIA   *[Sings]*

> *How should I your true love know*
> *From another one?*
> *By his cockle hat and staff,*   25
> *And his sandal shoon.*

QUEEN   Alas! sweet lady, what imports this song?

ACT IV, SCENE 5

Elsinore. A room in the castle.

[Enter QUEEN, HORATIO, and a Gentleman]

QUEEN   I won't talk to Ophelia.

GENTLEMAN   She begs and seems out of her wits. Pity her state of mind.

QUEEN   What does she want?

GENTLEMAN   She talks about Polonius. She says she hears rumors of trickery. She mutters and beats her chest. She strikes at trifles and makes little sense. Her words are worthless, but her incoherent mutterings cause people to wonder if there is deception. Listeners distort her meaning to make it match their guesses. Her gestures and nods seem sensible, but there is no way to know for sure. Whatever the cause, it is sad.

HORATIO   It is important to speak to her, for she may start rumors in evil minds.

QUEEN   Show her in. *[Courtiers go out]* Guilt is so naive a suspicion that it spills out in trying to remain hidden. *[Re-enter Gentleman, with OPHELIA]*

OPHELIA   Where is the beautiful queen of Denmark?

QUEEN   What are you saying, Ophelia!

OPHELIA   *[Sings] How can I know a sincere love from any other? By the shell on his hat and his walking stick and sandals, he resembles a holy pilgrim.*

QUEEN   Sweet lady, what does this song mean?

ACT IV

TRANSLATION

OPHELIA	Say you? nay, pray you, mark. *[Sings]*

> *He is dead and gone, lady,*
> *He is dead and gone;* 30
> *At his head a grass-green turf;*
> *At his heels a stone.*

O, ho!

QUEEN	Nay, but Ophelia,—
OPHELIA	Pray you, mark. 35 *[Sings] White his shroud as the mountain snow,—* *[Enter KING]*
QUEEN	Alas! look here, my lord.
OPHELIA	*[Sings]*

> *Larded all with sweet flowers;*
> *Which bewept to the grave did not go*
> *With true-love showers.* 40

KING	How do you, pretty lady?
OPHELIA	Well, God 'ild you! They say the owl was a baker's daughter. Lord! we know what we are, but know not what we may be. God be at your table!
KING	Conceit upon her father. 45
OPHELIA	Pray you, let's have no words of this; but when they ask you what it means, say you this: *[Sings]*

> *To-morrow is Saint Valentine's day,*
> *All in the morning betime,*
> *And I a maid at your window,* 50
> *To be your Valentine:*
> *Then up he rose, and donn'd his clothes*
> *And dupp'd the chamber door;*
> *Let in the maid, that out a maid*
> *Never departed more.* 55

KING	Pretty Ophelia!

OPHELIA	What did you say? Please, listen. *[Sings] He is dead and buried, lady, he is dead and buried. Green grass grows over his head. A stone marks his feet.*
QUEEN	But, Ophelia.
OPHELIA	Please, listen. *[Sings] His grave garment is as white as snow on the mountain. [Enter KING]*
QUEEN	Look at her, Claudius.
OPHELIA	*[Sings] Sprinkled all over with fresh flowers, he went to his grave without the tears of those who loved him.*
KING	How are you, pretty lady?
OPHELIA	God reward you! There is a story that the baker's daughter turned into an owl. Lord, we are aware of what we are, but we don't recognize what we could become. God bless your table!
KING	She is disturbed by Polonius's death.
OPHELIA	Please, don't talk about his death. When I ask you to interpret, you should reply: *[Sings] Tomorrow is Saint Valentine's day. In the morning, I will stand at your window and become your sweetheart. Then, her lover rose, dressed, and opened the door. She was a virgin when she entered, but not when she left.*
KING	Pretty Ophelia!

TRANSLATION

OPHELIA   Indeed, la! without an oath, I'll make
                 an end on 't:
                 [Sings]

> By Gis and by Saint Charity,
>   Alack, and fie for shame!   60
> Young men will do 't, if they come to 't;
>   By Cock they are to blame.
> Quoth she, before you tumbled me,
>   You promis'd me to wed:
>   He answers:
> So would I ha' done, by yonder sun,   65
>   An thou hadst not come to my bed.

KING   How long hath she been thus?

OPHELIA   I hope all will be well. We must be patient:
                 but I cannot choose but weep, to think they
                 should lay him i' the cold ground. My brother shall   70
                 know of it: and so I thank you for your good counsel.
                 Come, my coach! Good-night, ladies; good-night,
                 sweet ladies; good-night, good-night. *[Exit]*

KING   Follow her close; give her good watch, I
                 pray you. *[Exit HORATIO]*   75
                 O! this is the poison of deep grief; it springs
                 All from her father's death. O Gertrude, Gertrude!
                 When sorrows come, they come not single spies,
                 But in battalions. First, her father slain;
                 Next, your son gone; but he most violent author   80
                 Of his own just remove: the people muddied,
                 Thick and unwholesome in their thoughts and whispers,
                 For good Polonius's death; and we have done but greenly,
                 In hugger-mugger to inter him: poor Ophelia
                 Divided from herself and her fair judgment,   85
                 Without the which we are pictures, or mere beasts:
                 Last, and as much containing as all these,
                 Her brother is in secret come from France,
                 Feeds on his wonder, keeps himself in clouds,
                 And wants not buzzers to infect his ear   90
                 With pestilent speeches of his father's death;
                 Wherein necessity, of matter beggar'd,
                 Will nothing stick our person to arraign
                 In ear and ear. O my dear Gertrude! this,
                 Like to a murdering-piece, in many places   95
                 Gives me superfluous death. *[A noise within]*

ORIGINAL

OPHELIA	Indeed, I will come to the end of my song: *[Sings]*

By Jesus and holy charity, shame on you! Young men will take advantage of girls, if they can. By God, they are to blame. Said she, "Before you seduced me, you promised to marry me." He replies, "I would have married you if you hadn't given in to my seduction."

KING	How long has she been like this?
OPHELIA	I hope things turn out all right. We must be patient. But I must weep to think of burying my father in the cold earth. My brother will hear of Polonius's murder. I thank you for your advice. Come, my carriage is waiting! Good night ladies; good night, sweet ladies; good night, good night. *[She goes out]*
KING	Stay with her and watch out for her, please. *[HORATIO goes out]* Oh, this is the result of sorrow. It derives from Polonius's death. O, Gertrude, Gertrude, when sadness comes, it arrives not one at a time, but in armies. First, her father is killed. Then, Hamlet leaves for England. But Hamlet deserved to be removed. After Polonius died, the Danish people were confused and spread rumors arising from their evil thoughts. And I acted foolishly by burying Polonius in secret. Poor Ophelia, separated from her sanity, is like a picture, an animal. Then, while we dealt with these problems, Laertes arrived secretly from France. He feeds on imagination, shrouds himself in gloom, and lets gossip poison his mind with accusations about Polonius's death. Lacking facts, rumors charge me with the crime. O dear Gertrude, like a cannon loaded with a loose charge, this scandal wounds me in many places when one bullet would have killed me. *[A noise within]*

ACT IV

QUEEN	Alack! what noise is this?
	[Enter a Messenger]
KING	Where are my Switzers? Let them guard the door.
	What is the matter?
MESSENGER	Save yourself, my lord;

The ocean, overpeering of his list,
Eats not the flats with more impetuous haste   100
Than young Laertes, in a riotous head,
O'erbears your officers. The rabble call him lord;
And, as the world were now but to begin,
Antiquity forgot, custom not known,
The ratifiers and props of every word,   105
They cry, 'Choose we; Laertes shall be king!'
Caps, hands, and tongues, applaud it to the clouds,
'Laertes shall be king, Laertes king!'

QUEEN	How cheerfully on the false trail they cry!
	O! this is counter, you false Danish dogs! 110
KING	The doors are broke. *[Noise within]*
	[Enter LAERTES, armed; Danes following]
LAERTES	Where is the king? Sirs, stand you all without.
DANES	No, let's come in.
LAERTES	I pray you, give me leave.
DANES	We will, we will. *[They retire without the door]*
LAERTES	I thank you: keep the door. O thou vile king! 115
	Give me my father.
QUEEN	Calmly, good Laertes.
LAERTES	That drop of blood that's calm proclaims me bastard,
	Cries cuckold to my father, brands the harlot
	Even here, between the chaste unsmirched brows
	Of my true mother.
KING	What is the cause, Laertes, 120
	That thy rebellion looks so giant-like?
	Let him go, Gertrude; do not fear our person:
	There's such divinity doth hedge a king,
	That treason can but peep to what it would,
	Acts little of his will. Tell me, Laertes, 125
	Why thou art thus incens'd. Let him go, Gertrude.
	Speak, man.
LAERTES	Where is my father?

QUEEN	What caused that noise? *[Enter a Messenger]*
KING	Where is my Swiss guard? Let them watch the door. What has happened?
MESSENGER	Save yourself, my lord. A flood over the dikes does not spread over the low country any faster than Laertes overcomes your officers. Commoners call him lord. People forget Danish history and customs. In support of Laertes's revolt, the rabble cry, "We want Laertes to be king!" With caps, applause, and cries, they shout to heaven, "Laertes should be king, Laertes the king!"
QUEEN	How gladly they shout false mottoes! Oh, this is wrong, you Danish traitors!
KING	They have broken down the doors. *[Noise within] [Enter LAERTES, armed; Danes following]*
LAERTES	Where is the king? Sirs, leave the room.
DANES	Let us in.
LAERTES	Please, do as I say.
DANES	We will obey you. *[They retire outside the door]*
LAERTES	Thanks to you all. Guard the door. O you treacherous king. Give me back Polonius.
QUEEN	Stay calm, Laertes.
LAERTES	Any part of me that is calm betrays my father and calls my mother a whore.
KING	Why are you leading a revolt, Laertes? Let go of him, Gertrude. Don't worry about me. A king is so surrounded by God's grace that rebels can glance at the king but do no harm. Tell me, Laertes, why are you so angry? Let go of him, Gertrude. Tell me.
LAERTES	Where is my father?

ACT IV

TRANSLATION

KING	Dead.
QUEEN	But not by him.
KING	Let him demand his fill.

LAERTES   How came he dead? I'll not be juggled with.   130
To hell, allegiance! vows, to the blackest devil!
Conscience and grace, to the profoundest pit!
I dare damnation. To this point I stand,
That both the worlds I give to negligence,
Let come what comes; only I'll be reveng'd   135
Most throughly for my father.

KING   Who shall stay you?

LAERTES   My will, not all the world:
And for my means, I'll husband them so well,
They shall go far with little.

KING   Good Laertes,
If you desire to know the certainty   140
Of your dear father's death, is't writ in your revenge,
That, swoopstake, you will draw both friend and foe,
Winner and loser?

LAERTES   None but his enemies.

KING   Will you know them then?

LAERTES   To his good friends thus wide I'll ope my arms;   145
And like the kind life-rendering pelican,
Repast them with my blood.

KING   Why, now you speak
Like a good child and a true gentleman.
That I am guiltless of your father's death,
And am most sensibly in grief for it,   150
It shall as level to your judgment pierce
As day does to your eye.

DANES   *[Within]*   Let her come in.

KING	Dead.
QUEEN	But Claudius did not kill him.
KING	Let Laertes ask all the questions he wants to.
LAERTES	What caused his death? Don't toy with me. I will pledge to the worst demon. I will cast conscience and goodness into the deepest hell. I am risking damnation. Whatever happens on earth or in the afterlife, I will face anything. I demand revenge for my father's murder.
KING	Who is stopping you?
LAERTES	I will do as I want, not as the world wants. I will use my means so carefully that they will go far.
KING	Laertes, if you want the truth about Polonius's death, do you intend to avenge him by killing his friends and his enemies in one swoop?
LAERTES	Only his enemies.
KING	Can you identify them?
LAERTES	I will welcome his friends and, like the nurturing pelican, feed them with my blood.
KING	Now you are talking like a good son and a true gentleman. As the day goes by, you will learn that I am innocent of Polonius's death and that I grieve for his loss.
DANES	*[Within]* Let her come in.

ACT IV

LAERTES	How now! what noise is that?
	[Re-enter OPHELIA]
	O heat, dry up my brains! tears seven times salt,
	Burn out the sense and virtue of mine eye! 155
	By heaven, thy madness shall be paid by weight,
	Till our scale turn the beam. O rose of May!
	Dear maid, kind sister, sweet Ophelia!
	O heavens! is 't possible a young maid's wits
	Should be as mortal as an old man's life? 160
	Nature is fine in love, and where 'tis fine
	It sends some precious instance of itself
	After the thing it loves.

OPHELIA   *[Sings]*

> *They bore him barefac'd on the bier;*
> *Hey non nonny, nonny, hey nonny;*   165
> *And in his grave rain'd many a tear;—*

Fare you well, my dove!

LAERTES   Hadst thou thy wits, and didst persuade revenge,
It could not move thus.

OPHELIA
> *You must sing, a-down a-down,*   *170*
> *And you call him a-down-a.*

O how the wheel becomes it! It is the false steward
that stole his master's daughter.

LAERTES   This nothing's more than matter.

OPHELIA   There's rosemary that's for remembrance;   175
pray, love, remember: and there is pansies, that's
for thoughts.

LAERTES   A document in madness, thoughts and
remembrance fitted.

OPHELIA   There's fennel for you, and columbines;   180
there's rue for you; and here's some for me; we may
call it herb of grace o' Sundays. O! you must wear
your rue with a difference. There's a daisy; I would
give you some violets, but they withered all when my
father died. They say he made a good end,—   185
[Sings] For bonny sweet Robin is all my joy.

LAERTES   Thought and affliction, passion, hell itself,
She turns to favour and to prettiness.

LAERTES	What was that noise? *[Re-enter OPHELIA]* Oh anger, consume my thoughts! Salty tears burn the sight from my eyes! By heaven, your insanity shall be avenged until the family's woes bend the scale. Oh rosebud, dear girl, kind sister, sweet Ophelia! Oh heavens, can a young girl's sanity be as vulnerable as an old man's life? The nature of love is delicate and, because of its delicacy, it loses some of itself in the person it loves.
OPHELIA	*[Sings] They carried him uncovered on the bier; hey non nonny, nonny, hey nonny. And tears fell in his grave.* Farewell, my dove!
LAERTES	If you were sane and urging me to avenge Polonius, you could not be more persuasive than is your insanity.
OPHELIA	*You must sing, a-down a-down, and you call him down to the grave.* Oh how the spinning wheel keeps time with the song. A false manager kidnapped his master's daughter.
LAERTES	This nonsense is more moving than sense.
OPHELIA	I give you rosemary, which symbolizes remembrance. Please, my love, remember Polonius. And here are pansies, which symbolize thoughts.
LAERTES	A lesson in madness in which thoughts and remembrance are fitting.
OPHELIA	I give you fennel for flattery and columbines for disloyalty. I give you rue for regret and save some for myself. On Sundays, we call it a gracious herb. Oh, you must wear your regret for a different reason. Here is a daisy for trickery. I would give you violets for loyalty, but faithfulness dried up when my father died. They say he died well. *[Sings] For handsome sweet Robin brings me joy.*
LAERTES	She turns from thought and suffering, grief, hell itself, to charming and pretty things.

ACT IV

TRANSLATION

OPHELIA	*[Sings]*

> *And will a' not come again?*
> *And will a' not come again?*   190
> *No, no, he is dead;*
> *Go to thy death-bed,*
> *He never will come again.*
> *His beard was as white as snow*
> *All flaxen was his poll,*   195
> *He is gone, he is gone,*
> *And we cast away moan:*
> *God ha' mercy on his soul!*

And of all Christian souls I pray God. God be wi'ye!
[Exit]

LAERTES	Do you see this, O God?	200

KING	Laertes, I must commune with your grief,

Or you deny me right. Go but apart,
Make choice of whom your wisest friends you will,
And they shall hear and judge 'twixt you and me.
If by direct or by collateral hand   205
They find us touch'd, we will our kingdom give,
Our crown, our life, and all that we call ours,
To you in satisfaction; but if not,
Be you content to lend your patience to us,
And we shall jointly labour with your soul   210
To give it due content.

LAERTES	Let this be so:

His means of death, his obscure burial,
No trophy, sword, nor hatchment o'er his bones,
No noble rite nor formal ostentation,
Cry to be heard, as 'twere from heaven to earth,   215
That I must call 't in question.

KING	So you shall;

And where the offence is let the great axe fall.
I pray you go with me. *[Exeunt]*

OPHELIA	*[Sings] And will he not return? And will he not return? No, no, Polonius is dead. Go to your death, Polonius will never return. His beard was snowy white and his head was covered in flax-colored hair. He is dead, he is dead. And we who are left behind can only grieve. God have mercy on his soul!* and on all Christian souls, I pray God! God go with you! *[She departs]*
LAERTES	Oh God, do you see Ophelia's mental state?
KING	Laertes, I must investigate your grievance. I have a right to find out the truth. You go alone and select your most knowledgeable friends and they shall judge between us. If your friends find me guilty of killing Polonius or of abetting the crime, I will forfeit my realm, crown, life, and all that I own to you. But if they find me innocent and you agree with their decision, we shall join forces to learn the truth about the crime.
LAERTES	I agree to your proposal. I must then question how he died, why he was secretly buried without awards, sword, coat of arms, ceremony, and formal ritual. These neglected honors deserve to be proclaimed from heaven to earth.
KING	You shall restore these rites to him. Let punishment fall on your father's killer. Please, follow me. *[They go out]*

ACT IV

TRANSLATION

ACT IV, SCENE 6

Another room in the same.

[Enter HORATIO and a Servant]

HORATIO   What are they that would speak with me?

SERVANT   Sailors, sir: they say they have letters
for you.

HORATIO   Let them come in. *[Exit Servant]*
I do not know from what part of the world   5
I should be greeted, if not from Lord Hamlet.
[Enter Sailors]

FIRST SAILOR   God bless you, sir.

HORATIO   Let him bless thee too.

SECOND SAILOR   He shall, sir, an't please him.
There's a letter for you, sir;—it comes from the   10
ambassador that was bound for England;—if your
name be Horatio, as I am let to know it is.

HORATIO   *[Reads]* Horatio, when thou shalt have
overlooked this, give these fellows some means to the
king: they have letters for him. Ere we were two   15
days old at sea, a pirate of very war-like appointment
gave us chase. Finding ourselves too slow of sail, we
put on a compelled valour; in the grapple I boarded
them. On the instant, they got clear of our ship, so I
alone became their prisoner. They have dealt with   20
me like thieves of mercy, but they knew what they
did; I am to do a good turn to them. Let the king
have the letters I have sent; and repair thou to me
with as much haste as thou wouldst fly death. I have
words to speak in thine ear will make thee dumb, yet   25
are they much too light for the bore of the matter.
These good fellows will bring thee where I am.
Rosencrantz and Guildenstern hold their course for
England: of them I have much to tell thee. Farewell.
                    He that thou knowest thine,   30
                                   Hamlet.
Come, I will give you way for these your letters;
And do't the speedier, that you may direct me
To him from whom you brought them. *[Exeunt]*

ACT IV, SCENE 6

Another room in the castle.

[Enter HORATIO and a Servant]

HORATIO   Who wants to speak to me?

SERVANT   Some sailors have letters for you.

HORATIO   Let them enter. *[The Servant goes out]* The only person who would be sending me mail by sea is Hamlet. *[The Sailors enter]*

FIRST SAILOR   God bless you, sir.

HORATIO   And God bless you as well.

SECOND SAILOR   He will bless me if he chooses. Here's a letter addressed to you, if you are Horatio. It comes from an ambassador who was on his way to England.

HORATIO   *[Reads] "Horatio, when you have read this, send these sailors to the king. They have messages for him. Two days after we left Denmark, a dangerous pirate pursued our ship. Because we couldn't outrun the pirate ship, we were forced to fight. In the struggle, I boarded their ship. At that moment, the pirates left our ship. I was their only prisoner. They have been merciful to me because they know I am a royal prince. I must do a favor for the pirates. Give the other letters to the king and hurry to me as though you were running from a killer. I have information for you that will leave you speechless. Written words can't communicate so important a message. These sailors will bring you to me. Rosencrantz and Guildenstern are still bound for England. I have information about them to tell you. Farewell. Your faithful friend, Hamlet."* Come with me to the king with your letters. And do it quickly so you can lead me to the man who gave you the messages. *[They depart]*

ACT IV

TRANSLATION

ACT IV, SCENE 7

Another room in the same.

[Enter KING and LAERTES]

KING   Now must your conscience my acquittance seal,
And you must put me in your heart for friend,
Sith you have heard, and with a knowing ear,
That he which hath your noble father slain
Pursu'd my life.

LAERTES   It well appears: but tell me   5
Why you proceeded not against these feats,
So crimeful and so capital in nature,
As by your safety, wisdom, all things else,
You mainly were stirr'd up.

KING   O! for two special reasons;
Which may to you, perhaps, seem much unsinew'd,   10
But yet to me they are strong. The queen his mother
Lives almost by his looks, and for myself,—
My virtue or my plague, be it either which,—
She's so conjunctive to my life and soul,
That, as the star moves not but in his sphere,   15
I could not but by her. The other motive,
Why to a public count I might not go,
Is the great love the general gender bear him;
Who, dipping all his faults in their affection,
Would, like the spring that turneth wood to stone,   20
Convert his gyves to graces; so that my arrows,
Too slightly timber'd for so loud a wind,
Would have reverted to my bow again,
And not where I had aim'd them.

LAERTES   And so have I a noble father lost;   25
A sister driven into desperate terms,
Whose worth, if praises may go back again,
Stood challenger on mount of all the age
For her perfections. But my revenge will come.

KING   Break not your sleeps for that; you must not think   30
That we are made of stuff so flat and dull
That we can let our beard be shook with danger
And think it pastime. You shortly shall hear more;
I lov'd your father, and we love ourself,
And that, I hope, will teach you to imagine.—   35
[Enter a Messenger]
How now! what news?

ORIGINAL

ACT IV, SCENE 7

Another room in the castle.

[Enter KING and LAERTES]

KING   Now you must stop suspecting me of killing Polonius. You must regard me as a friend. The investigation proves that Hamlet killed your father.

LAERTES   The evidence proves you innocent. Tell me why you didn't punish Hamlet for his crimes. The murder was so criminal, so deserving the death penalty, for your own safety and prudence.

KING   There were two reasons not to arrest Hamlet. You may think them weak, but they were important to me. The queen, Hamlet's mother, dotes on him. As for me, for good or bad, I need her so much that, like a star restricted to its orbit, I can do nothing without considering her welfare. The other reason that I didn't arrest Hamlet is his popularity with Danes. I could not try him in a public trial. If I did present his case in court, like mineral water that turns wood to stone, the people would see his faults as assets. My accusations against Hamlet, like arrows blown by the wind back to the bow, would not justify his arrest.

LAERTES   And so I have lost a worthy father and seen my sister driven insane. Ophelia, whom others praised in the past, stood out from other girls for her qualities. I will get my revenge for them both.

KING   Don't lose sleep over your anger. You must not think that I am so weak and dull-witted that I ignore danger. I revered your father and I revere myself. That statement should inspire your thoughts. *[Enter a Messenger]* Do you bring news?

ACT IV

MESSENGER	Letters, my lord, from Hamlet: This to your majesty; this to the queen.
KING	From Hamlet! who brought them?
MESSENGER	Sailors, my lord, they say; I saw them not: They were given me by Claudio, he receiv'd them 40 Of him that brought them.
KING	Laertes, you shall hear them. Leave us. *[Exit Messenger]* *[Reads]* 'High and mighty, you shall know I am set naked on your kingdom. To-morrow shall I beg leave to see your kingly eyes; when I shall, first 45 asking your pardon therunto, recount the occasions of my sudden and more strange return.—Hamlet.' What should this mean? Are all the rest come back? Or is it some abuse and no such thing?
LAERTES	Know you the hand?
KING	'Tis Hamlet's character. 'Naked,' 50 And in a postscript here, he says, 'alone.' Can you advise me?
LAERTES	I'm lost in it, my lord. But let him come! It warms the very sickness in my heart, That I shall live and tell him to his teeth, 55 'Thus diddest thou.'
KING	If it be so, Laertes, As how should it be so? how otherwise? Will you be rul'd by me?
LAERTES	Ay, my lord; So you will not o'er-rule me to a peace.
KING	To thine own peace. If he be now return'd, 60 As checking at his voyage, and that he means No more to undertake it, I will work him To an exploit, now ripe in my device, Under the which he shall not choose but fall; And for his death no wind of blame shall breathe, 65 But even his mother shall uncharge the practice And call it accident.
LAERTES	My lord, I will be rul'd; The rather, if you could devise it so That I might be the organ.

ORIGINAL

MESSENGER	I bring letters from Hamlet. One for you and one for the queen.
KING	From Hamlet! Who brought the letters?
MESSENGER	I am told that sailors brought the messages, but I did not see them. Claudio received them from the sailors.
KING	Laertes, you shall hear Hamlet's letters. Leave us in private. *[The Messenger goes out] [Reads]* "*Mighty king, you know that I am defenseless in your realm. I request an appointment with you for tomorrow. If you give me an opportunity, I will explain my unexpected return. Hamlet.*" What does Hamlet mean? Did Rosencrantz and Guildenstern also return? Or is Hamlet hatching a plot?
LAERTES	Do you recognize the handwriting?
KING	It is Hamlet's writing. He says "vulnerable" and, in the postcript, "alone." Can you explain his meaning?
LAERTES	It puzzles me, my lord. But let him come! This letter relieves the despair in my heart. If I live to see him tomorrow, I will charge him to his face, "This is the crime you have committed."
KING	If this letter speaks the truth, Laertes, how can Hamlet return alone from the voyage? How else would you respond? Will you do what I tell you?
LAERTES	Yes, my lord, if you don't make me abandon my vengeance.
KING	I want to satisfy your anger. If he is back in Denmark after halting his voyage and if he doesn't mean to go to England, I will assign him a task for my own purpose that will kill him. When he dies, no accusation will fall on me. Even his mother will call the death accidental.
LAERTES	My lord, I will obey you only if you let me be the one to kill Hamlet.

ACT IV

TRANSLATION

KING   It falls right.
You have been talk'd of since your travel much,   70
And that in Hamlet's hearing, for a quality
Wherein, they say, you shine; your sum of parts
Did not together pluck such envy from him
As did that one, and that, in my regard,
Of the unworthiest siege.

LAERTES   What part is that, my lord?   75

KING   A very riband in the cap of youth,
Yet needful too; for youth no less becomes
The light and careless livery that it wears
Than settled age his sables and his weeds,
Importing health and graveness. Two months since   80
Here was a gentleman of Normandy:
I've seen myself, and serv'd against the French,
And they can well on horseback; but this gallant
Had witchcraft in 't, he grew unto his seat,
And to such wondrous doing brought his horse,   85
As he had been incorps'd and demi-natur'd
With the brave beast; so far be topp'd my thought,
That I, in forgery of shapes and tricks,
Come short of what he did.

LAERTES   A Norman, was 't?

KING   A Norman.   90

LAERTES   Upon my life, Lamord.

KING   The very same.

LAERTES   I know him well; he is the brooch indeed
And gem of all the nation.

KING   He made confession of you,
And gave you such a masterly report   95
For art and exercise in your defence,
And for your rapier most especially,
That he cried out, 'twould be a sight indeed
If one could match you; the scrimers of their nation,
He swore, had neither motion, guard, nor eye,   100
If you oppos'd them. Sir, this report of his
Did Hamlet so envenom with his envy
That he could nothing do but wish and beg
Your sudden coming o'er, to play with him.
Now, out of this,—

KING	Everything is working out for me. Hamlet has heard Danes speak well of your character. Hamlet has grown envious of you and thinks you unworthy of praise.
LAERTES	What trait do people praise, my lord?
KING	Your youth. Young people deserve a reputation for light-heartedness and recklessness just as older people deserve to be known for vigor and seriousness. Two months ago, there was a man here from northwestern France. I observed in wartime how well Frenchmen ride horseback. This rider seemed one with his horse. He rode as though he were kin to his horse. He was so skillful that he surpassed anything I could imagine.
LAERTES	Was he a Norman?
KING	Yes, a Norman.
LAERTES	I know you must refer to Lamord.
KING	That was his name.
LAERTES	I know him well. He is the jewel of all France.
KING	He spoke of you and complimented your athleticism, especially your swordsmanship. He wanted to see you matched with your equal. He said you could out-perform any fencer in France in movement, self-defense, and aim. When Hamlet heard this compliment, he was so envious that he wanted you to come back to Denmark immediately to fence against him. Enough of this.

ACT IV

TRANSLATION

| LAERTES | What out of this, my lord? | 105 |

KING Laertes, was your father dear to you?
Or are you like the painting of a sorrow,
A face without a heart?

LAERTES   Why ask you this?

KING Not that I think you did not love your father,
But that I know love is begun by time,   110
And that I see, in passages of proof,
Time qualifies the spark and fire of it.
There lives within the very flame of love
A kind of wick or snuff that will abate it,
And nothing is at a like goodness still,   115
For goodness, growing to a plurisy,
Dies in his own too-much. That we would do,
We should do when we would, for this 'would' changes,
And hath abatements and delays as many
As there are tongues, are hands, are accidents;   120
And then this 'should' is like a spendthrift sigh,
That hurts by easing. But, to the quick o' the ulcer;
Hamlet comes back; what would you undertake
To show yourself your father's son in deed
More than in words?

LAERTES   To cut his throat i' the church.   125

KING No place indeed should murder sanctuarize;
Revenge should have no bounds. But, good Laertes,
Will you do this, keep close within your chamber.
Hamlet return'd shall know you are come home;
We'll put on those shall praise your excellence,   130
And set a double varnish on the fame
The Frenchman gave you, bring you, in fine, together,
And wager on your heads: he, being remiss,
Most generous and free from all contriving,
Will not peruse the foils; so that, with ease   135
Or with a little shuffling, you may choose
A sword unbated, and, in a pass of practice
Requite him for your father.

LAERTES	What happened next, my lord?
KING	Laertes, did you really love Polonius? Or are you posing as the sorrowing son?
LAERTES	How can you ask such a thing?
KING	I don't doubt your love for Polonius, but I know that, over time, affection diminishes. Love bears a quality that wears it down and keeps it from being constant over time. We should act on our emotions immediately before discussion, events, and unforeseen experiences lessen our intent. We should take action before our pain eases. We should strike to the heart of the matter. Hamlet is returning. Can you avenge Polonius's death with more than angry words?
LAERTES	I would cut his throat in church.
KING	No place should exonerate Hamlet for murder. Revenge should have no boundaries. Laertes, will you do as I ask and stay in your room? Hamlet will learn of your return when he arrives. I will have courtiers praise you and double the compliments that Lamord gave you. Finally, I will match you with Hamlet and bet on your duel. He, out of carelessness and his unsuspicious nature, will not inspect the unsharpened foils. You can easily select the foil with a sharp point and, during warm-up, kill Hamlet to avenge Polonius's murder.

ACT IV

TRANSLATION

LAERTES   I will do 't;
And, for that purpose, I'll anoint my sword.
I bought an unction of a mountebank,   140
So mortal that, but dip a knife in it,
Where it draws blood no cataplasm so rare,
Collected from all simples that have virtue
Under the moon, can save the thing from death
That is but scratch'd withal; I'll touch my point   145
With this contagion, that, if I gall him slightly,
It may be death.

KING   Let's further think of this;
Weigh what convenience both of time and means
May fit us to our shape. If this should fail,
And that our drift look through our bad performance   150
'Twere better not assay'd; therefore this project
Should have a back or second, that might hold,
If this should blast in proof. Soft! let me see;
We'll make a solemn wager on your cunnings:
I ha 't: 155
When in your motion you are hot and dry,—
As make your bouts more violent to that end,—
And that he calls for drink, I'll have prepar'd him
A chalice for the nonce, whereon but sipping,
If he by chance escape your venom'd stuck,   160
Our purpose may hold there. But stay! what noise?
[Enter QUEEN]
How now, sweet queen!

QUEEN   One woe doth tread upon another's heel,
So fast they follow: your sister's drown'd, Laertes.

LAERTES   Drown'd! O, where?   165

LAERTES I will do as you say. To assure a kill, I will put poison on my sword. I bought a concoction from a quack. The poison is so lethal that even one dip in the liquid will kill with a touch of the blade. I will poison the tip of my sword. If I only scratch Hamlet, he will die.

KING Let's discuss this further. We must choose a time and reason to suit our plot. If we fail to poison Hamlet and our plot is discovered, we shouldn't even try it. We need a backup plan if the duel doesn't kill him. Hush, let me think. I'll make a bet on the duel. I have it. When the two of you are hot and thirsty, to make the duel more lethal, when he asks for a drink, I will prepare a cup for the occasion that will kill him with a second poison. Halt! What was that noise? *[Enter QUEEN]* It is you, sweet queen!

QUEEN One sorrow follows another immediately. Your sister has drowned, Laertes.

LAERTES Drowned! Oh, where?

ACT IV

QUEEN	There is a willow grows aslant a brook.
	That shows his hoar leaves in the glassy stream;
	There with fantastic garlands did she come,
	Of crow-flowers, nettles, daisies, and long purples,
	That liberal shepherds give a grosser name, 170
	But our cold maids do dead men's fingers call them:
	There, on the pendent boughs her coronet weeds
	Clambering to hang, an envious sliver broke,
	When down her weedy trophies and herself
	Fell in the weeping brook. Her clothes spread wide, 175
	And, mermaid-like, awhile they bore her up;
	Which time she chanted snatches of old lauds,
	As one incapable of her own distress,
	Or like a creature native and indu'd
	Unto that element; but long it could not be 180
	Till that her garments, heavy with their drink,
	Pull'd the poor wretch from her melodious lay
	To muddy death.
LAERTES	Alas! then, she is drown'd?
QUEEN	Drown'd, drown'd.
LAERTES	Too much of water hast thou, poor Ophelia, 185
	And therefore I forbid my tears; but yet
	It is our trick, nature her custom holds,
	Let shame say what it will; when these are gone
	The woman will be out. Adieu, my lord!
	I have a speech of fire, that fain would blaze, 190
	But that this folly douts it. *[Exit]*
KING	Let's follow, Gertrude.
	How much I had to do to calm his rage!
	Now fear I this will give it start again;
	Therefore let's follow. *[Exeunt]*

QUEEN	There is a silver-leafed willow that leans over a brook and is reflected in the water. She came there with garlands of buttercups, nettles, daisies, and purple loosestrife, which shepherds call by a vulgar name. Our ladies call them dead men's fingers. She draped her garlands on willow boughs. A branch broke. She and her flowers fell into the stream. Her skirts filled with air and held her above the surface like a mermaid. While she floated, she sang snatches of old songs. She was incapable of rescuing herself. She seemed like a sprite that enjoys the water. Shortly, her skirts became water-soaked and pulled her under. She drowned in the mud.
LAERTES	Alas, can she be dead?
QUEEN	Drowned, drowned.
LAERTES	Poor Ophelia, you have had too much water. I will withhold my tears. But it is only human to follow our nature. Never mind the shame. When I lose control, I will cry like a woman. Goodbye, my lord. I want to blast with hot words, but my tears extinguish them. *[He goes out]*
KING	Let's follow him, Gertrude. I worked hard to calm his anger! Now I fear that Ophelia's death will enrage him again. Let's follow him. *[They go out]*

ACT IV

ACT V, SCENE 1

A churchyard.

[Enter two Clowns, with spades and mattock]

FIRST CLOWN   Is she to be buried in Christian burial
that wilfully seeks her own salvation?

SECOND CLOWN I tell thee she is: and therefore
make her grave straight: the crowner hath sat on
her, and finds it Christian burial.   5

FIRST CLOWN   How can that be, unless she drowned
herself in her own defence?

SECOND CLOWN Why, 'tis found so.

FIRST CLOWN   It must be *se offendendo*; it cannot
be else. For here lies the point: if I drown myself   10
wittingly it argues an act; and an act hath three
branches; it is, to act, to do, and to perform: argal,
she drowned herself wittingly.

SECOND CLOWN Nay, but hear you, Goodman
Delver,—   15

FIRST CLOWN   Give me leave. Here lies the water;
good: here stands the man; good: if the man go to
this water, and drown himself, it is, will he, nill he, he
goes; mark you that? but if the water come to him,
and drown him, he drowns not himself: argal, he   20
that is not guilty of his own death shortens not his
own life.

SECOND CLOWN But is this law?

FIRST CLOWN   Ay, marry, is't; crowner's quest law.

SECOND CLOWN Will you ha' the truth on 't? If this   25
had not been a gentlewoman she should have been
buried out o' Christian burial.

FIRST CLOWN   Why, there thou sayest; and the more
pity that great folk should have countenance in this
world to drown or hang themselves more than their   30
even Christian. Come, my spade. There is no ancient
gentlemen but gardeners, ditchers, and grave-makers;
they hold up Adam's profession.

SECOND CLOWN Was he a gentleman?

ACT V, SCENE 1

A churchyard.

[Enter two Fools carrying spades and a mattock]

FIRST CLOWN   Is Ophelia to be buried in holy ground even though she appears to have committed suicide?

SECOND CLOWN   She is accepted in consecrated ground. Dig the hole immediately. The coroner examined her body and declares her worthy of Christian burial.

FIRST CLOWN   How is that possible, unless she drowned while trying to save herself?

SECOND CLOWN   That was the coroner's findings.

FIRST CLOWN   The drowning must have occurred when she tried to save herself. That is the only explanation. This is the crux of the matter: if I knowingly drown myself, the act is obvious. Every deed has three parts—to take action, to do it, and to complete it. Therefore, she knowingly drowned herself.

SECOND CLOWN   No. Listen, good digger.

FIRST CLOWN   Let me finish. Here is water; here is a person. If the person enters the water and drowns himself, he goes in willy-nilly. Do you follow my argument? But if the water should cover him and drown him, the person is not at fault. Therefore, the person who is innocent of suicide does not cut short his own life.

SECOND CLOWN   Is this how the law reads?

FIRST CLOWN   Yes. It is called the coroner's inquest law.

SECOND CLOWN   Have you quoted it exactly? If Ophelia had been a peasant, she would not have received a Christian burial.

FIRST CLOWN   Just as you say. It is unfair that aristocrats are free to drown or hang themselves when fellow Christians are condemned for suicide. Let me get to my spade. The only worthy gentlemen are gardeners, ditch diggers, and grave makers. They follow Adam's profession.

SECOND CLOWN   Was he a gentleman?

TRANSLATION

FIRST CLOWN	A' was the first that ever bore arms.	35

SECOND CLOWN Why, he had none.

FIRST CLOWN What! art a heathen? How dost thou
understand the Scripture? The Scripture says, Adam
digged; could he dig without arms? I'll put another
question to thee; if thou answerest me not to the   40
purpose, confess thyself—

SECOND CLOWN Go to.

FIRST CLOWN What is he that builds stronger than
either the mason, the shipwright, or the carpenter?

SECOND CLOWN The gallows-maker; for that frame   45
outlives a thousand tenants.

FIRST CLOWN I like thy wit well, in good faith; the
gallows does well, but how does it well? it does well to
those that do ill; now thou dost ill to say the gallows
is built stronger than the church: argal, the gallows   50
may do well to thee. To 't again; come.

SECOND CLOWN Who builds stronger than a mason, a
shipwright, or a carpenter?

FIRST CLOWN Ay, tell me that, and unyoke.

SECOND CLOWN Marry, now I can tell.   55

FIRST CLOWN To 't.

SECOND CLOWN Mass, I cannot tell.
[Enter HAMLET and HORATIO at a distance]

FIRST CLOWN Cudgel thy brains no more about it, for
your dull ass will not mend his pace with beating;
and, when you are asked this question next, say,   60
'a grave-maker': the houses that he makes last till
doomsday. Go, get thee to Yaughan; fetch me a
stoup of liquor.
[Exit Second Clown. First Clown digs, and sings]

> *In youth, when I did love, did love,*
>   *Methought it was very sweet,*   65
>   *To contract o' the time, for-a my behove,*
>   *O! methought there was nothing meet.*

HAMLET Has this fellow no feeling of his business,
that he sings at grave-making?

FIRST CLOWN	He was the first to bear arms.
SECOND CLOWN	He had no coat of arms.
FIRST CLOWN	Are you a heathen? Do you understand the Bible? The Bible says that Adam dug. Could he dig without arms? Let me ask you another question. If you can't answer it correctly, go to confession.
SECOND CLOWN	Never mind.
FIRST CLOWN	Who builds stronger than a brick mason, shipbuilder, or carpenter?
SECOND CLOWN	The gallows maker. His framework outlasts a thousand hangings.
FIRST CLOWN	I like your sense of humor. The gallows serves well. But how can it be well? It does well against criminals. You are wrong to say that a gallows is stronger than a church. Therefore, the gallows may take care of you. Get back to digging.
SECOND CLOWN	Who builds stronger than a brick mason, shipbuilder, or carpenter?
FIRST CLOWN	Answer that one and you can quit for the day.
SECOND CLOWN	I can answer it.
FIRST CLOWN	Do it, then.
SECOND CLOWN	By the Holy Mass, I can't tell you. *[Enter HAMLET and HORATIO at a distance]*
FIRST CLOWN	Beat your brains no more, for your dull mule will not speed up if you whip him. When someone asks you this riddle, say, "a grave maker." The structures that he makes last until the end of time. Go to Yaughan's tavern and bring me a flagon of ale. *[The second fool goes out. The first fool continues digging and singing]* *When I was young and fell in love, I thought it was sweet. Over time, to my benefit I thought nothing was better than love.*
HAMLET	Has this man no dignity in his profession that he sings while digging graves?

ACT V

TRANSLATION

HORATIO	Custom hath made it in him a property of easiness.

70

HAMLET	'Tis e'en so; the hand of little employment hath the daintier sense.

FIRST CLOWN	*[Sings]*

> *But age, with his stealing steps,*
> *Hath claw'd me in his clutch,*
> *And hath shipped me intil the land,*
> *As if I had never been such.*
> *[Throws up a skull]*

75

HAMLET	That skull had a tongue in it, and could sing once; how the knave jowls it to the ground, as if it were Cain's jaw-bone, that did the first murder! This might be the pate of a politician which this ass now o'er-reaches, one that would circumvent God, might it not?

80

HORATIO	It might, my Lord.

HAMLET	Or of a courtier, which could say, 'Good morrow, sweet lord! How dost thou, good lord?' This might be my Lord Such-a-one, that praised my Lord Such-a-one's horse, when he meant to beg it, might it not?

85

HORATIO	Ay, my lord.

90

HAMLET	Why, e'en so, and now my Lady Worm's chapless, and knocked about the mazzard with a sexton's spade. Here's fine revolution, an we had the trick to see 't. Did these bones cost no more the breeding but to play at loggats with 'em? mine ache to think on 't.

95

FIRST CLOWN	*[Sings]*

> *A pick-axe, and a spade, a spade,*
> *For and a shrouding sheet;*
> *O! a pit of clay for to be made*
> *For such a guest is meet.*
> *[Throws up another skull]*

100

HORATIO	Over time, he has grown indifferent to graves.
HAMLET	I guess you are right. The person who has never dug a grave is more sensitive to death.
FIRST CLOWN	*Advancing age has grabbed hold of me. And has sunk me into the earth as if I had never been made of dirt.* *[Throws up a skull]*
HAMLET	That skull was the head of a man who sang. How that irreverent gravedigger tosses it to the ground as though it were the bone of Cain, who committed the first murder! These remains might have been the skull of a politician which this fool dishonors. The gravedigger might get around God.
HORATIO	He might, my lord.
HAMLET	Or of a courtier, who once said, "Good day, my lord. How are you, my lord?" This might be Lord so-and-so, the man who praised Lord so-and-so's horse when he wanted to borrow it.
HORATIO	Yes, my lord.
HAMLET	Similarly, my Lady Worm's skull is jawless. The church groundskeeper may have knocked her skull with a shovel. Here is a fine overturning, if we had the wit to understand it. Did these skeletons sink from their high stature to pegs for a game of lawn bowling? My bones ache to think about it.
FIRST CLOWN	*An ax and a shovel, a shovel, and a burial shroud. Oh, it is proper to dig a clay grave to receive the next graveyard guest. [Throws up another skull]*

ACT V

HAMLET	There's another; why may not that be the skull of a lawyer? Where be his quiddities now, his quillets, his cases, his tenures, and his tricks? why does he suffer this rude knave now to knock him about the sconce with a dirty shovel, and will not tell him of his action of battery? Hum! This fellow might be in 's time a great buyer of land, with his statutes, his recognizances, his fines, his double vouchers, his recoveries; is this the fine of his fines, and the recovery of his recoveries, to have his fine pate full of fine dirt? will his vouchers vouch him no more of his purchases, and double ones too, than the length and breadth of a pair of indentures? The very conveyance of his land will hardly lie in this box, and must the inheritor himself have no more, ha?
HORATIO	Not a jot more, my lord.
HAMLET	Is not parchment made of sheep-skins?
HORATIO	Ay, my lord, and of calf-skins too.
HAMLET	They are sheep and calves which seek out assurance in that. I will speak to this fellow. Whose grave's this, sir?
FIRST CLOWN	Mine, sir. *[Sings]*

> *O! a pit of clay for to be made*
> *For such a guest is meet.*

HAMLET	I think it be thine, indeed; for thou liest in't.
FIRST CLOWN	You lie out on 't, sir, and therefore it is not yours; for my part, I do not lie in 't, and yet it is mine.
HAMLET	Thou dost lie in 't, to be in 't and say it is thine; 'tis for the dead, not for the quick; therefore thou liest.
FIRST CLOWN	'Tis a quick lie, sir; 'twill away again from me to you.
HAMLET	What man dost thou dig it for?
FIRST CLOWN	For no man, sir.
HAMLET	What woman, then?
FIRST CLOWN	For none, neither.

Line numbers: 105, 110, 115, 120, 125, 130, 135

HAMLET	There's another skull. Couldn't it have been the head of a lawyer? Where are his questions, his quibbles, his cases, his property rights, and his subtle legal tricks? Why does the lawyer allow this lowly gravedigger to conk him in the head with a dirty shovel and not charge him with battery? Hmmm. At one time, this attorney may have been a land agent, a wielder of bonds, obligations, fines, multiple witnesses, and transfers. Is this the result of his fines and the sum of his recoveries to have his skull filled with dirt? Will his witnesses assure him none of his purchases, some at double price, but only duplicate contracts? The very sale of his land will hardly fill this coffin. Will his heir receive no more than this?
HORATIO	Not a bit more, my lord.
HAMLET	Isn't parchment made from sheepskin?
HORATIO	Yes, my lord, or of calfskin.
HAMLET	Men who rely on deeds are like sheep and calves. I want a word with this man. Whose grave is this, sir?
FIRST CLOWN	It is mine, sir. *It is a clay pit worthy of such a man.*
HAMLET	I think it is yours because you "lie" in it.
FIRST CLOWN	You lie about it, sir. Therefore, it isn't your grave. As for me, I don't lie in it, and yet it belongs to me.
HAMLET	You do "lie" in it when you stand in it and say it is yours. It is for a corpse, not for a living person. Therefore, you are lying.
FIRST CLOWN	It is a living lie, sir. It will pass from me to you.
HAMLET	For what man are you digging a grave?
FIRST CLOWN	For no man, sir.
HAMLET	For what woman, then?
FIRST CLOWN	For no woman, either.

ACT V

HAMLET	Who is to be buried in 't?
FIRST CLOWN	One that was a woman, sir; but, rest her soul, she's dead. 140
HAMLET	How absolute the knave is! we must speak by the card, or equivocation will undo us. By the Lord, Horatio, these three years I have taken note of it; the age is grown so picked that the toe of the peasant comes so near the heel of the courtier, he galls 145 his kibe. How long hast thou been a grave-maker?
FIRST CLOWN	Of all the days i' the year, I came to 't that day our last King Hamlet overcame Fortinbras.
HAMLET	How long is that since?
FIRST CLOWN	Cannot you tell that? every fool can tell 150 that; it was the very day that young Hamlet was born; he that is mad, and sent into England.
HAMLET	Ay, marry; why was he sent into England?
FIRST CLOWN	Why, because he was mad: he shall recover his wits there; or, if he do not, 'tis no great 155 matter there.
HAMLET	Why?
FIRST CLOWN	'Twill not be seen in him there; there the men are as mad as he.
HAMLET	How came he mad? 160
FIRST CLOWN	Very strangely, they say.
HAMLET	How strangely?
FIRST CLOWN	Faith, e'en with losing his wits.
HAMLET	Upon what ground?
FIRST CLOWN	Why, here in Denmark; I have been 165 sexton here, man and boy, thirty years.
HAMLET	How long will a man lie i' the earth ere he rot?
FIRST CLOWN	Faith, if he be not rotten before he die,—as we have many pocky corses now-a-days, that 170 will scarce hold the laying in,—he will last you some eight year or nine year; a tanner will last you nine year.

ORIGINAL

HAMLET	Who is going to be buried in it?
FIRST CLOWN	Someone who was a woman, sir. But, God rest her soul, she is dead.
HAMLET	How literal the rascal takes every phrase. We must address him precisely or else he will fool us with word tricks. By God, Horatio, for the past three years I have noticed something: The times have grown so refined that the peasant's toe walks on the aristocrat's heel and scrapes it raw. How long have you worked as a gravedigger?
FIRST CLOWN	I work every day. I began when King Hamlet defeated old Fortinbras, the king of Norway.
HAMLET	How long has that been?
FIRST CLOWN	Don't you remember? Every fool knows that day—the day that Prince Hamlet was born. He is insane and dispatched to England.
HAMLET	Why was he sent to England?
FIRST CLOWN	Because he is crazy. He will regain his sanity in England. If he doesn't, it doesn't matter.
HAMLET	Why do you say that?
FIRST CLOWN	No one in England will notice a madman. All the English are crazy.
HAMLET	Why is Hamlet crazy?
FIRST CLOWN	By odd circumstances, it is said.
HAMLET	How odd?
FIRST CLOWN	Truly, strange in the way he lost his wits.
HAMLET	On what grounds?
FIRST CLOWN	Here in Denmark. I have been the church sexton from boyhood for thirty years.
HAMLET	How long does a corpse remain in the ground before it rots?
FIRST CLOWN	Indeed, if he isn't rotten before death—we have many diseased bodies these days that will scarcely last for the viewing of the dead—a corpse will last eight or nine years. A tanner will last nine years.

ACT V

TRANSLATION

HAMLET	Why he more than another?
FIRST CLOWN	Why, sir, his hide is so tanned with his 175 trade that he will keep out water a great while, and your water is a sore decayer of your whoreson dead body. Here's a skull now; this skull hath lain you i' the earth three-and-twenty years.
HAMLET	Whose was it? 180
FIRST CLOWN	A whoreson mad fellow's it was: whose do you think it was?
HAMLET	Nay, I know not.
FIRST CLOWN	A pestilence on him for a mad rogue; a' poured a flagon of Rhenish on my head once. This 185 same skull, sir, was, sir, Yorick's skull, the king's jester.
HAMLET	This!
FIRST CLOWN	E'en that.
HAMLET	Let me see.—*[Takes the skull]*—Alas! 190 poor Yorick. I knew him, Horatio; a fellow of infinite jest, of most excellent fancy; he hath borne me on his back a thousand times; and now, how abhorred in my imagination it is! my gorge rises at it. Here hung those lips that I have kissed I know not 195 how oft. Where be your gibes now? your gambols? your songs? your flashes of merriment, that were wont to set the table on a roar? Not one now, to mock your own grinning? quite chapfallen? Now get you to my lady's chamber, and tell her, let her 200 paint an inch thick, to this favour she must come; make her laugh at that. Prithee, Horatio, tell me one thing.
HORATIO	What's that, my lord?
HAMLET	Dost thou think Alexander looked o' this 205 fashion i' the earth?
HORATIO	E'en so.
HAMLET	And smelt so? pah! *[Puts down the skull]*
HORATIO	E'en so, my lord.

HAMLET	Why does he last longer than another corpse?
FIRST CLOWN	Why, he has so much tanning solution on his skin that it keeps out water. Water is what rots dead bastards. Here is a skull that has been buried for years.
HAMLET	Whose was it?
FIRST CLOWN	A crazy bastard. Whose skull do you think it was?
HAMLET	I don't know.
FIRST CLOWN	A plague on him for being a rascal—he once poured red wine on my head. This skull belonged to Yorick, the king's jester.
HAMLET	This!
FIRST CLOWN	Yes.
HAMLET	Let me see it. *[Takes the skull]* Alas, poor Yorick. I knew him, Horatio. A funny man filled with imagination. I rode on his back a thousand times. And now, how grotesque it seems. It makes me queasy just looking at it. Here were his lips that I often kissed. Where are your jokes now? your frolics? your singing? your jolliness that once set banquet guests to laughing? There is no one to laugh at your grinning. Are you downcast? Now, go to my mother's room and tell her to put on thick makeup to improve her appearance. Make her laugh at the joke. Please, Horatio, tell me something.
HORATIO	What, my lord?
HAMLET	Do you think Alexander the Great looked like this when he was buried?
HORATIO	Just like this.
HAMLET	And smelled like this? Ugh! *[Puts down the skull]*
HORATIO	Just like this, my lord.

ACT V

HAMLET	To what base uses we may return, Horatio! 210 Why may not imagination trace the noble dust of Alexander, till he find it stopping a bung-hole?
HORATIO	'Twere to consider too curiously, to consider so. 215
HAMLET	No, faith, not a jot; but to follow him thither with modesty enough, and likelihood to lead it; as thus: Alexander died, Alexander was buried, Alexander returneth into dust; the dust is earth; of earth we make loam, and why 220 of that loam, whereto he was converted, might they not stop a beer-barrel? Imperious Caesar, dead and turn'd to clay, Might stop a hole to keep the wind away: O! that that earth, which kept the world in awe, 225 Should patch a wall to expel the winter's flaw. But soft! but soft! aside: here comes the king. *[Enter KING, QUEEN, LAERTES, and a coffin with Lords attendant and Priest]* The queen, the courtiers: who is that they follow? And with such maimed rites? This doth betoken The corse they follow did with desperate hand 230 Fordo its own life; 'twas of some estate. Couch we awhile, and mark. *[Retiring with HORATIO]*
LAERTES	What ceremony else?
HAMLET	That is Laertes, A very noble youth: mark.
LAERTES	Where ceremony else? 235
PRIEST	Her obsequies have been as far enlarg'd As we have warrantise: her death was doubtful, And, but that great command o'ersways the order, She should in ground unsanctified have lodg'd Till the last trumpet; for charitable prayers, 240 Shards, flints, and pebbles should be thrown on her; Yet here she is allow'd her virgin crants, Her maiden strewments, and the bringing home Of bell and burial.
LAERTES	Must there no more be done?

HAMLET	To what corruption we return, Horatio! Could we follow Alexander's decay all the way to stopping up the hole in a barrel?
HORATIO	That is too morbid to think about.
HAMLET	No, indeed. It would be interesting to follow him from life to death and burial. It works like this: Alexander died, Alexander was buried, and Alexander's body decayed. The decay mixes with the earth. We turn earth into plaster and, of that plaster that once was Alexander, why couldn't we stop up a beer barrel? Even Julius Caesar, once he died and decayed, might stop up a hole to keep away drafts. Imagine that—the decay that once was a great ruler might serve now to patch a wall to keep out the winter wind. Silence. Here comes the king. *[Enter KING, QUEEN, LAERTES, and a coffin with Lords attendant and Priest]* Who is the dead person that the queen and courtiers follow? Why are the funeral rites so short? This unusual service means that the dead person committed suicide. It was a noble person. Let's hide and eavesdrop. *[Retiring with HORATIO]*
LAERTES	Is that the end of the service?
HAMLET	That is Laertes, a worthy youth. Listen.
LAERTES	Isn't there more ceremony?
PRIEST	The girl's service is as long as is allowed. There are questions about her death. But the king overruled the church custom of burying suicides in unhallowed ground until the end of time. Instead of generous prayers, mourners might have thrown pieces of glass, flint, and stones on her grave. But she was allowed wreaths and blossoms suited to a dead maiden along with a procession, tolling of the bell, and standard burial.
LAERTES	Is that all she deserves?

ACT V

TRANSLATION

PRIEST	No more be done: 245
	We should profane the service of the dead,
	To sing sage requiem, and such rest to her
	As to peace-parted souls.
LAERTES	Lay her i' th' earth;
	And from her fair and unpolluted flesh
	May violets spring! I tell thee, churlish priest, 250
	A ministering angel shall my sister be,
	When thou liest howling.
HAMLET	What! the fair Ophelia?
QUEEN	Sweets to the sweet: farewell! *[Scattering flowers]*
	I hop'd thou shouldst have been my Hamlet's wife;
	I thought thy bride-bed to have deck'd, sweet maid, 255
	And not have strew'd thy grave.
LAERTES	O! treble woe
	Fall ten times treble on that cursed head
	Whose wicked deed thy most ingenious sense
	Depriv'd thee of. Hold off the earth awhile,
	Till I have caught her once more in mine arms. 260
	[Leaps into the grave]
	Now pile your dust upon the quick and dead,
	Till of this flat a mountain you have made,
	To o'ertop old Pelion or the skyish head
	Of blue Olympus.
HAMLET	*[Advancing]* What is he whose grief
	Bears such an emphasis? whose phrase of sorrow 265
	Conjures the wandering stars, and makes them stand
	Like wonder-wounded hearers? this is I,
	Hamlet the Dane. *[Leaps into the grave]*
LAERTES	The devil take thy soul! *[Grapples with him]*
HAMLET	Thou pray'st not well.
	I prithee, take thy fingers from my throat; 270
	For though I am not splenetive and rash
	Yet have I in me something dangerous,
	Which let thy wisdom fear. Away thy hand!
KING	Pluck them asunder.
QUEEN	Hamlet! Hamlet!
ALL	Gentlemen,—

PRIEST	We can't do more. We would violate the burial ritual if we sang a Requiem Mass and left her to the eternal rest that Christians deserve.
LAERTES	Place her in the grave and from her beautiful, pure flesh, may violets grow. I inform you, rude priest, my sister will be an angel when you lie howling in hell.
HAMLET	What? Is it Ophelia?
QUEEN	Sweet blossoms to a sweet girl. *[Scattering flowers]* I had hopes that you would marry Hamlet. I intended to put flowers on your bridal bed, sweet girl, and not on your grave.
LAERTES	O triple harm fall ten times on that accursed villain whose evil deed drove you insane. Stop putting soil in the grave until I have embraced her one more time. *[Leaps into the grave]* Now pile in dirt on the living and the dead until you turn this flat ground into a mountain taller than Mount Pelion or Mount Olympus in Greece.
HAMLET	*[Advancing]* How dare you say such a thing in your grief? Your sorrowful words summon the planets and make them stand awe-stricken by the grave. It is I, Prince Hamlet. *[Leaps into the grave]*
LAERTES	Satan take your soul! *[They wrestle]*
HAMLET	You make an evil curse. Please, take your hand off my throat. I am not usually reckless and angry, but I am capable of a harm that you should fear. Take your hand off me!
KING	Separate them.
QUEEN	Hamlet! Hamlet!
ALL	Gentlemen.

ACT V

TRANSLATION

HORATIO	Good my lord, be quiet. 275
	[The Attendants part them, and they come out of the grave]
HAMLET	Why, I will fight with him upon this theme
	Until my eyelids will no longer wag.
QUEEN	O my son! what theme?
HAMLET	I lov'd Ophelia: forty thousand brothers
	Could not, with all their quantity of love, 280
	Make up my sum. What wilt thou do for her?
KING	O! he is mad, Laertes.
QUEEN	For love of God, forbear him.
HAMLET	'Swounds, show me what thou'lt do:
	Woo't weep? woo't fight? woo't fast? woo't tear thyself? 285
	Woo't drink up eisel? eat a crocodile?
	I'll do't. Dost thou come here to whine?
	To outface me with leaping in her grave?
	Be buried quick with her, and so will I:
	And, if thou prate of mountains, let them throw 290
	Millions of acres on us, till our ground,
	Singeing his pate against the burning zone,
	Make Ossa like a wart! Nay, an thou'lt mouth,
	I'll rant as well as thou.
QUEEN	This is mere madness:
	And thus a while the fit will work on him; 295
	Anon as patient as the female dove,
	When that her golden couplets are disclos'd,
	His silence will sit drooping.
HAMLET	Hear you, sir;
	What is the reason that you use me thus?
	I lov'd you ever: but it is no matter; 300
	Let Hercules himself do what he may,
	The cat will mew and dog will have his day. *[Exit]*
KING	I pray you, good Horatio, wait upon him.
	[Exit HORATIO]
	[To LAERTES] Strengthen your patience in our last
	night's speech;
	We'll put the matter to the present push. 305
	Good Gertrude, set some watch over your son.
	This grave shall have a living monument:
	An hour of quiet shortly shall we see;
	Till then, in patience our proceeding be. *[Exeunt]*

ORIGINAL

HORATIO	My lord, be silent. *[The Attendants part them, and they come out of the grave]*
HAMLET	I will fight him over this issue until my eyes close forever.
QUEEN	My son, what issue?
HAMLET	I loved Ophelia. Forty thousand brothers could not equal my love for her. What can you do for her?
KING	He is insane, Laertes.
QUEEN	For God's love, ignore him.
HAMLET	God's wounds, show me how you will mourn her. Will you weep? fight? go hungry? rip yourself apart? drink vinegar? eat a crocodile? I will do those things. Do you come here to whimper? To make me look bad by jumping into her grave? Be buried with her and I will join you. And if you brag about mountains of dirt, let them throw millions of acres on us till the cemetery burns against the sun and makes Mount Ossa look like a wart! As long as you rage on, I will match your ranting with mine.
QUEEN	This is insane talk. The seizure will control him for a while. Eventually, like a patient female dove, when someone discovers her two eggs, Hamlet will droop into silence.
HAMLET	Are you listening to me? Why do you belittle me like this? I was always your friend. But it doesn't matter. Let Hercules the strongman do what he wants. Every cat meows. Every dog has its day. *[He goes out]*
KING	I beg you, Horatio, go with him. *[HORATIO goes out] [To LAERTES]* Be patient by remembering what we talked about last night. We will soon test our plot. Gertrude, put guards around your son. This tomb will have a living memorial. I want a quiet hour. Until then, let us postpone all action. *[They go out]*

ACT V

TRANSLATION

ACT V, SCENE 2

A hall in the castle.

[Enter HAMLET and HORATIO]

HAMLET So much for this, sir: now shall you see the other;
       You do remember all the circumstance?

HORATIO Remember it, my lord?

HAMLET Sir, in my heart there was a kind of fighting
       That would not let me sleep; methought I lay   5
       Worse than the mutines in the bilboes. Rashly,—
       And prais'd be rashness for it, let us know,
       Our indiscretion sometimes serves us well
       When our deep plots do pall; and that should teach us
       There's a divinity that shapes our ends,   10
       Rough-hew them how we will.

HORATIO   That is most certain.

HAMLET Up from my cabin,
       My sea-gown scarf'd about me, in the dark
       Groped I to find out them, had my desire,
       Finger'd their packet, and in fine withdrew   15
       To mine own room again; making so bold—
       My fears forgetting manners—to unseal
       Their grand commission; where I found, Horatio,
       O royal knavery! an exact command,
       Larded with many several sorts of reasons   20
       Importing Denmark's health, and England's too,
       With, ho! such bugs and goblins in my life,
       That, on the supervise, no leisure bated,
       No, not to stay the grinding of the axe,
       My head should be struck off.

HORATIO   Is't possible?   25

HAMLET Here's the commission: read it at more leisure.
       But wilt thou hear me how I did proceed?

HORATIO I beseech you.

HAMLET Being thus be-netted round with villainies,—
       Ere I could make a prologue to my brains   30
       They had begun the play,—I sat me down,
       Devis'd a new commission, wrote it fair;
       I once did hold it, as our statists do,

ORIGINAL

ACT V, SCENE 2

A hall in the castle.

[Enter HAMLET and HORATIO]

HAMLET   Enough of this topic, sir. Now you will see the other thing that I mentioned. Do you remember the details?

HORATIO   Recall it, my lord?

HAMLET   Sir, in my heart is a quarrel that keeps me awake. I thought it worse than rebels locked in chains. Recklessness—and recklessness deserves praising. My outrages are sometimes useful when my more sensible plot fails. And that should indicate that God directs our fate, despite our crude beginnings.

HORATIO   You are right.

HAMLET   I left my cabin, draped in my night clothes, groped around the ship in the dark in search of Rosencrantz and Guildenstern, did what I wanted to, lifted their letter pouch, and returned to my cabin again. I dared—forgetting good manners—to unseal the king's orders. I discovered, Horatio, a royal crime. The king's command, shored up by several justifications involving the survival of Denmark and England. He ordered such intervention to my life that, as he directed, immediately without honing the ax, the headsman should execute me.

HORATIO   Is it possible he would do that?

HAMLET   Here's his command. Read it later. Listen to what I did next.

HORATIO   Please go on.

HAMLET   Being trapped in plots—before I could retaliate, they had set the plot in motion. I drew up a new command and wrote it neatly.

ACT V

TRANSLATION

	A baseness to write fair, and labour'd much
	How to forget that learning; but, sir, now 35
	It did me yeoman's service. Wilt thou know
	The effect of what I wrote?

HORATIO   Ay, good my lord.

HAMLET   An earnest conjuration from the king,
As England was his faithful tributary,
As love between them like the palm should flourish,   40
As peace should still her wheaten garland wear,
And stand a comma 'tween their amities,
And many such-like 'As'es of great charge,
That, on the view and knowing of these contents,
Without debatement further, more or less,   45
He should the bearers put to sudden death,
Not shriving-time allow'd.

HORATIO   How was this seal'd?

HAMLET   Why, even in that was heaven ordinant.
I had my father's signet in my purse,
Which was the model of that Danish seal;   50
Folded the writ up in form of the other,
Subscrib'd it, gave 't th' impression, plac'd it safely,
The changeling never known. Now, the next day
Was our sea-fight, and what to this was sequent
Thou know'st already.   55

HORATIO   So Guildenstern and Rosencrantz go to 't.

HAMLET   Why, man, they did make love to this employment;
They are not near my conscience; their defeat
Does by their own insinuation grow.
'Tis dangerous when the baser nature comes   60
Between the pass and fell-incensed points
Of mighty opposites.

HORATIO   Why, what a king is this!

HAMLET   Does it not, thinks't thee, stand me now upon—
He that hath kill'd my king and whor'd my mother,
Popp'd in between the election and my hopes,
Thrown out his angle for my proper life,   65
And with such cozenage—is 't not perfect conscience
To quit him with this arm? and is 't not to be damn'd
To let this canker of our nature come
In further evil?   70

HORATIO   It must be shortly known to him from England
What is the issue of the business there.

I once believed, as statesmen do, that it was lowly to write neatly. I tried to forget that prejudice. But, good handwriting came in handy. Do you want to know what I wrote?

HORATIO Yes, my lord.

HAMLET In a serious request from King Claudius to his ally the king of England, to prolong their good relations and maintain peace, as soon as he read the letter, he was to execute Rosencrantz and Guildenstern immediately.

HORATIO How did you seal the message?

HAMLET It just so happened that I had King Hamlet's signet ring in my pouch, which is a copy of the Danish royal seal. I folded the page like the other, signed and sealed it, and replaced the stolen letter without creating suspicion. The next day, we fought the pirates. The rest of the story you already know.

HORATIO So Guildenstern and Rosencrantz go to their deaths.

HAMLET They deliberately sought this mission. I suffer no pangs of conscience. Their deaths result from their own testimony against me. It is deadly when lowly people stand between the clashing blades of mighty fighters.

HORATIO What a king you would make!

HAMLET Doesn't this prove that Claudius murdered my father, debased my mother, and stood in the way of my crowning? He was fishing for my life and with such cunning—is it not just that I defeat him with my own arm? Is it not proper to halt this infection before it causes more disease?

HORATIO He will soon learn from the king of England that you switched the letters.

ACT V

TRANSLATION

HAMLET	It will be short: the interim is mine;
	And a man's life's no more than to say 'One.'
	But I am very sorry, good Horatio, 75
	That to Laertes I forgot myself;
	For, by the image of my cause, I see
	The portraiture of his: I'll court his favours:
	But, sure, the bravery of his grief did put me
	Into a towering passion.
HORATIO	Peace! who comes here? 80
	[Enter OSRIC]
OSRIC	Your lordship is right welcome back to Denmark.
HAMLET	I humbly thank you, sir. *[Aside to HORATIO]*
	Dost know this water-fly?
HORATIO	*[Aside to HAMLET]* No, my good lord.
HAMLET	*[Aside to HORATIO]* Thy state is the more 85
	gracious; for 'tis a vice to know him. He hath much
	land, and fertile: let a beast be lord of beasts, and
	his crib shall stand at the king's mess; 'tis a chough;
	but, as I say, spacious in the possession of dirt.
OSRIC	Sweet lord, if your lordship were at leisure, I 90
	should impart a thing to you from his majesty.
HAMLET	I will receive it, sir, with all diligence of spirit.
	Put your bonnet to his right use; 'tis for the head.
OSRIC	I thank your lordship, 'tis very hot.
HAMLET	No, believe me, 'tis very cold; the wind is 95
	northerly.
OSRIC	It is indifferent cold, my lord, indeed.
HAMLET	But yet methinks it is very sultry and hot for
	my complexion.
OSRIC	Exceedingly, my lord; it is very sultry, as 100
	'twere, I cannot tell how. But, my lord, his majesty
	bade me signify to you that he has laid a great wager
	on your head. Sir, this is the matter,—
HAMLET	I beseech you, remember—
	[HAMLET moves him to put on his hat]

HAMLET	I have a brief time. I must use it to my advantage. A man's life lasts no longer than the count of one. I regret, Horatio, that I challenged Laertes. In my vengeance I see a duplicate in his. I will court his friendship. But note that his boastful grief can rile my anger.
HORATIO	Quiet! Who is coming? *[Enter OSRIC]*
OSRIC	I welcome you back to Denmark, Hamlet.
HAMLET	I thank you, sir. *[Privately to HORATIO]* Do you know this trifler?
HORATIO	*[Privately to HAMLET]* No, my lord.
HAMLET	*[Privately to HORATIO]* You are the better man for not knowing Osric. It would be degrading to know him. Any man who owns rich land, even if he is a beast, earns a place at the king's table. He's a bluejay, but he owns much property.
OSRIC	If you have time, my lord, I want to tell you something from the king.
HAMLET	I will listen carefully. Put your hat back on your head.
OSRIC	I thank you, my lord. It is hot today.
HAMLET	Believe me, I think it is cold. The wind is coming from the north.
OSRIC	It is somewhat cold, as you say, my lord.
HAMLET	But I think it is humid and too hot for my skin.
OSRIC	Very hot, my lord. It is humid, but I don't know why. The king reports that he has placed a bet on you. This is the wager.
HAMLET	I beg you, put on your hat. *[HAMLET moves him to put on his hat]*

ACT V

TRANSLATION

OSRIC	Nay, good my lord; for mine ease, in good faith. Sir, here is newly come to court Laertes; believe me, an absolute gentleman, full of most excellent differences, of very soft society and great showing; indeed, to speak feelingly of him, he is the card or calendar of gentry, for you shall find in him the continent of what part a gentleman would see.	105 110
HAMLET	Sir, his definement suffers no perdition in you; though, I know, to divide him inventorially would dizzy the arithmetic of memory, and yet but yaw neither, in respect of his quick sail. But, in the verity of extolment, I take him to be a soul of great article; and his infusion of such dearth and rareness, as, to make true diction of him, his semblable is his mirror; and who else would trace him, his umbrage, nothing more.	 115 120
OSRIC	Your lordship speaks most infallibly of him.	
HAMLET	The concernancy, sir? why do we wrap the gentleman in our more rawer breath?	
HORATIO	Is 't not possible to understand in another tongue? You will do 't, sir, really.	125
HAMLET	What imports the nomination of this gentleman?	
OSRIC	Of Laertes?	
HORATIO	His purse is empty already; all's golden words are spent.	130
HAMLET	Of him, sir.	
OSRIC	I know you are not ignorant—	
HAMLET	I would you did, sir; in faith, if you did, it would not much approve me. Well, sir.	
OSRIC	You are not ignorant of what excellence Laertes is—	135
HAMLET	I dare not confess that, lest I should compare with him in excellence; but, to know a man well, were to know himself.	
OSRIC	I mean, sir, for his weapon; but in the imputation laid on him by them in his meed, he's unfellowed.	140
HAMLET	What's his weapon?	

ORIGINAL

OSRIC	No, my lord, for my comfort, I should leave it off. Sir, Laertes has recently arrived at court. Believe me, he is a gentleman blessed with distinction, polite behavior, and an impressive appearance. To say the best of him, he is a model of good breeding. You can find in him all that a gentleman should be.
HAMLET	Sir, your description lacks nothing. To take stock of his character would tax the memory, but he does not veer from his course. In his praise, I think him worthy of a list of accomplishments. And his qualities are so unusual and rare, to speak clearly, only his mirror could reflect them. Anyone who tries to summarize his qualities draws only his shadow.
OSRIC	You speak correctly of him.
HAMLET	Why are you telling me this? Why do we assess him with our coarse words?
HORATIO	Can you understand your words when someone else speaks them? Try it, sir.
HAMLET	Why do you name this gentleman?
OSRIC	Do you mean Laertes?
HORATIO	His word treasury is empty. He has used all his golden words.
HAMLET	Of Laertes, sir.
OSRIC	I know you are knowledgeable—
HAMLET	I wish you did know me well, sir. Truly, if you did, you wouldn't approve of me. Well?
OSRIC	You surely know how excellent Laertes is.
HAMLET	I can't claim to know him well enough to compare his excellence. To know a man that well would be to know him as well as he knows himself.
OSRIC	I am referring to his skill with the sword. According to those on his staff, he has no equal.
HAMLET	What weapon is his best?

ACT V

OSRIC	Rapier and dagger.
HAMLET	That's two of his weapons; but, well. 145
OSRIC	The king, sir, hath wagered with him six Barbary horses; against the which he has imponed, as I take it, six French rapiers and poniards, with their assigns, as girdle, hangers, and so: three of the carriages, in faith, are very dear to fancy, very 150 responsive to the hilts, most delicate carriages, and of very liberal conceit.
HAMLET	What call you the carriages?
HORATIO	I know you must be edified by the margent, ere you had done. 155
OSRIC	The carriages, sir, are the hangers.
HAMLET	The phrase would be more germane to the matter, if we could carry cannon by our sides; I would it might be hangers till then. But, on; six Barbary horses against six French swords, their assigns, 160 and three liberal-conceited carriages; that's the French bet against the Danish. Why is this 'imponed,' as you call it?
OSRIC	The king, sir, hath laid, sir, that in a dozen passes between yourself and him, he shall not exceed 165 you three hits; he hath laid on twelve for nine, and it would come to immediate trial, if your lordship would vouchsafe the answer.
HAMLET	How if I answer no?
OSRIC	I mean, my lord, the opposition of your 170 person in trial.
HAMLET	Sir, I will walk here in the hall; if it please his majesty, 'tis the breathing time of day with me; let the foils be brought, the gentleman willing, and the king hold his purpose, I will win 175 for him an I can; if not, I will gain nothing but my shame and the odd hits.
OSRIC	Shall I re-deliver you e'en so?
HAMLET	To this effect, sir; after what flourish your nature will. 180
OSRIC	I commend my duty to your lordship.

OSRIC	Sword and dagger.
HAMLET	You have named two weapons. But, no matter.
OSRIC	The king is wagering six Arabian horses. Laertes has matched his bet with six French swords and daggers, with their holsters, belt, straps, and so forth. Three of the holsters are handsome, well matched to their hilts, delicately encased, and of imaginative design.
HAMLET	What do you call the holsters?
HORATIO	I knew you would have to read the marginal notes before you finished with Osric.
OSRIC	The holsters, sir, are the straps.
HAMLET	The term would be better suited to straps for carrying cannon by our sides. I prefer to call them hangers until that happens. But continue—six Arabian horses versus six French swords, their equipage, and three imaginatively decorated holsters. That's the French bet against the Danish. Why is this promised?
OSRIC	The king has bet that, in a dozen clashes between you and Laertes, he will not hit you more than three times. Laertes is betting that he will outfight you nine times out of twelve. The duel is set for now, if your lordship will answer.
HAMLET	Suppose I say no?
OSRIC	I mean, sir, if your lordship will answer to Laertes in a duel.
HAMLET	Sir, I am walking in the hall. If the king does not mind, it is my usual exercise. Let the dueling foils be brought out, if Laertes is willing, and let the king keep his bet. I will win his bet if I can. If I lose, I will acquire shame and the losing number of hits.
OSRIC	Shall I report your message as you state it?
HAMLET	Exactly, sir. Decorate my words however you want.
OSRIC	I pledge my duty to you.

ACT V

TRANSLATION

HAMLET	Yours, yours. *[Exit OSRIC]* He does well to commend it himself; there are no tongues else for 's turn.
HORATIO	This lapwing runs away with the shell on 185 his head.
HAMLET	He did comply with his dug before he sucked it. Thus has he—and many more of the same bevy, that I know the drossy age dotes on—only got the tune of the time and outward habit of encounter, 190 a kind of yesty collection which carries them through and through the most fond and winnowed opinions; and do but blow them to their trial, the bubbles are out. *[Enter a Lord]*
LORD	My lord, his majesty commended him to you by young Osric, who brings back to him, that you attend 195 him in the hall; he sends to know if your pleasure hold to play with Laertes, or that you will take longer time.
HAMLET	I am constant to my purposes; they follow the king's pleasure: if his fitness speaks, mine is 200 ready; now, or whensoever, provided I be so able as now.
LORD	The king, and queen, and all are coming down.
HAMLET	In happy time. 205
LORD	The queen desires you to use some gentle entertainment to Laertes before you fall to play.
HAMLET	She well instructs me. *[Exit Lord]*
HORATIO	You will lose this wager, my lord.
HAMLET	I do not think so; since he went into 210 France, I have been in continual practice; I shall win at the odds. But thou wouldst not think how ill all's here about my heart; but it is no matter.
HORATIO	Nay, good my lord,—
HAMLET	It is but foolery; but it is such a kind of 215 gain-giving as would perhaps trouble a woman.
HORATIO	If your mind dislike any thing, obey it; I will forestal their repair hither, and say you are not fit.

HAMLET	Yours, too. *[OSRIC goes out]* He is wise to carry the message himself. There are no others who speak like Osric.
HORATIO	This baby bird runs from his nest with the shell still on his head.
HAMLET	He was polite to the breast before he sucked it. He—and others like him in this overdecorated age—has recently learned fashionable wording and showiness of address. His mannered speech is a frothy topping for the most foolish and thinned-out opinions. His words blow away like foam. *[Enter a Lord]*
LORD	My lord, the king sent Osric to you and has learned from Osric that you await him in the hall. The king wants to know if you will duel with Laertes or if you want to face him later.
HAMLET	I keep my word. I am at the king's service. If it is convenient for him, I am ready. Now or later, if I am able to fight later.
LORD	The king and queen and other courtiers are assembling in the hall.
HAMLET	Good.
LORD	The queen wants you to speak kindly to Laertes before you duel.
HAMLET	She advises me well. *[The Lord goes out]*
HORATIO	You will lose this bet, my lord.
HAMLET	I disagree. Since he left for France, I have practiced continually. I will win the bet. You are worried about my depression, but it won't stop me from dueling.
HORATIO	No, my lord.
HAMLET	The duel is just frippery. It is a kind of ego builder that a woman would like.
HORATIO	If you doubt you are ready for this duel, don't go. I will delay the match and say you are not well.

ACT V

TRANSLATION

HAMLET	Not a whit, we defy augury; there's a special 220
	providence in the fall of a sparrow. If it be
	now, 'tis not to come; if it be not to come, it will be
	now; if it be not now, yet it will come: the readiness
	is all. Since no man has aught of what he leaves,
	what is 't to leave betimes? Let be. 225
	[Enter KING, QUEEN, LAERTES, Lords, OSRIC, and
	Attendants with foils]
KING	Come, Hamlet, come, and take this hand from me.
	[The KING puts the hand of LAERTES into that of HAMLET]
HAMLET	Give me your pardon, sir; I've done you wrong;
	But pardon 't, as you are a gentleman.
	This presence knows, and you must needs have heard,
	How I am punish'd with a sore distraction. 230
	What I have done
	That might your nature, honour and exception
	Roughly awake, I here proclaim was madness.
	Was't Hamlet wrong'd Laertes? Never Hamlet:
	If Hamlet from himself be ta'en away, 235
	And when he's not himself does wrong Laertes,
	Then Hamlet does it not; Hamlet denies it.
	Who does it then? His madness. If't be so,
	Hamlet is of the faction that is wrong'd;
	His madness is poor Hamlet's enemy. 240
	Sir, in his audience,
	Let my disclaiming from a purpos'd evil
	Free me so far in your most generous thoughts,
	That I have shot mine arrow o'er the house,
	And hurt my brother.
LAERTES	I am satisfied in nature, 245
	Whose motive, in this case, should stir me most
	To my revenge; but in my terms of honour
	I stand aloof, and will no reconcilement,
	Till by some elder masters, of known honour,
	I have a voice and precedent of peace, 250
	To keep my name ungor'd. But till that time,
	I do receive your offer'd love like love,
	And will not wrong it.
HAMLET	I embrace it freely;
	And will this brother's wager frankly play.
	Give us the foils. Come on.
LAERTES	Come, one for me. 255

ORIGINAL

HAMLET	Not a bit sick. I challenge bad omens. There is God's hand in a sparrow's fall. If I don't fight him now, I never will. If the duel takes place, it must be now. If I don't die now, I will someday. Readiness is the most important factor. Since no one keeps his property when he dies, why should I worry about dying. Don't worry. *[Enter KING, QUEEN, LAERTES, Lords, OSRIC, and Attendants with foils]*
KING	Come here, Hamlet, and shake Laertes's hand. *[The KING puts the hand of LAERTES into that of HAMLET]*
HAMLET	I apologize, Laertes. I have wronged you. Please pardon me, if you are a gentleman. Everyone here knows—and you must have heard—that I am deeply troubled. Whatever I have done that arouses your pride and anger, I claim was insanity. Did Hamlet do wrong to Laertes? Not Hamlet. If Hamlet is out of his mind when he wrongs Laertes, then Hamlet is not responsible for the fault. Hamlet denies wrongdoing. Who committed the fault? Insanity. If this be the case, Hamlet is the one who is slighted. Insanity has become Hamlet's enemy. Sir, I deny deliberately wronging you. I have not recklessly shot an arrow over a house and struck my friend.
LAERTES	I accept the fact that my nature stirred my anger. But I will defend my honor by accepting no reconciliation until I have talked to wise elders, who will protect my reputation. Until that time, I accept your affection as true and I will not spurn it.
HAMLET	I accept your offer willingly and will duel honestly under this wager. Give us each a foil. Let's duel.
LAERTES	Hand me a foil.

ACT V

TRANSLATION

HAMLET	I'll be your foil, Laertes; in mine ignorance Your skill shall, like a star i' the darkest night, Stick fiery off indeed.
LAERTES	You mock me, sir.
HAMLET	No, by this hand.
KING	Give them the foils, young Osric. Cousin Hamlet, 260 You know the wager?
HAMLET	Very well, my lord; Your Grace hath laid the odds o' the weaker side.
KING	I do not fear it; I have seen you both; But since he is better'd we have therefore odds.
LAERTES	This is too heavy; let me see another. 265
HAMLET	This likes me well. These foils have all a length?
OSRIC	Ay, my good lord. *[They prepare to play]*
KING	Set me the stoups of wine upon that table. If Hamlet give the first or second hit, Or quit in answer of the third exchange, 270 Let all the battlements their ordnance fire; The king shall drink to Hamlet's better breath; And in the cup an union shall he throw, Richer than that which four successive kings In Denmark's crown have worn. Give me the cups; 275 And let the kettle to the trumpet speak, The trumpet to the cannoneer without, The cannons to the heavens, the heavens to earth 'Now the king drinks to Hamlet!' Come, begin; And you, the judges, bear a wary eye. 280
HAMLET	Come on, sir.
LAERTES	Come, my lord. *[They play]*
HAMLET	One.
LAERTES	No.
HAMLET	Judgment.
OSRIC	A hit, a very palpable hit.
LAERTES	Well; again.
KING	Stay; give me drink. Hamlet, this pearl is thine; Here's to thy health. Give him the cup. *[Trumpets sound; and cannon shot off within]*

ORIGINAL

HAMLET	I will be your opponent, Laertes. Without knowing your abilities, your skill, like a star on a dark night, will glitter.
LAERTES	You ridicule me, sir.
HAMLET	No, I guarantee you.
KING	Hand me the foils, Osric. Kinsman Hamlet, you know the bet?
HAMLET	Very well, my lord, You have placed your bet on the weaker fighter.
KING	I am not worried. I have seen you both in action. Since he outranks you in reputation, we have better odds of winning.
LAERTES	This foil is too heavy. Let me try another.
HAMLET	I like this one. Are they all the same length?
OSRIC	Yes, my lord. *[They prepare to play]*
KING	Set wine cups on the table. If Hamlet achieves the first or second hit, or scores a return hit, let the cannon fire on the battlements. The king will drink to Hamlet's rest. I will throw a pearl in the cup more valuable that any of Denmark's last four kings have worn in their crown. Hand me the wine cups. Let the timpani alert the trumpeter. Let the trumpeter signal the cannoneer outside. Let the cannon alert the sky and the sky notify the earth. People will know that the king toasts Hamlet. Come, begin the duel. Judges, watch carefully.
HAMLET	Let's begin, sir.
LAERTES	Come at me, my lord. *[They play]*
HAMLET	One hit.
LAERTES	It wasn't.
HAMLET	What do the judges say?
OSRIC	It was a hit, a very evident hit.
LAERTES	Let's go again.
KING	Halt. Let me have wine. Hamlet, this pearl is yours. I toast your health. Hand him the cup. *[Trumpets sound; cannon fire from the castle]*

ACT V

TRANSLATION

HAMLET	I'll play this bout first; set it by awhile. 285 Come—*[They play]* Another hit; what say you?
LAERTES	A touch, a touch, I do confess.
KING	Our son shall win.
QUEEN	He's fat, and scant of breath. Here, Hamlet, take my napkin, rub thy brows; The queen carouses to thy fortune, Hamlet. 290
HAMLET	Good madam!
KING	Gertrude, do not drink.
QUEEN	I will, my lord; I pray you, pardon me. *[Drinks]*
KING	*[Aside]* It is the poison'd cup! it is too late.
HAMLET	I dare not drink yet, madam; by and by.
QUEEN	Come, let me wipe thy face. 295
LAERTES	My lord, I'll hit him now.
KING	I do not think 't.
LAERTES	*[Aside]* And yet 'tis almost 'gainst my conscience.
HAMLET	Come, for the third, Laertes. You but dally; I pray you, pass with your best violence. I am afeard you make a wanton of me. 300
LAERTES	Say you so? come on. *[They play]*
OSRIC	Nothing, neither way.
LAERTES	Have at you now. *[LAERTES wounds HAMLET; then, in scuffling, they change rapiers, and HAMLET wounds LAERTES]*
KING	Part them! they are incens'd.
HAMLET	Nay, come, again. *[The QUEEN falls]*
OSRIC	Look to the queen there, ho!
HORATIO	They bleed on both sides. How is it, my lord? 305
OSRIC	How is it, Laertes?
LAERTES	Why, as a woodcock to mine own springe, Osric; I am justly kill'd with mine own treachery.
HAMLET	How does the queen?

ORIGINAL

HAMLET	I will finish this first bout. Put my cup back on the table. Come. *[They play]* I scored another hit, didn't I?
LAERTES	A touch, I admit it.
KING	Hamlet will win.
QUEEN	He's out of shape and breathless. Here, Hamlet, take my handkerchief and rub your face. The queen bets on your good luck, Hamlet.
HAMLET	Good lady!
KING	Gertrude, do not drink from Hamlet's cup.
QUEEN	I will drink from it, my lord. Please, excuse me. *[Drinks]*
KING	*[To himself]* It is too late to stop her from drinking from the poisoned wine.
HAMLET	I don't want to stop yet for a drink, madam. Shortly, I will.
QUEEN	Come, let me wipe the sweat from your face.
LAERTES	My lord, I will strike Hamlet now.
KING	I don't think you can.
LAERTES	*[To himself]* And yet my conscience forbids me to strike Hamlet.
HAMLET	Come, Laertes, try for a third hit. You are wasting time. Please, give me your best lunge. I think you are playing with me.
LAERTES	Do you think so? Come at me. *[They play]*
OSRIC	No hit on either side.
LAERTES	I have you now. *[LAERTES wounds HAMLET; then, in scuffling, they change rapiers, and HAMLET wounds LAERTES]*
KING	Separate them. They are angry.
HAMLET	No. Come at me once more. *[The QUEEN falls]*
OSRIC	Help the queen.
HORATIO	Both duelers are bleeding. Are you all right, my lord?
OSRIC	How badly are you wounded, Laertes?
LAERTES	As a game bird in my own snare, Osric. I am poisoned by my own plot.
HAMLET	How is the queen?

ACT V

TRANSLATION

KING	She swounds to see them bleed.
QUEEN	No, no, the drink, the drink,—O my dear Hamlet! 310 The drink, the drink; I am poison'd. *[Dies]*
HAMLET	O villainy! Ho! let the door be lock'd: Treachery! seek it out. *[LAERTES falls]*
LAERTES	It is here, Hamlet. Hamlet, thou art slain; No medicine in the world can do thee good; 315 In thee there is not half an hour of life; The treacherous instrument is in thy hand, Unbated and envenom'd. The foul practice Hath turn'd itself on me; lo! here I lie, Never to rise again. Thy mother's poison'd. 320 I can no more. The king, the king's to blame.
HAMLET	The point envenom'd too!— Then, venom, to thy work. *[Stabs the KING]*
ALL	Treason! treason!
KING	O! yet defend me, friends; I am but hurt. 325
HAMLET	Here, thou incestuous, murderous, damned Dane, Drink off this potion;—is thy union here? Follow my mother. *[KING dies]*
LAERTES	He is justly serv'd; It is a poison temper'd by himself. Exchange forgiveness with me, noble Hamlet: 330 Mine and my father's death come not upon thee, Nor thine on me! *[Dies]*
HAMLET	Heaven make thee free of it! I follow thee. I am dead, Horatio. Wretched queen, adieu! You that look pale and tremble at this chance, 335 That are but mutes or audience to this act, Had I but time,—as this fell sergeant, death, Is strict in his arrest,—O! I could tell you— But let it be. Horatio, I am dead; Thou liv'st; report me and my cause aright 340 To the unsatisfied.
HORATIO	Never believe it; I am more an antique Roman than a Dane: Here's yet some liquor left.

KING	She fainted at the sight of blood.
QUEEN	No, the drink—Oh my dear Hamlet! The drink. I am poisoned. *[She dies]*
HAMLET	Oh crime! Lock the doors. A plot. Investigate it. *[LAERTES falls]*
LAERTES	The cause is on my foil, Hamlet. You are dying. No antidote in the world can save you. You have only a half hour to live. The poisoned murder weapon is in your hand. My evil plot has turned against me. I will never get up from the floor. Your mother died of poison. I can say no more. The king did it.
HAMLET	The foil is also poisoned!— Then, poison, do your work. *[HAMLET stabs the KING]*
ALL	Hamlet has committed treason!
KING	Defend me, friends. I am hurt.
HAMLET	Here, you adulterous, murdering, damned Dane, drink the rest of the poisoned wine. Is your mate here? Follow her into death. *[CLAUDIUS dies]*
LAERTES	He got what he deserved. He mixed the poison himself. Let us forgive each other, noble Hamlet. My death and my father's death were not your fault. Nor is your death my fault. *[LAERTES dies]*
HAMLET	Heaven forgive you for it. I will die next. I am dying, Horatio. Wretched queen, goodbye! You courtiers turn pale and tremble at these multiple deaths. If I had time— death is strict in allotting time—I could tell you the truth. But leave it as it is. Horatio, I am dying. Because you are still alive, report the reason for my vengeance to those who don't believe it.
HORATIO	I don't want to live. I want to die like ancient Romans. There is poison left in the cup.

ACT V

TRANSLATION

HAMLET   As thou'rt a man,
Give me the cup: let go; by heaven, I'll have 't.
O God! Horatio, what a wounded name,   345
Things standing thus unknown, shall live behind me.
If thou didst ever hold me in thy heart,
Absent thee from felicity awhile,
And in this harsh world draw thy breath in pain,
To tell my story.
[March afar off, and shot within]
                              What war-like noise is this?   350

OSRIC   Young Fortinbras, with conquest come from Poland,
To the ambassadors of England gives
This war-like volley.

HAMLET   O! I die, Horatio;
The potent poison quite o'er-crows my spirit:
I cannot live to hear the news from England,   355
But I do prophesy the election lights
On Fortinbras: he has my dying voice;
So tell him, with the occurrents, more and less,
Which have solicited—The rest is silence. *[Dies]*

HORATIO   Now cracks a noble heart. Good-night, sweet prince, 360
And flights of angels sing thee to thy rest!
Why does the drum come hither? *[March within]*
*[Enter FORTINBRAS, the English Ambassadors
and Others]*

FORTINBRAS   Where is this sight?

HORATIO   What is it ye would see?
If aught of woe or wonder, cease your search.

FORTINBRAS   This quarry cries on havoc. O proud death!   365
What feast is toward in thine eternal cell,
That thou so many princes at a shot
So bloodily hast struck?

FIRST   The sight is dismal;
AMBASSADOR   And our affairs from England come too late:
The ears are senseless that should give us hearing,   370
To tell him his commandment is fulfill'd,
That Rosencrantz and Guildenstern are dead.
Where should we have our thanks?

HAMLET	Give me the cup. Let go of it. By heaven, I won't let you drink it. Oh God, Horatio, my reputation will never be clear. If you were ever my friend, give up your own welfare, and in this troubled place painfully tell my story. *[Marching sounds in the distance and a shot in the castle]* What noise of battle do I hear?
OSRIC	Young Fortinbras, who triumphed in Poland, reports to the English with a victorious round of fire.
HAMLET	Oh, I am dying, Horatio. This poison saps my strength. I won't live long enough to hear England's response to the Norwegian victory. I do predict that the Danish people will elect Fortinbras to the throne. He has my recommendation. Tell him what has happened here. The rest will remain untold. *[HAMLET dies]*
HORATIO	Now breaks a worthy heart. Good night, sweet prince, and flights of angels sing you to heaven. Why is there drumming in the castle? *[Marching soldiers in the castle]* *[Enter FORTINBRAS, the English Ambassadors, and Others]*
FORTINBRAS	What has happened here?
HORATIO	What do you want to see? If it is tragedy or amazement, you have found it.
FORTINBRAS	This carnage is evidence of slaughter. Oh death, what feast are you preparing in your eternal quarters that you have killed so many royal people at one time?
FIRST AMBASSADOR	This is a woeful sight. I come too late to bring a message from the king of England. The ones are dead who would hear the message that Rosencrantz and Guildenstern are dead. Who is there to thank us for bringing the message?

ACT V

TRANSLATION

HORATIO   Not from his mouth,
                    Had it the ability of life to thank you:
                    He never gave commandment for their death.   375
                    But since, so jump upon this bloody question,
                    You from the Polack wars, and you from England,
                    Are here arriv'd, give order that these bodies
                    High on a stage be placed to the view;
                    And let me speak to the yet unknowing world   380
                    How these things came about: so shall you hear
                    Of carnal, bloody, and unnatural acts,
                    Of accidental judgments, casual slaughters;
                    Of deaths put on by cunning and forc'd cause,
                    And, in this upshot, purposes mistook   385
                    Fall'n on the inventors' heads; all this can I
                    Truly deliver.

FORTINBRAS   Let us haste to hear it,
                    And call the noblest to the audience.
                    For me, with sorrow I embrace my fortune;   390
                    I have some rights of memory in this kingdom,
                    Which now to claim my vantage doth invite me.

HORATIO   Of that I shall have also cause to speak,
                    And from his mouth whose voice will draw on more:
                    But let this same be presently perform'd,   395
                    Even while men's minds are wild, lest more mischance
                    On plots and errors happen.

FORTINBRAS   Let four captains
                    Bear Hamlet, like a soldier, to the stage;
                    For he was likely, had he been put on,
                    To have prov'd most royally: and, for his passage,   400
                    The soldiers' music and the rites of war
                    Speak loudly for him.
                    Take up the bodies: such a sight as this
                    Becomes the field, but here shows much amiss.
                    Go, bid the soldiers shoot.   405
                    [A dead march. Exeunt, bearing off the bodies;
                    after which a peal of ordnance is shot off]

ORIGINAL

HORATIO   Not the king, who would have thanked you if he were still alive. King Claudius did not order their execution. But since you arrived from the war in Poland to this bloody scene, and the messenger arrived from England, order that these corpses be viewed on a platform. I will tell everyone why these people died. I will tell you of evil murders, of accidental death, of casual slaughter, of deaths caused by plotting and deliberation. And, of the latter, of conniving that turned against the plotter. All this information I will truly explain.

FORTINBRAS   Let us hear it at once. Call the nobles to hear it too. As for me, I welcome my good luck with sorrow. I have some rights to claim in Denmark and this is a good opportunity.

HORATIO   Of your claim I will also speak. I will speak the words from Hamlet's mouth, which will never again draw breath. Let me do this immediately while citizens are disrupted. I want to circumvent other plots and false assumptions.

FORTINBRAS   Let four officers carry Hamlet military style to the platform. He was a worthy heir to Denmark's throne. For his death, play military music. So many deaths are normal in battle, but it is unusual for a king's castle. Tell the soldiers to fire a respectful volley. *[A funeral march. They depart, carrying the corpses. Afterward, soldiers fire a salute]*

ACT V

TRANSLATION

Questions for Reflection

1. How does Shakespeare use irony in the final scene? Consider how multiple deaths derive from Claudius's and Laertes's evil plots, as well as why Fortinbras's arrival is a fortunate coincidence for himself and for Denmark.

2. How does the death of King Hamlet compare with that of Polonius? Consider the responses of their children to loss, sorrow, and outrage. How does Polonius's death contribute to the immediacy and seriousness of the task that the ghost demands of Prince Hamlet?

3. What lines from the play give clues to Hamlet's age, especially the dialogue in the graveyard? Why is his youth a factor in his tragedy? Why does Horatio conclude that Hamlet has the makings of a king?

4. How do King Hamlet, Polonius, and Gertrude compare as parents? Discuss Claudius's failings as a stepfather. How does King Hamlet's charge to "leave her to heaven" accurately describe Gertrude's accidental poisoning? Why is old Norway a poor choice of surrogate parent for young Fortinbras?

5. How would you describe the deaths of two sons and the drowning of a daughter in the play? Why does Shakespeare stress the parent-child relationship? What does he suggest about Prince Hamlet's future as heir apparent to the Danish crown? How does Prince Hamlet's death elevate both Horatio and Fortinbras?

6. Why does Hamlet choose suspicious behavior, pacing, quibbling, a journey to England, dueling, and a re-enactment of King Hamlet's murder rather than a straightforward accusation of Claudius for regicide, adultery with his sister-in-law, and a plot to kill the heir apparent? Why does Shakespeare stress Prince Hamlet's dilemma rather than his actions?

7. What forms of spying supply information to Claudius, Rosencrantz and Guildenstern, Prince Hamlet, Horatio, Reynaldo, and Polonius? Which spy is the most effective? The most inept? The least rewarded? The most suitably punished?

8. How does Shakespeare present the causes and symptoms of insanity and emotional collapse? How does a guilty conscience contribute to King Hamlet's torments, Claudius's guile, Prince Hamlet's delay, and Gertrude's regrets? How does Ophelia turn disconnected bits of song into veiled accusations?

9. What strengths do Horatio, young Fortinbras, and Laertes have that Prince Hamlet lacks? Why does Laertes regret setting up the duel to kill Hamlet? Why does Horatio fail to commit suicide by drinking from the poisoned wine cup?

10. How does King Hamlet pressure his son and heir to seek vengeance from Claudius? Why do Horatio and the night watch fear for Prince Hamlet?

11. How would you summarize the play's advice to actors? Consider how Shakespeare honors drama as a noble endeavor and a valuable part of the humanities.

12. Why does Prince Hamlet fail to kill Claudius during prayer? Why must Claudius die with his sins unforgiven? Which characters die in a similar state in the final scene?

13. What are some of the plant images in the play? Why is yew sap deadly? What do daisies, rosemary, pansies, and rue symbolize? In what way are Ophelia's garlands instructive as well as deadly? How does her flower monologue foreshadow Gertrude's grave gift to Ophelia?

14. How would you predict the strengths of Fortinbras's reign? Consider the shock of arriving at Elsinore and finding the royal family dead.

15. Why does Prince Hamlet knowingly accept a challenge to a duel that he will most likely lose? Why does he accept the inevitability of death? How does Horatio respond to the prince's hasty acceptance of the challenge?

16. How would you compare the leadership qualities in Laertes, King Hamlet, old Norway, young Fortinbras, Claudius, Gertrude, the king of England, Polonius, old Fortinbras, Horatio, and Prince Hamlet? Note the qualities that they share or lack.

17. What are Gertrude's, Ophelia's, and Polonius's roles in locating the cause of Hamlet's madness?

18. How would you explain the theme of mortality? How do the gravediggers, Yorick, Julius Caesar, Ophelia, Polonius, King Hamlet, and Alexander the Great supply examples of human frailty?

19. Are Hamlet's theft of a royal dispatch and his forgery of a new order for the execution of Rosencrantz and Guildenstern justified? Why or why not?

20. How would you compose an extended definition of courtship ritual based on the relationship between Ophelia and Prince Hamlet? Why does Gertrude grieve that Ophelia died unwed? What are the implications of "sweets to the sweet"?

21. What is the tone of the priest at Ophelia's burial. Consider why he seems unwilling to eulogize a woman who may have committed suicide. How does Laertes scorn church dogma on the subject of Christian burial?

22. How does each death bring down the Danish royal family? How does Claudius set in motion a weakening of national power and the destruction of a dynasty?

23. How would you define Gothic convention using examples from the graveyard scene and from Prince Hamlet's interaction with his father's ghost? What do the floating dress on the stream and the concealment of "the guts" contribute to Shakespeare's Gothicism? Why is hand-to-hand fighting in Ophelia's grave a favorite scene for actors and audiences?

24. How does Shakespeare depict Gertrude and Ophelia as weaker and less influential than male characters? What actions make Gertrude seem easily led? Why does Ophelia seem gullible and unworthy of Prince Hamlet's devotion?

25. How does Shakespeare reveal that Claudius suffers for his deception and murder? Does Claudius deserve what he gets?

26. What does Shakespeare imply about the cause and spread of royal scandal? Is Claudius wrong to bury Polonius secretly and without honor? Why do Danes welcome Laertes and proclaim him king?

27. How does the last scene typify human failing? What aspects of the duel derive from pride, vengeance, conniving, and despair? Why does Prince Hamlet wish that he had more time?

28. Why does Prince Hamlet pretend to comment on "The Mouse Trap"? How does his commentary delight Ophelia, unsettle Claudius, and alarm Gertrude? Why does Hamlet's made-up title for the play focus on vermin?

29. How does Shakespeare please both groundlings and more discerning playgoers with *Hamlet?* What aspects of the play would please both extremes of drama appreciation? What themes are universal? poignant? puzzling? existential?

30. How does Shakespeare justify the downfall of Denmark's royal family? Why does Fortinbras appear to stumble onto good fortune?

31. What roles do Lamord, old Norway, old Fortinbras, and pirates play in Prince Hamlet's plot? Why does Shakespeare present these episodes through narrative rather than action?

32. What aspects of Prince Hamlet's character appeal to stage actors? Which speeches reveal nobility, wit, vulnerability, and humanity?

33. Is Laertes's insistence that Prince Hamlet is guilty of killing both Polonius and Ophelia valid? Does Laertes have evidence to support his accusations?

34. How do Horatio and Prince Hamlet complement each other's strengths and weaknesses? Why does their friendship thrive? Why does the play depict Horatio as the rescuer of Hamlet's reputation?

35. How does Hamlet ridicule Osric's presentation of the wager? How does the gift of a pearl sweeten Claudius's bet of six Arabian horses on Hamlet?

36. How does Shakespeare use lowly people in a drama about kings, queens, princes, and lords? How do cast members like Osric, servants, messengers, sailors, the night watch, an acting troupe, and Norwegian soldiers contribute to the action?

No more "Double, double, toil and trouble…"

You can learn Shakespeare on the Double!™

Shakespeare on the Double!™ books make understanding the Bard as easy and painless as this one does. The most comprehensive guides available, they include an easy-to-understand translation alongside the original text, *plus:*

- A brief synopsis of the basic plot and action that provides a broad understanding of the play
- A character list with an in-depth description of the characteristics, motivations, and actions of each major player
- A visual character map that identifies the major characters and how they relate to one another
- A cycle-of-death graphic that pinpoints the sequence of deaths in the play, including who dies, how they die, and why
- Reflective questions that help you identify and delve deeper into the themes and meanings of the play

All *Shakespeare on the Double!* Books
$8.99 US/$10.99 CAN/£5.99 UK • 5½ x 8½ • 192–264 pages

The next time you delve into the Bard's masterpieces, get help—on the double!

Available wherever books are sold.

WILEY
Now you know.